DEATH OF FATHERS

Death of Fathers

C. J. DRIVER

faber and faber

This edition first published in 2010
by Faber and Faber Ltd
Bloomsbury House, 74–77 Great Russell Street
London WC1B 3DA

Printed by Books on Demand GmbH, Norderstedt

All rights reserved
© C. J. Driver, 1972

The right of C. J. Driver to be identified as author of this work
has been asserted in accordance with Section 77 of the
Copyright, Designs and Patents Act 1988

This book is sold subject to the condition that it shall not, by way of
trade or otherwise, be lent, resold, hired out or otherwise circulated
without the publisher's prior consent in any form of binding or cover other than
that in which it is published and without a similar condition including this
condition being imposed on the subsequent purchaser

A CIP record for this book is available from the British Library

ISBN 978–0–571–26050–8

But you must know your father lost a father;
That father lost, lost his; and the survivor bound,
In filial obligation, for some term
To do obsequious sorrow. But to persever
In obstinate condolement is a course
Of impious stubbornness; 'tis unmanly grief,
It shows a will most incorrect to heaven,
A heart unfortified, a mind impatient,
An understanding simple and unschool'd;
For what we know must be, and is as common
As any the most vulgar thing to sense,
Why should we in our peevish opposition
Take it to heart? Fie! 'tis a fault to heaven,
A fault against the dead, a fault to nature,
To reason most absurd; whose common theme
Is death of fathers, and who still hath cried
From the first corse till he that died today,
'This must be so' . . .

Hamlet, I ii

The secret of a man is not his Oedipus complex nor his
inferiority complex; it is the limit of his own freedom;
his capacity for standing up to torture and death.

Sartre, *Situations III*

For Richard Hanson, Alan Hurd and John Adams

For your sakes as well as my own, I must make it clear that the school of my novel has nothing to do with the school in which we all teach, and that my characters – teachers, pupils, parents – are fictitious and 'bear no resemblance to any living person', or dead for that matter.

This is not an ironic disclaimer; it is a simple truth, since
> "The artist lies
> For the improvement of truth."*

And his friends have to bear with him, as you have done with me.

C. J. D.

*Charles Tomlinson, "A Meditation on John Constable."

Contents

PROLOGUE   11

PART ONE: Call   17

PART TWO: Response   149

PART THREE: Silence   215

Prologue

The guide stopped suddenly, then looked carefully to his right. The trees were thinner there. He took a few hesitant steps forward before turning back to stare at the prisoners.

"Ist das der Platz hier?" he asked sharply; but the prisoners looked steadily forward into the sunlit trees and made not a sign that they had heard. The guide watched them for a moment and then, as if he had made up his mind from their silence, walked quickly forward, leading the party towards the clearing.

"What did he say?" John Detheridge asked the interpreter at his side quietly.

"He wanted to know if this was the place." The interpreter was pale and whenever he took his hands from his pockets John noticed their shaking. He was very young and had only arrived a week before; he had been warned about what he would find but this was his first time out.

John Detheridge looked round at the three prisoners behind him; they too were pale, but he knew that it was only the pallor of months of hiding. The six military policemen guarding them were old hands now; they knew what they were going to find, somewhere in this wood, and though the sickness did not change, they had learned to hold themselves still. Behind them came the villagers, ten or twelve men, each one carrying a spade, and three women, middle-aged, with their heads covered. Occasionally one of them would whisper something to another, and the whisper would carry forward like the sound of feet through leaves. A little way to their right walked the Russian observer; for once he had taken off his great-coat. What he watched was the prisoners, especially the young one, the one called Holze.

The guide stopped at the edge of the clearing, and the party fanned out each side of him. "Das ist der richtige Platz," he said and, unnecessarily, the interpreter translated it. The ground was suddenly uneven there, and the weeds were high, not like the smooth leaf-moulded wood they had walked through. While they stood there waiting, the Russian observer moved suddenly over to one of the trees flanking the clearing. John Detheridge saw him take a pocket-knife from his great-coat pocket, open it, and dig fiercely into the bark of the tree. After a moment or two he levered something out and walked over to Detheridge to show him. It was the misshapen lead of a bullet, which he dropped into Detheridge's hand. John looked at it for a moment or two, uncertain what to do with it—it was no good as evidence, certainly—and then handed it back to the Russian.

"All right," he said to the interpreter. "Will you ask the villagers to . . . to get started, please?" What did you say? Start work? Dig their dead up? Dig their sons and daughters and grandchildren out of the quiet earth? Usually, he brought troops in to do this work, volunteers who knew what they would have to do, what they would find; but the villagers had come to him this time, and they had said that they wanted to do the work themselves. For their own.

The graves were not deep, no more than two feet of earth over the bodies. Sometimes they had been very careful to conceal the bodies, but here they had not bothered. John Detheridge knew enough to stay away for as long as he could; and when he finally went to look, he covered his mouth and nose with a handkerchief. The bodies were buried neatly,

PROLOGUE

methodically; they must have been shot away from the graves at the edge of the clearing, judging by the marks on the trees. And they were naked. They must have been made to undress beforehand. There was a young girl there, the third body in the first trench.

He turned away from the graves and called to the guards who stood around the prisoners at the edge of the clearing. "Bring them here, sergeant," he called, and slowly the group came over. "Tell them to look," he said to the interpreter.

"Er sagt, dass Sie dort hinsehen müssen, in die Gräber hinein," the young man said and, when they did not, he said again, his voice breaking, "Seht her, Ihr Scheisskerle."

"No," Detheridge said to him sharply.

The interpreter looked at him. "Sorry, sir," he said, "it's just..."

"I know," he interrupted. "But there's no good doing that. Ask them if they still refuse to answer."

"Er mochte wissen, de Sie sich immis noch weigern Alles von diesem Ereignis zu wissen," the interpreter asked the prisoners. The two older men, looking away from the graves, shook their heads, but the young one, standing a full head taller than the men each side of him, looked down now steadily at the bodies in the graves, almost, thought Detheridge, as if he were inside a museum looking at the bones of dead animals.

"All right," he said. "Ask them what they did with the clothes."

"Was machten Sie mit der Bekleidung, die Sie von Ihren nahmen?"

One of the older prisoners looked at Detheridge then, cleared his throat, hesitated and said, very quietly, "Wir schichten sie zum Hauptquartier."

"Halts Maul," the young prisoner said, but the old man went on wearily. "Es wurde uns befohten, das zu tun."

"Wer befahl es?"

The older prisoner gestured with his head to Holze, who said again, fiercely, "Sie ruhig, Sie alter Idiot."

"It's the old line of the orders from above, above being Holze again," the interpreter said, turning to John Detheridge.

"Yes," he answered.

"We should shoot them now," said the Russian observer in his heavy English. John looked at him carefully, though he was getting used to the invariable remark; he had been with them nearly a month now. He was after Holze; he was wanted in the Russian sector.

"No," he answered automatically, then turned to the interpreter. "Look," he said, "there's no point in our staying any longer. We've got more than enough now. Will you tell the villagers that?" He watched him walk carefully round the first trench to where the men were standing and heard him speak to them. One of the men asked a question, and the interpreter turned to call across the trench. "Colonel Detheridge, they want to know what's going to happen to the prisoners now."

"Tell them that we'll take them back for trial. Oh, and say that we may need one or two of them for witnesses."

The interpreter turned and Detheridge could hear him explaining carefully. He turned to the sergeant in charge of the guard and said, "You can start back to the truck now. We've got what we need. Don't let them talk, please."

"Sir," the sergeant acknowledged his order; you could see the relief on all their faces, even on the prisoners'. The smell was very bad; you got used to looking, but the smell stayed the same. The guard closed round the prisoners and began to move them off; one of the older prisoners was slow and one of the guards prodded him forward angrily, but the sergeant held the guard's arm and spoke quietly to him, "No," Detheridge heard him say, "no, that's no good."

PROLOGUE

Detheridge walked round the trenches to where the villagers stood, looking down at their dead. He shook hands with all of them but said nothing. They would do the rest, he knew; they had already taken one of the bodies from the trench and two of the women were sewing it into the canvas shrouds he had given them. There were carts coming from the village and he had seen in the village that morning another party of men preparing graves in the churchyard.

Walking back through the wood to where they had left the truck, he let the interpreter and the Russian observer walk on ahead of him. There were a thousand woods like this in Europe, perhaps tens of thousands; in how many now were there these graves? And how many men were there who knew these graves and knew how they came to be there? And how many of them would be found, even in the end? Perhaps the Russian was right. Perhaps you should just shoot the ones you found, and let them lie in the same graves. Perhaps that would be the best and quickest way; the judgement could be left then.

He stopped for a moment to take a cigarette from his breast pocket and to light it. His hands, he noted, were quite steady. For a while at least you had to stop feeling; you shut these things out, and went back to the traditional simplicities. You stopped being angry. You learned not to connect. You learned not to notice that the young girl in her trench was the same age as your own daughter. More important even, you learned to forget that Holze, who looked so steadily at his own handiwork, and who cursed his comrades, could have been your own son. There was such arrogance in feeling; what could you possibly feel about a Holze with his steady eyes and steady hands? Not anger. Not even pity. Nothing could comprehend such corruption. Except God. Therefore God, and therefore one of the simplicities was to pray, and therefore one of the prayers was: Later, let me feel more than I do now. But you also prayed that it would not be now.

Part One

Call

*. . . forgetting the bright speed he had
In his high mountain cradle in Pamere,
A foil'd circuitous wanderer: – till at last
The long'd-for dash of waves is heard, and wide
His luminous home of waters opens, bright
And tranquil, from whose floor the new-bath'd stars
Emerge, and shine upon the Aral Sea.*

                Matthew Arnold, "Sohrab and Rustum"

I

The footpath led him along the top of the cliff, then a few yards inland across a stile and around the edge of two fields, over a wall of piled stones, and dropped him suddenly and muddily through the low thick trees and bushes of a gully, so quiet that it could have been miles from the sea. He stopped for a moment in the trees to listen—for anything, bird-song, a stream falling through rocks, the sea breaking—but the sight of the path dipping away to his left and the knowledge that the gully must open on to the beach itself drew him quickly down out of the silence so that, when he reached the open, he was running and nearly tripped and fell on the stones above the high-water line. Stones gave way to soft sand and then to hard, and soon he stood at the water's edge, looking back at the hidden path down the gully and wondering why he had run at all. There was no one up there and no one on the beach.

Though the sun was shining, the wind of early spring came sharply off the sea, and the sweat round the collar of his jersey dried coldly. The tide was on the ebb but every now and again a bigger wave would break and would push a low line of foam unevenly and hesitatingly towards his feet.

He had not meant to come this far; he had told his wife that he would walk only as far as the ruined lookout on the promontory—three hours today, he had told her, and now he would be back at least an hour later than he had said. Still, he was glad; this beach couldn't be seen from the village and, as far as he could see, there were no houses above it and no ways down other than the gully, though the footpath must lead on over the fallen rocks at the northern end of the beach. He could not see the headland from here but he would walk here tomorrow and he would climb over those rocks to see the sweep of the bay and culmination of headland; in the meantime, he would stand here at the edge of the sea for a moment by himself.

* * *

"Look," she had said, "Look at that . . . that thing in the sea."

"Where?"

"Look. Can't you see?" She had pointed again to somewhere out in the bay. "There, where the gulls are."

He had seen then; she was right, there was something out there, something that moved sluggishly and clumsily, something which held its own motion in opposition to the waves, something that the gulls swooped down on and pecked at and flapped away from. He had opened the window and had stepped out into the cold of the small balcony.

"What is it?" his wife had called from the window.

"I can't see properly; it looks like something dead—a seal, perhaps . . . or a dead dolphin. I don't know. The gulls are eating it, anyway." He came back through the french windows and closed them behind him. He did not look at his wife.

"Galer," she said, coming up to him. "Galer, are you sure it isn't someone drowned out there, a sailor or fisherman or someone?"

"I don't know."

"It looks horrible." She was close enough for him to feel her shudder.

"Yes—but it won't worry now. The tide will bring it in."

"Shouldn't we go down to the harbour and tell someone?

Just in case it is a dead person—it looks too big to be a seal."

He looked out of the window again towards the harbour. "There are fishermen down there," he said. "Look; they must be able to see it out there, and they don't seem to be worried. We are probably just imagining things."

"Probably," Skarfe said, but shuddered again as she turned away from the window.

Galer had gone on standing at the window, waiting for the tide to bring the dead thing in; but it had come so slowly and the gulls' excited tearing and pecking had been so obscene that he could not bear to watch and, by the time he had gone back to the window again, the thing had disappeared. Whatever it was must have washed up on to the rocks and if it had really been a drowned man someone would have found him by now—there were children playing down there in the pools just about where the tide would have washed him to.

Stone in water, stone from water, stone from home of waters; no voice there, or did stones find a voice in the water, at least to the dead? No, that was no choice now. Not by any means. Therefore without change; and if you moved away, it wasn't away at all, but closer.

* * *

His wife was waiting for him at the cottage, but she said nothing about his being late. Only after she had given him his tea, she said, "Oh, I forgot to tell you. A letter came from Jim this afternoon. I fetched it from the Post Office in the village."

"What's he say?" Galer asked.

"He says he's bored. Naturally." She smiled across the room at Galer and then fetched the letter from the bedroom for him. He read it through once quickly, then re-read it slowly, but there was nothing much in it beyond a few facetiously funny remarks about aged friends and some poor ignorant clergyman who had dared lecture him on the octagon of Ely Cathedral. Reading the letter, Galer was glad that he and Skarfe had decided not to ask Jim to come on holiday to Cornwall with them; he would not have suited the mood and he would have disrupted John's need to be alone for a while. You needed time away from everything to do with a school, even where school meant your friends, though perhaps the holiday would have been easier for Skarfe if Jim had been there; he was no good at talking idly himself, and Jim loved chattering and gossip. Certainly, though this letter was addressed to both of them, most of it was intended for Skarfe, since it was written in the vein of bantering facetiousness which the pair of them used almost as a private language. So he put the letter down on the arm of the chair and looked out at the steadily darkening evening outside; he must, he knew, give some time specially to Skarfe before they left Cornwall for St Michaels – they must have a day out together. But soon the darkness caught his attention fully and he forgot wife and friend and the need for words as he looked out at sea and wind and the darkness sweeping in on him.

* * *

Skarfe said suddenly into the near-dark of the room, "Oh, Galer, you remember that thing we saw in the sea this morning?" He nodded and looked at her. "Well, this afternoon, while you were out walking, I went down to the rocks and looked for it – it was only an old dead tree; it must have been uprooted in a flood or something, but it had been in the sea a long time, because it was all covered with sea-weed and stuff. It must have been that the gulls were eating. I found it in one of the pools and the gulls were still pecking at it."

When he didn't reply, she said again, "It was only a dead tree-trunk after all; isn't that strange?" But even now he said only "Yes," and she realised that he didn't want to talk. The sea slowly turned from grey to black, and his wife looked at the sea too, but sometimes at him. When it was completely dark, Galer went upstairs to find a book from his suitcase and Skarfe turned on the television.

*   *   *

He dreamed: it was summer somewhere – he knew that because of the light on the walls of the room, light falling through the windows cleanly, hard-edged, as if the shadows were permanently in one position, and he was there, as a child or a very old man, for he could not move. Nothing happened in the dream. He sat, not moving, not looking out of the window, looking at the light on the wall, looking at the light alive on the wall. He could not move, but he did not feel trapped, for he was not a prisoner; he was passive in his stillness, as if he had gone on some long journey past the concerns of action, beyond choice, to a place where he could watch the flux of things, the eddying and burning and air-dancing.

Someone else in his dream, nameless, trying to force him back into feeling, showed him a still vision of a dead woman holding a dead child at the side of a road in some far country, but he would not see that at all, refused to guess at the presence of an armed soldier invisible at the edge of the vision, would not connect the blood on the mother's face with her dead eyes, or the dead eyes of the child with the gashes across his chest. He saw only colour and shape and line and form, the red, the brown, the green, the plane of this face and the curve of that, everything broken down into light and degrees of light, a million separate dancing molecules and, at the centre of each dance, something very still, something peaceful, something exactly in the state that he was. The dance of light comprehended everything.

Yet somehow there was terror in the dream too, as if the

air itself, for all its brilliance, had been out of order. The passive gradually became a terror, inaction a threat, not moving an illness, and the vision that he did not see became itself an armed soldier, invisible behind him. He did not wonder at the terrible light, he submitted to it; and that was the worst terror of all.

* * *

Awake very early, he could see that the light on the wall was only fractionally less grey than the shadow on the same wall. He looked across the bed to where his wife was still sound asleep; was she ever in his dreams, he wondered momentarily – certainly she didn't appear in the dreams he remembered. But then he didn't dream very often of the living; if people appeared at all, they were dead or imagined. Oh, it was nonsense to suppose that you never dreamed of the faces of the dead, because you did – sometimes you dreamed of people who didn't even exist until you dreamed them.

Holding the dream in his mind still, Galer got quietly out of bed and walked, still in pyjamas, to the drawing-room, where he drew the curtains and stood looking out to sea. After a moment or two, he opened one of the french windows, stepped out on to the balcony and stood there in the cold wind that swooped in past him, past the curtain, making it pulse like a heart beating, tug, tug, tug, the room behind him like his own heart steadily beating and the cold gathering like mist in the house and around his body, warm from the bed at first, soon shivering, and doors inside the cottage banging as the wind spread. But he did not move, even when his wife called out, "Galer, what are you doing? Galer, are you all right?" For a moment he didn't even realise that it was his wife calling, but thought that it was someone else calling, someone outside there in the sea-spray, in the cold, on the rocks below, someone tall and thin and gesticulating, or a child lost in a rainstorm, and then he knew that it was only his wife calling, and he did not bother to reply but looked out across the balcony into the grey light. He did not move even when Skarfe came from the bedroom to join him, and stood next to him in the cold on the balcony, shivering in her thin nightdress, not even looking at her when she put an arm around him.

"Aren't you cold?" she asked.

"No, not really."

"But it's freezing. Come back to bed."

"No. No, I don't want to." He turned away from her and stepped back through the window and, when she had followed him, closed it behind her. He turned away from the window but did not walk far before she caught him.

"Galer," she said, "Galer darling, what's wrong?"

"I don't know, not to say anyway."

"Are you still worrying? About that boy? About Nigel?"

He looked at her now. "Yes," he said.

"You mustn't go on, really you mustn't."

"He died, didn't he? He died and I should have prevented it."

"But you did everything possible; you did ten times as much as anyone else would have . . . anyone else *could* have done. It wasn't you at all, you know it wasn't."

But he only shook his head, pulled free of her hand on his arm, and walked away from her across the living-room.

2

Where to begin? Ladies and Gentlemen is a good place. But the self, I suppose, paramount reigns. Galer told me once that I was so self-conscious that I was almost invisible. I see everything so clearly from this little vantage place that I understand what he means; it is a kind of invisibility not to be able to act, even to speak, sometimes even to think, without detaching myself so far from the rest of me that the self floats away into the air like a balloon. Yet it is easier to speak what little truth I know now from that degree of detachment. How arrogant that sounds, said so coldly! But still I believe it. I must tell the truth, though I qualify it now as I would not have understood as a schoolboy – the truth as best I can, as I see it, with especial emphasis on 'I' – so that the limitation is 'I', not the nature of truth. Always the limitation, that 'I'.

I've known Galer Detheridge for fifteen or sixteen years. He is two years older than me, but because he had spent two years on National Service, we were contemporaries at Oxford. He had taken his first degree at a provincial university – Bristol, I think – and then came up to Trinity to read for a Diploma in Education. I had taken four years over my degree for much the same reason that I had avoided National Service; some time during my childhood my mother persuaded the family doctor that I suffered from what used to be called a 'nervous disorder' (in other words, that I was more or less permanently off my head). The Medical Board accepted it as sufficient reason to keep me out of the trenches, or whatever foulness they had in store for me; and of course I was delighted to have the excuse then. But in my third year of University when the pressure of exams became intolerable, I retreated from the childish disorder to a grown-up breakdown, which sent me to the Warneford for three months and delayed my finals for a year. Prophecy fulfilled.

I forget when we first met; it must have been at one of the champagne parties that our contemporaries gave after Schools. I knew that I had gone through comfortably and I was delighted to have survived without another breakdown. I had seen Galer around the college most of the year and I found myself talking to him. He listened, I talked. Within a few minutes I had established that he and I were both going to be suffering the Education Diploma the next year—at least, I called it suffering; I had no clear reason for wanting to be a teacher, except that the alternatives—business, advertising, public relations, one of the big corporations—were all god-awful, and of course the BBC, the higher civil service and the Foreign Service were out of my reach, god-awful too, away in the distance. Galer was a teacher with a vocation as large as a farmyard.

All the same, we became friends; I suppose that I needed friends badly then, because most of my contemporaries had already left Oxford and the few who were still around seemed distant, perhaps because they had been so embarrassed by my breakdown and its attendant lack of balance. I mean lack of balance literally; the material world seemed to take on some kind of vengeful hatred for me and kept on leaping out or up to hammer at me. So, when I reached up to take a book from the top shelf of the faculty library, the whole bookcase fell on me, and I thought that it had deliberately tried to kill me. So, I was walking along a road, and the whole world seemed suddenly to stand up on end in front of me, the road like a wall, and I went on walking straight into it. Onlookers probably thought that I was drunk or, if they were charitable, that I had tripped. But still the sensations was of the road rearing up to strike me, of the bookcase leaping down to crush me, and later, of the steering wheel twisting deliberately in my hands and plunging me at forty miles an hour straight into a high brick wall.

Anyway, I ended up, not in the Radcliffe, but in the Warneford, and though the doctors there taught me to see that what had gone wrong with the world was inside my head, not in the world outside, I kept, even when I was well, a sensory suspicion of the physical world that confirmed the old intellectual suspicion.

I don't suppose that Galer has once doubted the existence of the physical world. It's all there, waiting to be touched, held, cherished, and there's no question of it flying free. Partly it is because he is big, I guess; he can seldom feel threatened, certainly by people's bodies, and if he ever were, all he would need do is to stand up and let people see him. Or reach out and pick whoever it was up into the air, as if he were a ball that could be thrown or kicked or whatever variety of action Galer happened to feel like.

I saw him do that to two boys once; there were a couple of them fighting on the lawns outside the main school building and one of them was being hammered a little. Galer shouted across the lawn for them to stop; and the smaller boy tried to use the induced moment of hesitation to break away. But the other boy caught him again and threw him down on the grass. So Galer loped across the grass and, before the boys could get away, he grabbed both of them, one in each hand, and picked them both right off their feet, held them in the air for a moment or two, shook them, and then put them lightly down again. I don't suppose that I have ever seen a fight between two boys more effectively stopped; yet when Galer came back over the lawn again and saw me smiling, he apologised for the performance as if he were ashamed of it.

"I know I should explain to them," he said, "but it takes such a long time, and I just seem to act before I think. It's all wrong, of course."

CALL

I didn't have to ask why he thought it wrong; I had known for years that he felt that the stronger a person was, the more pacific he had to be, simply because he could do so much damage if he weren't—his assumption was that everyone was equally aggressive at heart, and the more effective one could be, the more careful one had to be. Because I am nearly as tall as he is, he pretends that I understand better than most people what he means; it's ridiculous, of course, but flattering, to belong to his coterie of the large aggressors who need to cultivate passivism.

I understand a little of it at least, what it is like to be large, I mean; Galer told me once that he didn't hear half of what most people said to him when he was standing up—they spoke to his chest, he said, and then supposed either that he was slightly deaf or too aloof to pay attention to them. It may be just an excuse for being aloof, though it's true that he likes to sit down to talk to people; I notice that he always sits down when he wants to talk to boys. I've developed an elegant aristocratic stoop myself to compensate for being tall; but I make myself stand straight to talk to Galer, because he can't help standing straight.

I don't mean that he flaunts his size; indeed, one doesn't notice how big he is, because he has a strange quality of self-effacement, or is it of merging into his background? I don't think I've ever seen him look uncomfortable in any kind of situation, whether it be a Lady Headmaster's ghastly polite sherry party for staff wives or the touch-line of a rugger field or even a Sixth Formers' dance. He's the kind of man, for instance, who never thinks about what he is going to wear, whatever the occasion, but who will always wear the right kind of thing; whereas I, faced with a social occasion, will spend an hour wondering what other people will wear and whether my choice will be the correct one—sometimes I will change two or three times while making up my mind and as often as not my choice will be ... well, not wrong, because I have thought, but just a little odd. I'll wear a suit where everyone else is wearing flannels and jackets, or a brightly coloured shirt when everyone else is soberly in white. Trivial, yes, but I will know and the edge of my enjoyment will be taken off in wondering what other people think of me. All except Galer, who would not notice, even if I attended a funeral in my underpants. Bless Galer.

Has a voice that sounds like a deep growl in the chest, very quiet, intended (I guess) to sound gentle but in fact threatening; the result is that he's not much good at teaching small boys, because he frightens them too much to get any spontaneous reaction from them. The older boys are better able to understand, though most of them still treat him very cautiously. I suppose it's the right kind of voice for Galer, the kind of voice a man might have who had been told once that he had a surprisingly light and high-pitched voice for so large a man and who decided at that moment to convert his voice to something that suited his size better. Not that Galer would function that way; that's my sort of explanation, Jenkyns the Self. Like the Amateur Dramatic version of a Welsh accent I adopt at times, though, see you, I have never been near my presumably ancestral home in my life. Galer of course always sticks to his own voice and talks the same way to everyone: the intellectual aristocrat defined; yet still there's something odd about the voice, though it suits him—something odd, almost as if every time he spoke he was a little surprised to find that he had a voice at all. Wordless man, Galer the gruff, distrustful of speech.

I suppose that the honest thing to say is that there are two or three people whom I have loved in my life; one of them is Galer. And of those two or three, he is the only one I have not bothered to deceive. I mean that very carefully because, in a traditional way, I have cheated him in many ways, the worst ways possible perhaps. Yet I say again that I have never needed to deceive him. And that I love him. Nor is this some kind of confession of a homosexual passion. In that sense, I love Skarfe a great deal more than I love Galer.

And he towards me? I don't think Galer ever thinks about me—I don't mean he does not regard me; perhaps he even loves me, but he almost never thinks about me. I'm just Jim Jenkyns, a friend, oldest friend perhaps, but only friend. Not brother, because that's different, nor son, nor son's image, as it was with Nigel. In his eyes I'm part of the world, like tree, or mountain. Jenkyns the rickety tree. Elm with no deep roots, that the wind will topple during the night. Or Jenkyns the Mole-Hill.

He was staying with me in my mother's house when the news about his father came. He had told me he hadn't ever seen the cathedral, and so I invited him to come for the weekend; on the Sunday a telegram called him back home and his father died later that week; somehow it seems to have made Galer think that I was special in his life, as if I was associated with his father. Only the chance of time, of course, but Galer doesn't work that way. Because I was there when he got the telegram, I understood—or so Galer seemed to think. If thinking is the right way to describe what Galer does in his head.

Actually, I suppose our friendship is odd. We are in so many ways different, yet it is the differences themselves which create the friendship, somehow: a sort of meeting of polarities. Not Lawrentian, of course—I'd hate to wrestle Galer, clothed or naked, not least because I'd break up in his hands—but still polarities. Dark he, fair me; mindless he, mindful me; wordless he, wordy me. Though the need is only mine, I suppose: I love, he accepts love.

And—or should it be 'but'?—who is this 'I', this limiting, asserting 'I'? My family name, as I've said, is Jenkyns, oh yes, with a 'y'; that's very significant, that 'y'. It means that the name is old, or rather that the family is old. How my mother used to stress that! J-E-N-K-Y- yes, Y, not I-N-S, she would spell it out at every genteel little shop where she opened her genteel little accounts, Jenkyns with a 'y', Mrs Raymond Jenkyns, as proudly as if Raymond Jenkyns had been the most magnificent land-owner in England, instead of a man who had inherited some land from his father and who had, before his death, managed it cautiously and sensibly, finally selling it to a Town Council for the building of three rows of suburban houses. I still get four hundred a year from that carefully nurtured capital, and how comfortable to be a teacher with a small private income!

My first name is officially John, though I am called Jim as often as I am called John. Jim/John Jenkyns. I'm still not sure where the Jim comes from; I think that it must be a relic of school, where someone probably muddled me up with a Jim Jenkins. With a small 'i'. A sloppy little jingle, Jim/John Jenkyns. Galer told me once that I had a habit of talking about myself in the third person and he asked if I sometimes thought of myself in the same way. You know: *Jim Jenkyns thinks*, not *I think*, or *John Jenkyns says*, not *I say*. True, very true. Jim/John Jenkyns says, True, very true. Not that the insight extends to himself or Skarfe. Nor did it to Nigel, for that matter. There it was all blind acceptance. So says Jim/John Jenkyns.

I was thinking in the third person long before Mailer made it respectable, Dark Night of the American Dream, or whatever, formidable sentence running to its scatological end, or is it eschatological? Never can remember the difference, scatology or eschatology, all points of final departure. But of course cisatlantic in my instance; Jenkyns gave up demonstrating at Oxford, gave up voting ten years ago—poor old England, Wales, Northern Ireland, and Scotland; what a loss of loss.

Passivity is all. How I anger Galer by that, always writing/ saying Passivist not "Pacifist". The Passivic Sea stretches from shore to shore. Holidays in Cornwall at Easter-tide and a deep growl in the chest. Concealing the passive. The passive is concealed.

Idiocy too: for instance, Galer has never learned to drive a car. Relies on me to drive him when he can't walk or go by train. Very convenient is my car, a relic of pre-war days that the boys call the Green Monster, with a maximum speed of 35 mph and a noise like a series of hand-grenades exploding. It diverts attention from me, does the Green Monster, and it serves its purpose of getting me from place to place. I told Galer once, more or less joking, that the only reason he and I were friends was that he needed a chauffeur. Not at all funny, I saw him react. Not funny, though being Galer he didn't try to refute my argument by defining reasons for our friendship; doesn't like things mechanical (including definitions) and that's deadly serious. Friendship he lets be, that's all. When his father died, he was inconsolable, almost mad. Perhaps that was what helped friendship to grow, because he saw in me a little of what might happen to him if he let himself loose for a moment. So he helped pick me up on his way back to being the first-born Detheridge.

Thus Galer ... Have I destroyed him? Has writing him down like that destroyed him? Has writing down that I love him destroyed love? Loved? Was loving? Am in the process of loving? Certainly, I know that he joined the staff at St Michaels because I was there. He went from his Dip. Ed. year at Oxford full of bright ideas and enthusiasms to Dornford's School in Shropshire; it had a reputation then of being one of the three or four really progressive schools in England, and Galer, being Galer, stuck it for five years – most of the other members of staff lasted a year at the longest, not necessarily because the ideas were all that wrong or because the pupils were more or less nasty than most pupils, but because the Headmaster was a religious megalomaniac. Galer told me once how the man settled business at staff meetings. Believing in the efficacy of prayer, whenever he had to face the staff with a difficult decision, he used to go into the meeting hall that served the school as chapel and pray for an hour or so, depending on the gravity of the decision. God would, of course, answer his prayers, and the Headmaster would go straight on into the staff meeting to tell them what the problem was and what God had advised him to do. It must have been bloody having to argue with God as well as a Headmaster.

Anyway, after five years, Galer wrote to me asking if I would ask the Headmaster of St Michaels–it was King Lyons the Headstrong who governed us in those days–if there was a job going. Lyons believed me when I said Galer was a brilliant teacher and, although there wasn't in fact a job going, he called in the Head of the History Department to tell him that his Department was understaffed and since he had the opportunity of getting a good new man, he was going to appoint Galer. Marvellous man in that way, Lyons was. He probably had a god-awful row with the Board of Governors for doing it, but he was scared of no one. So Galer joined the staff, as an additional History teacher with special responsibilities for the Sixth Form. Thank God for Galer. Bless Galer. Protect Galer. Though too late now, maybe ...

I suppose that I should have seen what was going to happen, the first part of it anyway. I knew Nigel Westcott and I knew his father. I should have been able to see what a combination of Galer and Nigel would do. I suppose that I did in a way see it, because, God help me, I sent Nigel to him in the first place. Galer, what he is or used to be; Nigel, what he is; old Father Westcott, what he will go on being. The stars, dear Brutus. Or the Furies perhaps. Eumenides rampant. The bookcase tumbling down around my half-educated confused head. Poor ambiguous Jim/John alliterative Jenkyns reports to the Eumenides...

3

Galer had heard about the boy before he met him; it was easy not to know all the boys in a school the size of St Michaels, but, because people in the common-room talked about the 'problems' especially, you often knew a certain amount about a difficult boy before you met him, sometimes knew about him even when you never once saw him consciously the whole of his time in the school. Nigel Westcott was one of these: "brilliant, quite brilliant", the senior English master would say, shaking his head sadly to show that the brilliance was unstable, and "a confounded nuisance", his tutor, Shafter, the Geography man, would reply, "always in trouble, always skipping classes and games, always in the wrong uniform", and gently Tremone, the very liberal French teacher, would murmur, "but such a charming boy, so charming, all the same, and so talented".

As usually happens, it was not so much the boy who was a 'problem' but his parents, or rather, his father, because his mother was dead and his stepmother left decisions to the father; and here even the most liberal member of staff agreed with the most reactionary, that old Adamson Westcott was almost impossible.

Yet, when the common room had been told that a son of Adamson Westcott was coming to St Michaels, there had been great excitement. Adamson Westcott was a social anthropologist of world reputation; his double-volumed work on the Bapedi, written when he was only twenty-four, was still a major authority, and his later work, on age-groupings in Central African tribes, was even more celebrated, because it was less technical and drew parallels with European society wherever possible. Recently, his work had begun "to acquire a certain wildness" as one academic reviewer put it; his almost mystical account of the relics of tribalism in modern British society had been greeted derisively by most academic historians and sociologists, but the Sunday newspapers vied madly with each other for the serialisation rights—for some of Westcott's ideas about sexual customs in particular were sensational—and so a great many people read at least some extracts from the work, and it was much discussed at dinner parties and in correspondence columns.

He was now an old man, in years at least, though he was on his fourth wife, and she was nearly forty years younger than him. His first wife had been a fellow anthropologist who had helped him with his study of the Bapedi and who had died of malaria with complications while they were in Central Africa; his second had been a doctor who had divorced him on grounds of his adultery two years after the marriage, when she was pregnant with their second child; as soon as the divorce became final, he had married the woman named as co-respondent in the divorce case—she was an actress, by all accounts very beautiful, who gave up her career for him (not a man to have a careerist wife was Westcott) and who, a year later, gave him his son, Nigel, and who then died. A year later Westcott married again, the young widow of a farmer who had been killed in a shooting accident; she had given him two stepdaughters and then had given him two more daughters and, perhaps more importantly to him, had given him a comfortable home on the farm which she had inherited from her husband and which she continued to run profitably—for she was a most competent woman—while Westcott got on with his research and writing.

Galer had met the old man only once, at a dinner party given by the Headmaster soon after Nigel joined the school. There were twenty or more people there, and Galer did not feel like joining the circle which paid court to the old man in the corner of the Headmaster's drawing-room. So he stood in the corner of the room, large and aloof, holding a drink but not drinking it, and refusing to talk to anyone, not even to Jim Jenkyns, who saw his mood and tried to drive him out of it by standing next to him and making salacious comments about the various women in the room. But, in the end, the old man, seeing the tall young man who was virtually the only person in the room who dared to ignore his presence—except his wife, who always talked about him as if he were deaf—standing alone in the corner, called him over and made him sit down next to him and, for the next hour, talked solely to him, despite the Headmaster's efforts to bring more people into the conversation. Not that it was really a conversation at all, for once Adamson Westcott had discovered that Galer was a teacher of History he launched into a monologue on the rise of capitalist ideas about the ownership of property, their foolishness, and the need to return to the direct democracy of the African tribes, by which his imagination had been caught when young and for always. At one stage Galer tried to argue with him, and got as far as calling the old man a romantic; but the old man would not listen, tore his remark down in a sentence or two, and went on hectoring and lecturing. Although Galer did not like the old man, he found himself drawn to him and even when he lost track of all the words upon words, the high-pitched emphatic voice with its passionate love of the past and loathing of the present stayed with him; he was not easy to like, despite his charm and directness, for his voice said plainly that the only thing in the world that mattered was what he thought and the only person who mattered was himself, but Galer found a magnificence in that even, and by the end of the evening was half-hoping that he might be invited to the Westcott's house, though no invitation came, then at any rate.

The next morning in the common-room the Headmaster asked Galer what he had thought of the 'guest . . . of honour' (he paused carefully to show that he was speaking ironically). "He was obviously very taken with you, Detheridge," said the Headmaster, smiling the compliment, for it was a compliment; but Galer ignored what he thought flattery and tried to explain the conflict in his feelings between admiration for the old man's vitality and disgust at his egocentricity. The Headmaster nodded and then, still smiling, said, "You know, all the time that those two were trying to charm my wife and me and the rest of us here, Adamson had a letter in his pocket which he gave me just as they were leaving, a real stinker of a letter about the futility of organised games and asking if his blessed Nigel might be excused from all games from the rest of his time here. D'you know the boy?"

Galer shook his head, but the Headmaster went on, "He's always in trouble and I bet he goes on being a trouble-maker throughout the school—but with that father who can blame him? Though I expect he's inherited his father's brains. I had the boy in my study this morning and asked him if he knew about his father's request. He said yes. So I asked him if he wanted to give up playing games; I made it clear, of course, that there was no question of his doing so, because we can't make exceptions for one boy unless we are prepared to make them for everyone." Galer knew that the apparent digression was intended especially for him, for although he spent almost every afternoon coaching rugger or cricket or tennis, he always argued vehemently for an end to compulsory games; he was about to say something but the Headmaster went on rapidly:

"Do you know what the boy replied? He said that he enjoyed games and was blowed if he was going to give them up. The truth is that the old man doesn't give a damn what the boy wants..." and, before Galer had time to reply, he turned away to repeat the story to another member of staff who had been there the evening before.

Standing in the middle of the common-room, drinking his mid-morning tea, and listening to the Headmaster, now with a group of staff gathered round him as he used Westcott's letter to demonstrate the dangers of allowing parents to have anything to do with the upbringing of their children, and remembering the old man's face, untidy grey hair and badly shaven cheeks, and the fanatical eyes as he had demonstrated the virtues of the past, Galer heard, out of the jumble of words and images, D'Arcy, the senior English master, who taught Nigel and knew the Westcott family, describe the old man. "Like an oak," he said. The image hurt. There came, drifting up on the tide of his mind, something his mother had said to him once about his father—"He's like a tree," she had said. "You can hold on to him. You can shelter there. He doesn't change, he just goes on growing stronger."

It was impossible not to compare his own dead father with this immortal; the image worked for both, yet his father had been ... well, loving, without any sense of self in his love, where this man was egocentric; oh, no doubt he was capable of love, where it was love on his own terms. His father had loved on wider terms, had been gentle to the point of stillness, to the point of letting his children run wild if they wanted to rather than trample down their independence. Oh, it was true that Adamson Westcott gave his son independence in some senses; he had heard Shafter say that when the boy was thirteen he had been allowed to go off to France for a holiday entirely on his own. But allowing a child to do whatever he wanted was not giving him the tools to use his own independence. No, thought Galer, if this was love, it was love without care.

* * *

Galer's early reactions were confirmed by what he heard of Nigel Westcott during his next few years in the school. Once, very late one night, his tutor was phoned by the police in Camberwell and asked if he would come and take the boy out of their cells; he had been picked up on suspicion of some offence, vagrancy or drunkenness, though the police told his tutor confidentially, and his tutor told the common-room loudly, that it was on suspicion of having drugs. It turned out that his father had gone off on a lecture tour of the States and that his stepmother had gone out for the evening, leaving the boy at home alone with his stepsisters, and he had decided that it was a good chance to try out the delights of South London. Once, he arrived at school one evening to see a play with a bottle of whisky in his pocket and nearly ruined the whole performance by trying to get the lead tight. Once, he told one of his French tutors that he was a "slimy little busybody" and, when haled before the Headmaster, repeated the description and defended himself by asserting that it was an accurate and hence permissible one. Galer secretly approved of this, because Nigel was quite right in his description.

Every summer, Nigel would go off travelling, still entirely on his own, to France, or Spain or Italy; he spoke French like a native and was reputed by Jim Jenkyns to know more Italian than he did himself, and over the summer he picked up a smattering of Spanish, German and even Swedish. But invariably, there would be trouble in the first week of the new term; Nigel would be found selling duty-free cigarettes he had brought back, or he would be handing round a collection of pornographic photographs, or he would simply be talking of his experiences in such a way that some poor master, overhearing, would feel constrained to report the matter to the Headmaster. Not Galer, of course, who liked to deal with such things on his own if he ever heard or saw them, or Jim Jenkyns, who satirised the school's fear of drugs, drink, sex and tobacco as the very worst evils a boy could fall into.

Certainly it was something marvellous that the expulsion that the Headmaster regularly threatened Nigel with was never fulfilled. But Nigel had three great advantages: he had charm (even Shafter, who loathed the boy for the trouble he caused, admitted this), he had great intelligence (he was, by common agreement, probably the brightest boy of his age-group in the school) and he was the son of a famous man. The first enabled him to take punishment gracefully, even, sometimes, to make masters feel that they were being very unkind to punish him at all; the second enabled him to calculate very carefully just how far he could go in trouble; and the third meant that the school wanted not to expel him if it could possibly avoid doing so.

All this Galer knew without ever having come across Nigel Westcott and indeed without being able to identify him. Then, one afternoon while Galer was sitting in his classroom after lessons for the day had ended, marking a pile of Upper Sixth essays that he had been avoiding for weeks, a boy had come in and had stood at Galer's desk waiting for him to finish the essay he was reading. Galer did not look up but signalled the boy to the bookcase to browse while he read the last page, scribbled a few comments down and the titles of three or four books that the essayist should use for further reference. Only then did he turn to the boy to ask what he wanted; he did not know him, though it was apparent from the blazer he wore that he was not in the Sixth Form yet.

"What can I do for you?" Galer asked.

"Mr Jenkyns sent me to you."

"Oh really," Galer smiled. "Why should he do that?" It

was a kind of game that he and Jim played on each other, sending boys between them, usually when for some reason or the other they were angry or bored with the particular boy.

"He said that you might be able to help me with a project that I am doing for English."

Blast Jim, thought Galer; here he was up to his eyes in work, and now Jim was loading more on to him. "What's your project about?" he asked.

"Names... the origin of names. Mr Jenkyns told me not to do place-names, but to look at Christian names and surnames. He gave me something from the *Golden Bough* as epigraph." Galer nodded but the boy went on, "About savages treating names as sacred..."

"I know the passage," Galer interrupted and stood up; he went over to the bookcase that stood behind his desk; he moved quickly along it, looking at the top shelf where he kept his reference books and, after a moment, spotted what he wanted and took it down. He checked that his name was written in the front of it, then handed it to the boy, saying as he did so, "You'll find a lot of material in that; it's *The Origin of English Surnames*. Let me have it back when you are finished with it and, if you don't mind, I'll just write its title and your name down so that..."

The boy interrupted him by handing the book back and saying, "It's all right; I've got a copy of it already – or rather my father has, and I use it. He's also got a *Dictionary of English Surnames* by the same man."

"Oh," said Galer, a little nonplussed. "If you've got that already, what do you want from me?"

"Well, actually, I wanted to know about your own name; and Mr Jenkyns said that your wife had an unusual name too. I looked up Detheridge, and I know about that; but it's really your first name I want to know about." The boy grinned at him across the desk. "If you don't mind, that is."

Galer smiled back at him. "Well, if I am going to tell you about my name, hadn't you better tell me yours first?" he said.

The boy did not smile now. "Westcott," he said. "Nigel Westcott. Son of Adamson Westcott."

"I know," Galer said. "I've met your father. Well . . ." He sat back in his chair and looked at the boy. He was tall, very thin, with dark hair that flopped over his forehead and around his ears; his mother's son, Galer guessed, the one who had been an actress, because no one would have guessed that this was Adamson Westcott's child. But hang on, he thought; if you looked more carefully, you could see it, there in the setting of the eyes and the shaping of the forehead. There was something of the look of his father there, not much, but something.

The boy looked back at Galer; he smiled lopsidedly, then said, "I don't look like my father, that's what you're thinking, isn't it?" Galer nodded and the boy went on, "My stepmother says that I look like my real mother used to; my father doesn't talk about her." He turned away from Galer's desk and wandered over to the bookcase to stand idly looking at the titles. "She was very beautiful," he went on after a moment or two. "I've been shown photographs of her." He turned round suddenly and grinned at Galer. "That isn't meant to mean that I think I'm beautiful."

Well, what does it mean, wondered Galer. No, not beautiful, too thin that face, too nervous those perpetually twisting hands. "Look," he said carefully. "I'm in a bit of a hurry and I've got an enormous amount of work to do; so why don't you sit down and let me answer your questions?" He was not in fact in any particular hurry but he had a sense that Nigel wanted to talk and he did not feel that he wanted to hear, not at that moment—he was tired, he did have work to do, and he had not seen Skarfe all day, because he had been dragged off to a meeting at lunch time. He was intrigued by the boy, yes, but he did not particularly want to make friends with him at this moment.

Nigel brought one of the chairs from behind the long table that served boys as a desk and sat down next to Galer's desk. "What I really want to know," he said, "is about your first name. It's Galer, isn't it?"

Galer nodded, then asked, "You know about my surname, do you?"

"Yes. I looked it up—it's sort of 'death-ridge' isn't it? Like a grave-yard on a hill or something. I thought I'd told you that."

"Yes, you did. It's something like that anyway," smiled Galer at the boy.

"And Galer?"

"Well, it's a puzzle really; my father told me once that it was a family name from way back—but as far as I know I've never come across it anywhere else, or in the family bible or anything like that."

"Have you really got a family bible with all the names of your family in?"

"No," said Galer. "I meant it as a metaphor. I mean that I've never come across it written down."

"And its meaning?" The boy had taken out a little notebook from his blazer pocket and was writing something into it.

"Again, I haven't a clue; I suppose that it may have started as a nickname originally—perhaps for a child who bawled the whole time, or for a windy, woffly man, but I think it may more probably have been a surname that someone used as a first name."

"That happens quite often, doesn't it?"

"Quite often. I think especially when a man wants to keep his mother's surname going. That's where my wife's name comes from."

"Mr Jenkyns says there is something funny about it. What is it?"

"I don't think it's particularly funny, though Jim Jenkyns has a different sense of humour to mine." Galer could not resist the crack at Jim, but the boy did not seem to notice, because he did not smile. "It's Skarfe," Galer went on and spelt it out to the boy. "It means 'cormorant'–her father's mother was from Scandinavia originally, and so she was named after that part of the family."

"I think it's a beautiful name," the boy said suddenly.

"So do I," said Galer, "but then I'm biased." The boy was beginning to interest him more and more, and especially the directness with which he spoke–how many boys would dare to use the word 'beautiful' as easily and freely as he did? He leaned back in his chair, swinging it back on its legs until the back touched the wall, and looked carefully at Nigel Westcott.

"Well," he said, "is that all?"

"No, actually; this is a question I'm asking everyone–can you tell me what names you are going to give your children when you have them?"

"That's simple," Galer replied. "My daughter will be Kimberley, after my own mother, and my son will be Unwen."

" 'Son born beyond hope'," the boy murmured.

"How do you know that?" exclaimed Galer, astonished.

"I don't know–it just came out," the boy said, looking as surprised as Galer was at what his mind had made him say. "I expect that I've heard my father say it, or read it somewhere."

"I didn't know that your father was a scholar of Anglo-Saxon as well as the other things."

"Unwen is Anglo-Saxon, is it? I must write it down. Well, it's most things with my father. He seems to know something about almost everything I've ever heard of."

"Almost everything," Galer probed, "almost everything, except . . ."

"Almost everything," the boy repeated and Galer left his question.

"What about that other name you mentioned?" the boy asked. "Kimberley, was that it? That's a place in Africa, isn't it? A diamond place, or is it gold?"

"Diamonds," said Galer. "Oh, that's just a bit of family history too. Shall I tell you the story?"

"If you want to."

"My mother's name was Kimberley. Her father, my grandfather–he was a greengrocer–went off to Africa during one of the diamond rushes, to make his fortune, he thought. He didn't of course; he died out there, of some disease, or hunger or something. The name is just about the only thing he left; his wife called the daughter who was born after he went away Kimberley; they had called the other children straightforward things like Alfred and James and . . . oh well, Nigel too, I suppose."

"Wasn't his wife angry with him for giving up greengroceries and pushing off like that? I mean, why did she call her daughter after what he was doing?"

"I don't know; perhaps she believed in what he was doing. I don't think he was much of a businessman–probably much better suited to being an adventurer than a greengrocer." Galer, looking across the desk at the boy, remembered clearly how much the story had appealed to him when he was a boy, how he had dressed it up for himself with details and excitement. How marvellous it had seemed then, to give up everyday things for the sake of a great final adventure. His mother had shown him a photograph once, and he could still remember the disappointment of seeing that ordinary man peering out of the past at him; he had expected someone massive, wild-eyed, with one of those great white beards and flowing hair, and all he had seen was a pleasant-faced man with short grey hair and blurred eyes. "You must get Mr Jenkyns to tell you all about the ideas of establishing a Utopia, you know, going away from everything mundane to make a new kind of life where everything will be perfect." That will pay Jim back, he thought, for sending this boy to me; yet he was grateful—there were things about the boy that he did not fully understand yet but that excited him. Yes, get Jim to tell him about the failures, and then later he would tell the boy himself that the real journeys were inside the mind, and that the new life would be found there as well as anywhere.

*   *   *

That had been the start. Once Galer had met Nigel Westcott, he seemed to see him everywhere. They would meet as Galer was leaving the common-room and would stop to exchange pleasantries; Nigel would tell Galer what he had discovered about Utopia, and Galer would ask how his project on names was getting on. Or Nigel would enquire if Galer had such and such a book, and they would walk back to Galer's classroom to find it or some other. Galer would be standing on the edge of the rugger pitch, exhorting the Ist XV forwards on to greater efforts and violence, and Nigel would come to stand next to him and ask questions about the quality of the game. Nigel would be watching the school play, and during the interval Galer would see him and would leave his wife for a minute or two to stroll over to ask Nigel what he thought of the performance. It was worthwhile talking to Nigel because he had the sophistication to talk to grown-ups on their terms; some of the staff hated this, because it threatened their authority, but Galer, who was never threatened, enjoyed the feeling—it was his ideal as a teacher that the taught and the teachers were both sharers in a process, rather than two sides in a battle.

Then, a year later, Nigel Westcott elected to take History as one of his major subjects in the Sixth Form and Galer, seeing his name on the list in the common-room, asked his Head of Department if Westcott might join his class rather than the parallel class that Fraser taught.

Nearly all his pupils regarded Galer as a very good teacher; certainly he seemed to get them through exams and regularly to university without spending every lesson dictating pre-digested notes or force-feeding them with facts or bullying for written work, but he knew, in a strict sense, he was not a teacher at all – he had one great quality, which was an ability to get his pupils to read on their own; and he was not self-conscious enough to realise that it was his own enthusiasm for his subject, an enthusiasm so strong that it would never allow him to suppose that any aspect of the subject might be boring, that made the boys willing to work for him. His own idea of his method was that he simply put his pupils together with interesting books and then left them to teach themselves, with a little guidance, it was true, but independently of his own judgement. Often he didn't teach a class as a class for weeks on end. He would suggest to each boy individually a subject which he might find worth exploring, would suggest a reading list, would lend the boy a pile of his own books, and then would leave the boy to get on on his own, until he was ready to come to his teacher for advice or until he himself realised that the boy was lost and needed help; but it was amazing how seldom the boys did get lost, for they knew that they were on their own, and they wanted to be independent of authority. Since he assumed their interest, he seemed to get it without effort; and since he assumed that no one would ever question his authority, he never had to raise his voice, never had to punish anyone, and very seldom had to tell a boy more than once that it was time he produced some written work to demonstrate the extent of his exploration. He was always slightly surprised when he heard that such and such a master had trouble in controlling his classes or in getting his pupils to work hard; but he had the grace to acknowledge that his methods as a teacher was only one method among many. It wouldn't, for instance, have worked for Jim Jenkyns, who liked to talk to his classes and liked them to talk and who seemed to remember almost everything he read; for Galer refused to clutter his memory with his subject, with the details of history—he had more important things to remember and he could always get what he had forgotten from a reference book; no, it was the sway and scope of history that mattered to him, not the details, it was the underlying themes and the constructed patterns, not the finite details. His pupils had to learn certain basic details for their exams, it was true (though a pity, when they could easily have taken reference books into exams with them), but it was not that which mattered in the end.

Still, his method seemed to work, even in exam results, and St Michaels was a sensible enough school to allow its staff their oddities of teaching method. So Galer, unlike the rest of the staff, was allowed a classroom to himself, and he made the classroom into his study, lined it with his books, and taught as a university teacher might. He was lucky too in that his first Headmaster at St Michaels, Lyons, had recognised that his innate sense of his own authority and his relaxation with the boys made him an ideal man to take a special interest in Sixth Formers, and he was not only given his classroom-study in the new Sixth Form Studies Centre, but after his marriage, was offered by Lyons's successor the flat on the third floor of the Studies Centre. That meant that he could use his classroom as his study during the evening as well as during teaching time, as if his classroom were part of his private home. So, if ever Galer wanted to speak privately to one of his pupils during class-time, he would take the boy upstairs to his sitting-room and would ask Skarfe to bring them in a couple of cups of coffee, while the rest of the class went on reading downstairs (which they usually did, because Galer believed that they always would). So too in the evenings when Galer had work to do, Skarfe would often come downstairs to his classroom and would sit at one of the pupil's tables reading or writing letters or mending clothes, while Galer sat at his desk preparing new topics and reading-lists or reading new books and re-reading old ones, or marking essays – for the drawback of his system was that it meant that he had an enormous amount of marking to do, since no time was dissipated in talk. So too, in the summer Galer and Skarfe would have the use of the old walled garden that was the only survival of the Victorian building that had stood on the site of the Studies Centre; and they never had to waste time looking after its lawns and flower-beds or pruning the flowering shrubs that stood under the old brick walls or even sweeping up the leaves that fell from the oaks and elms at the bottom of the garden. It was, Galer believed, an ideal arrangement; and Skarfe, who knew that he needed to work like that, so that home and work were united, never voiced her occasional feeling that she was married to a man who was so thoroughly a teacher that he hardly had time to be a husband. Most of the time Galer didn't even seem to notice whether she was there or not; but she loved him, and he was a passionate man who needed to work passionately.

4

At one point along the footpath over the rocks at the far end of the beach there had been a small landslide, and Galer had to scramble a little way up the cliff and then around the loose rocks and pebbles to get past. After that there was no obstacle for half a mile or more, and he let the path lead him on over the slow rise and fall of the cliff top, where the sea curved beautifully and dangerously below him, and the fields curved safely and greenly above.

He had walked the first part of the afternoon very quickly and had made his first stage, the sheltered beach, in half an hour less than the day before. He had been a little tired but exultant, as if he had taken half an hour of his life back from death; but now he was on new ground. Today was better than it had been all holiday; the wind had almost dropped and had hardly the force to stir the cliff-top grass left unmown from the summer before, and the sun, if not quite shining, was at least visible through the thin clouds – a day to be savoured carefully. Yet he was not tempted to find somewhere to sit and watch the sea curving and edging below him; he had stopped already on the beach for longer than he had intended and now he wanted to keep moving for at least another half hour. The headland was clear of mist today; in a mile or so he would have reached a point high enough to be able to see the whole way around the coast to the headland. If it were possible, if there were not some stream or gully cutting into the coast line and diverting the footpath miles inland, he would, before the holiday was over, walk the whole way round to the headland; he was determined to do that – it would probably take him most of a day but he had already told Skarfe that he would like to spend a whole day walking on his own.

He would have got further today if he had not stopped on the beach. He had needed to rest for a moment or two, but he must have stayed there nearly a quarter of an hour. Strange what had happened, he thought, yet not strange, for it suited his mood these days. He had been about to begin his climb up the footpath to where the landslide had obscured the path when, suddenly, without thinking, he had stopped to pick out of the thousands lying there half buried in the sand one particular stone, round, smooth, mottled white and grey, quartz perhaps, tumbled smooth. Why do that, he had thought, even as he did it. So many actions now turned out to be repetitions of the past; could he remember doing this before? He had shut his eyes carefully and had cupped the stone in his hands as if it had been alive, a bird say, something that suffered and needed comfort. He could feel the difference in temperature between the sun-warmed top and the sand-cold underneath; yet this too he knew must come from memory, because he had been taught to recognise the difference. He searched back into the past for a start to the pattern, and then it was suddenly easy. It must have been his father. He must have done this to amuse or educate a child, to explain the working of the world and the warmth of the sun, the nature of light and dark. That was the story, yes, for the pattern started there always. He could put that carefully back in his memory now, where it would be easily accessible, where it would obscure what was not important.

But what had his father done then? Had he turned to throw the stone across the beach, a high lofted throw across the waves and into the smooth curve before the breakers began? Had he explained that it would not, in time, make any difference, since the stone would complete its journey again, in a week or in a year or in a century? Or had he put the stone back into its little hollow in the sand, carefully?

Galer had shut his eyes again then and had tried to remember, but there was nothing there, no story, not even to be guessed at, nothing except the memory of a tall man bending over his first-born son and that voice, explaining carefully. So Galer had spoken aloud to the stone, ironically yes, because he was not mad and knew that the stone could not hear and would not, in any case, reply, but seriously too, just in case it did reply. "Well, stone," he said aloud, "do you remember now that I remind you? Did he treat you as sacred too?" He listened, but there was no reply. He hesitated for a moment, not sure himself what to do with the stone, whether to throw it back to its home in the water—and what would it say there?—or return it to the home it had made in the sand. He looked down at the sand again, then at the sea and, as if he had made up his mind, slowly fitted the stone back into its place.

Yards away, in the first slight breath of wind above the shelter of the beach, he had stopped and half-turned back. Wait, he thought; wait, and hear if it speaks now. But he could hear nothing except the wind and the slight grass moving and, below him now, the breakers; the footpath drew him up to the cliff-top and into the open again. Tomorrow, he thought, he would understand more. Tomorrow he would understand better what had not changed. Stones did not speak, however much you wanted to hear them.

Of course, many things did not change; some things were simply there, fixed, definite, and there was no going back over them searching for a change. For instance, his father was dead. For instance, Nigel was dead. Perhaps if he had loved them more they would not have died. Perhaps if you wanted enough to hear a stone speak, it would. Skarfe was wrong about that; he had not done enough for Nigel and of course she did not understand about his father's death; she couldn't understand, even if he were able to tell her what his father had said during those hours before he died. Why, he had not even been able to tell his brother Harry that. It had to be a secret between him and his dead father, just as what had passed between Nigel and him had to be a secret; yet it had to be put out of mind too, where it would not destroy. He had loved both of them, and perhaps if he had loved better he would have understood better; perhaps if he had understood better, he could have held off death for a time, even if only for half an hour.

Yet Galer did not, today, feel the kind of misery that had driven him from his bed two mornings before; he was content with what he had decided to remember. True, his father was dead. True, Nigel was dead. But he had loved them part of the way at least; that had been the only action possible and though it might be as unsure as breathing itself, it would not undo any man's death. He would have to learn to be content with what he had – to love better, but to be content.

There were times when Galer had, in the sense that a tree must have a vision of its own roots, a vision of what lay below the surface of his own consciousness – you could not know it, because you could not be conscious of it, nor could you translate it into symbols as you did in a dream, but you could feel it, as if giant sliding doors had been drawn back and you were peering down into that apparent darkness; and then, in splashes and flashes of light, you could see the leaping and writhing things that appeared and melted and fused and separated, like dancers in hell; except that it was heaven as well as hell down there, for some of the things were in ecstasy, some in agony, some asleep, some drunk, some icy-closed, some open and as warm in their colour as the flowers of an enormous rhododendron tree. There were things down there which could not be remembered, which you did not dare to remember, but there all the same; out of the range of words, senses, the feelings of everyday; but there.

You would peer down through the great unshuttered doors

and stare down, aware that 'you' were somewhere down there, but not the 'you' whom other people looked at and called Galer Detheridge, rather a 'you' who was a dance of the things, a temporary glittering agonising ecstatic dance of separation and fusion, flowers and ice.

Yet far below all that unknown, there was a known; but a known that was terrible, a great drum that beat out the sound of your own birth and death and re-birth, ancestral knowledge, knowledge of the flimsy self, knowledge of children unborn, great grandchildren unborn, a drum that beat too slow for dancing, too slow for marching, that beat more slowly than an athlete's heart, yet more strongly and certainly than the pulse itself. Terrible yes, but not terrifying, because it was there and could not be prevented.

Then he would draw back and, almost by an effort of will, force the doors to slide closed again. It was not a place to live, down there, because it transcended choice and action; it moved, yes, it moved continually, but it was also totally passive. Passivity made it almost a temptation—but it was not available, however attractive it was, because you did not choose to give up consciousness. Consciousness was as necessary as action.

So he would walk; he would let the footpath lead him on over the cliffs and eventually round to that massive headland. He would let his legs drive him forward, over the sheep-paths and the tangle of bracken, around fallen rocks and over half-broken wooden stiles, until it seemed almost that his body was working quite separately of his will, a great driving body that ignored time and distance and let every step dominate the next. This was what it was to be complete in your own power, so that it was no longer a matter of control, no longer the body doing what it was told, but the body totally alive. There was no thought here, no memory, no father walking in front to remind him of the way, no friend behind him to call out, *Beware, Galer, the soil there is loose.* His wife was back at the cottage in the village, sitting out on the balcony probably, reading or looking at the gulls wheeling and the cormorants diving, and every pace drove him outwards, complete in his own strength. Nor was here any muddle with purpose; it did not matter how far you went, you were not walking to keep healthy, to find peace of mind, or to reach any target now; you were beyond purpose, because this was its own purpose, the path leading the body onwards, the body its own purpose.

5

My own father died when I was four. People say that what happens in the first five years is all important; and of course if I say that I don't remember it may mean nothing, because whatever having a father for four years and lacking him for the rest of my childhood – indeed, for the rest of my life – did mean, it would have meant to my unconscious mind. Now, I don't have any evidence that I don't have an unconscious and therefore I should, I suppose, assume that I have. But I have decided to assume that I don't; and anyway I can't know – by definition – what happens in my own unconscious. Nor am I an adept at remembering what I dream, so even that source is cut off from me, which is, in my terms, my self. So I don't know what not having a father for most of my life meant to me. Pointless to wonder, you see, what Jenkyns Jim/John might have been in another kind of life.

I do know what having a mother meant. I don't know how long it takes a body to corrupt in the ground, but I guess that five years is long enough for ash to become part of the earth again. My mother was burnt–dead, of course–and so became ash, which is now . . . how does it go? 'A small quantity of Christian dust.' And I shan't live to see it resurrected. Neither really nor symbolically. She tried so hard to be father as well as mother; she asked all the right questions, she told me all the right things at the right times, and it made not a damn difference. Would it have changed if she had remarried? Would she have remarried if I had not been around? I don't know, but I bet that she thought very carefully about it simply because I was around. To give me another father. But weighing it up, she must have decided that a stepfather might be as disastrous as no father. Probably had no candidate either. But, all the same, fruitless to wonder what I might have been if my father had not died or if my mother had married again. I am (ho, ho, Jah) what I am. Jim/John Jenkyns. What's in a name? My self. Nothing more, nothing less.

Galer, unlike me, is both more and less than himself. It's his great strength and his great weakness, nice moral names. I do wish that I had known his father, the great John, not because it could have given me what I may have lacked, but so that I had another way to judge him than his sons' opinion. Opinion, I say? Hardly the right word. Vision is more like it. Matthew Arnold in that long graveyard piece had nothing on Galer Detheridge. We must have talked about that vision early on, because I have lived with it a long time; and again I don't mean that we discussed–Galer doesn't discuss visions, he doesn't even tell you them, he assumes that you see them because he does. Galer and his blessed father. But of what he was like before he was filtered through his son's mind I have little idea, though, of course, I do have some, because the stories haven't always been word for word–wordless for wordless–the same; and I have heard the other brother talking too. Harry Detheridge, that's his name. The Canadian brother. A doctor of some kind, not a G.P., but something to do with research. Obviously prosperous and probably more intelligent than Galer in most ways, even though he is a scientist. I heard them talking about their father once, not that it was the talking that mattered, just the way they looked at each other before and after they talked; and anyone could see that, inside them, they were just the same. Let me reconstruct the memory. Filtered through my own mind, of course: one way of looking at a father, so to say.

Harry had come down to St Michaels to stay with Galer for a couple of days; he was over from Canada, not on holiday, but on a course of some kind at the Medical Research Institute in London, something to do with new techniques of statistical analysis, I seem to remember. That was before Galer married, in the days when we lived next to each other in the bachelors' quarters. Harry was sleeping on a divan in Galer's study and he said it was so uncomfortable that he had to be drunk before he could sleep. So the three of us went off to a shining pub in Burston and we talked—good talk it was, Galer talking because his brother was there and understanding what he had to say almost before he said it, Harry talking, and Jenkyns being himself. In other words, I was playing the Welsh nationalist that night, talking about the continuing imperialism of bloody England, and Galer and Harry were being serious and intelligent about the colonial past and the post-colonial present. Until a man and wife called Peter and Sally Ladnum came in; Peter Ladnum was on the science side at St Michaels, a physicist or something like that, an enthusiastic young man who believed that everyone should know the difference between vectors and velocity and who thought I was joking when I said that his subject was a waste of time; Galer and Harry could understand his language, of course. Sally, the wife, was a former teacher of Physical Education, whatever that is; a pretty girl whose body and mind seemed to have been formed solely on the trampoline. They had just had their first baby, however, and their topics of conversation had changed: now it was all baby and what it was like to be parents. Anyway, when they came in, I groaned, Harry smiled – she was a very pretty girl until you talked to her – and Galer invited them to join us. I suppose that he felt he had to, because they looked a little lost in that shining pub. We went on talking about imperial England for a while, but then Harry obviously thought that he would have a go at entertaining the pretty girl on his right and began to engage her in conversation. And so to baby . . . poor bloke, he couldn't have had the slightest conception of what he was letting himself in for.

Baby, then; everything about baby, not the details of conception of course – they might have been interesting, perhaps – but from parturition onwards. Everything, in colourful detail. And so to the big statements. Said the young lady. "You have no idea, you can't have, without children of your own, what it is like to know that you have someone who is going to depend on you almost entirely for the next fifteen years, longer perhaps – to know that you have almost sole responsibility for his happiness, that you – us, I mean," turning to her proudly smiling husband, "absolutely hold that child's future in your hands..." Or words to that effect.

"Yes," interrupted proud young husband, "yes. It's only when you have a baby of your own that you realise how important the happiness of your marriage is going to be, not just for yourselves, I mean, but for the baby . . ." And so on *ad nauseam.*

I was just casting about for a way to get us back to more unnatural topics when Harry spoke. "You don't think that a child can have too much happiness when he is young?" he said gently; and if they hadn't been such fools they would have realised how dangerous Detheridge gentleness really is.

"No, of course not," Sally said. "How can that possibly be? I mean, there's no such thing as too much happiness..."

"For a child," Peter Ladnum added; he at least had the sense to keep the conversation away from abstract philosophy.

"Balls," said Harry. "Nonsense. Codswallop. Crap." Poor Peter, I don't suppose that he was used to people using words like that to his pretty little wife, and he looked darkly across the table at Harry. But being a physicist, he must have realised that to flare up at a man six inches taller than you and five stone heavier—for Harry is nearly as big as Galer— might be foolish. Still, Harry was a gentleman, and said, "Sorry, Sally, but it is nonsense. Of course I'm not saying that you should deliberately make a child unhappy, but they can have too much happiness."

"You mean the old silliness," Peter said, leaning forward, fierce in his desire to protect his wife, "the old stupidity of thinking that because most great men had unhappy childhoods, if you want your child to be great, treat him badly and make him unhappy..."

"Oh, for God's sake," Harry interrupted, "of course not. I'm not as stupid as I look. Unhappiness damages people; but too much happiness damages them too."

"Well, balls back to you," said Sally bravely.

"No," said Harry, "you don't understand." He was passionately involved now, determined to make this young man and wife see what he meant; he knew that Galer understood, and I suppose that he assumed that because I had known Galer for years I would understand too. I did too; I hadn't heard Galer ever say it, but I knew it already, I knew it simply because I could see Galer's face, looking gravely across the table at his clever young brother. "You see," Harry said, "if someone is too happy when he is young, if he loves his parents too much, it destroys him later on—destroys him in some ways, at least; because he is always looking for the same happiness, a model happiness, but it's a model, and it's in the past, and so you can't ever re-create it exactly. Because the people are different, because society is different, because the world changes around you." But Sally and Peter Ladnum, loving each other, loving the baby that lay in its cot at home, cared for by the loving grandmother, would not or could not believe him; and perhaps they were right not to, because Harry was making his own life, Galer's life, into a universal experience. But the Detheridge brothers were no good at seeing their own limitations, and so he turned to Galer for confirmation. "Aren't I right, Galer? Isn't what I say true?"

I knew Galer and I could see that he agreed; but he sat quiet for a long time before he replied. That's one of Galer's qualities; when you speak to him, and he doesn't reply, you usually know that it's not because he hasn't heard you or because he is being deliberately rude in not answering, but because he is trying to find the right words before he says them. Oh, he's articulate enough at times, but he's articulate slowly. I know him, you see, and I knew what he was thinking at that moment, as well as I know my own name: yes, his brother was right, you could have too much happiness too soon, and if it was given to you, if you didn't have to fight for it, if you didn't have to create your own happiness, you would spend the rest of your life dissatisfied with your own creations. Make heaven a place in the past, and the future was not only dark but impossible, because the future could not re-create the past. Yet how to explain to these stupid, earnest and loving people? How to explain the damage that had already been done and that the future would only compound?

Waiting for Galer to answer his brother, I saw the pub around us come alive again; it is one of those places where every surface is a mirror, either actual or so brightly polished that it reflects. So there always seems to be twice as much as there actually is, twice as many people, brightly coloured bottles, shining glasses, silver rails, barmen, boozers, girls in short skirts and bright jerseys, and twice as many reflections too, for that matter—appearance so much more magnificently multiplied than reality. Even voices seem to rebound off the bright surfaces, loud glass and silver, and the double doors rock heavily as double people come in and out.

"Look," said Galer, deeply in his chest, turning back to brother, friend and acquaintances. "You can't be certain; Harry and I, and the rest of our particular family, we just guess. You simply have to guess. But all of us believe, in ourselves, that we suffer from an excess of father. I don't mean that we don't love him; I mean the opposite, that we loved him too much. Perhaps because there was too much of him. Too much because it makes it so much more difficult to love other people, at least in terms of what they think love is . . ." Not articulate, you see, but if you listened, you got the point.

"But domination isn't love," Peter interrupted him, poor Peter in his moral clichés. "If your father dominated you . . ."

"Oh, no, he didn't, you see," Harry came in to defend Galer. It didn't really matter whether it was Galer or Harry who spoke, because their minds were working totally as one. This they knew, this they had lived through—were living through—this linked them in a way that no one would ever break. "He didn't dominate us at all; he gave us all the independence we wanted. We didn't want to be independent from him; we loved him too much. It wasn't that he dominated us, he dominated everyone, everything. Sort of like a god . . ."

"Yes," said Galer, and he meant "Enough, Harry," as well as "yes". You couldn't go any further than that, you see; if your father was "sort of like a god", you were the Sons of God. It's all been written down somewhere else, about the Sons of God and the Sons of Men. In the end, speech fails between them—no, I should say between us, because I know that I am a son of man. Without capital letters. I can talk to my own kind until kingdom come, and perhaps then I shall have speech with the others. At the moment I have love without words. One day perhaps, out of this place ... From the face of the earth, they said. But wrong, I tell you, wrong. From the face of the sons of men, perhaps, but only for a time.

The poor little Ladnums; they were lost in all that silence, Galer looking across the table to his brother, Harry looking back, both without smiling, the men of stone, like reflections in that bright room. And Jim/John Jenkyns, double-named Jenkyns, floating there, a neat little self with too much apprehension. Peter Ladnum tried to argue more; but Galer put him down gruffly, and I, to save myself and the others, began to tell a series of very dirty stories, which Harry laughed politely at and Galer ignored, and soon Peter took his pretty little trampoline away to feed their safe child. He didn't last long at St Michaels, poor Peter; ambition drove him to a Head of Department job at a grammar school in some city, where Sally breeds happily in the suburbs and Peter trampolines her once a night and twice on Sundays. I forgive them much, even their safe little loving, for the sake of what they enabled me to see that night.

Over the years that I have known Galer, I have gradually built up a biography of his father; it has taken a long time, because Galer talks about him as if everyone must have known him, and so the facts come few and far between. Of course, in one way Galer is quite right not to dwell on the facts; it's the image that matters, the vision of the man in his children's minds. But to the rest of us – ordinary mortals as we are – the facts remain.

John – *Johann*, 'Jah is gracious' – Detheridge must have been born round about 1890; at least, I know that he was a bit over forty when Galer was born, and I know that that was in

1932. He was the son of a farm labourer, or perhaps a smallholder, in the Cotswolds. Galer's grandparents died long before he was born, and I don't think he knows much about them; or if he does, he doesn't speak about what he knows, though he has talked once or twice about the "eleven known generations" of his family. But the closeness to the land is there, in his past, and he knows that and respects that; if, say, he knew that they had been illiterate, he would be proud of it, not out of inverted snobbery, but because it would help show how unimportant words were. Anyway, Father Detheridge was one of the young men who are made by wars; you always hear about the young men who are killed, seldom about the young men who are made—many less of them, of course, but still . . . Anyway, when the war started, John Detheridge was in his early twenties, an almost illiterate big-booted young farmer, and by the end he was something of a hero, held a commission, and had learned a great deal about men and books. Yes, books. You see, he joined up very early on, went to France, was wounded quite badly within a week or two, was shipped back to England, and somehow got himself attached to the Army Education Corps. In what capacity isn't quite clear, but certainly not as a safe billet, because he went back to France in 1916. I suppose that he must have been a very early version of the Psychological Warfare species, because he had the job of delivering books to the men in the trenches, carefully chosen books no doubt, Galsworthy and early Kipling, as well as the great masters, and he did his work so well that he was three times mentioned in dispatches and even got himself an MC or something like that, because on one of his delivery rounds he found himself involved in a battle and did a great deal of damage to the enemy. I suppose that a Galsworthy or a Dickens at a range of three feet can be a pretty deadly weapon, especially in the hands of a Detheridge. Or perhaps he borrowed a rifle.

CALL

Anyway, John Detheridge ended the war as something of a hero and with a commission; in between battles and deliveries he must have found time to read a good many of his own goods, and after the war he stayed on in the Education Corps. When he left it, in the mid-twenties it must have been, it was as a captain or major—I've heard both from Galer—and he went straight into a fairly senior post in the administration of adult education in the north. Came the depression, and John Detheridge threw up his job to work with the hunger-marchers. God knows exactly what he did, but a good many of the specific histories of those times, especially if they were written by participants, find room for a mention or two of him; from the sound of those, and from what Galer has told me, he was teacher, doctor, priest, cook, scavenger, agitator, politician, demagogue, the lot, and somewhere in the middle of all that he found time to marry—he was over forty then—and in 1932 Galer was born. John Detheridge went back to adult education at round about the same time, though he went on working with the labour movements, and he stayed on until 1936 or '7, when he was sacked, I gather mainly because he turned his office as well as his home into a sort of headquarters-hospital-school for the anti-Mosleyites; the Detheridges were living in the East End by then. Galer has told me that one of his earliest memories is of a gang of Mosley thugs throwing rocks through the windows of their house in the East End, and he, Harry and his mother lying under the dining-room table in terror until Father Detheridge, waving the pickaxe handle which one of his young men had left behind, charged out into the street and drove them away. Judging by his sons, he must have been a good man to run away from, a terrifyingly big man, damn near six and a half feet of him, with the hands and feet and shoulders of a farm labourer, and a great angry mop of grey hair. I've seen a photograph of him that Galer keeps carefully upstairs; it must have been taken at about this time—there's a group of men, some of them carrying their pickaxe handles, some Jews I would guess, some earnest young men from the universities, some workers, and in the middle of the unlikely mob towers the Detheridge—oh, there's no mistaking that head, those wide-set eyes and enormous jagged jawline, Detheridge archetypal.

Anyway again, when the war with the Nazis began, his anti-Mosleyite sympathies and actions became respectable, and he was called back into the army and was set to work in the War Office. Again, I'm not sure exactly what he did; nor, I suspect, is Galer, but I think that it was something specifically to do with Psychological Warfare. At any rate, at the end of the war, he was appointed a member of the British section of the War Crimes Commission, and spent the next two years digging things up in France, Belgium, Austria, visiting the death-camps, reading the files of the SS and the Gestapo.

Galer doesn't talk about that part of his father's life, almost as if it were a blank. Yet it couldn't have been, because Galer has hinted at various things; there was a story about some Gestapo man he half-started to tell me once, but he dried up into wordlessness. I suppose it was simple really, John Detheridge proving to himself that at the heart of every man there was a darkness without limit. Someone else's words but he did find out something, at any rate, because in 1948, after his release from the army and the War Crimes Commission, he 'took orders' as an Anglican clergyman.

'Took orders' is a funny phrase for any Detheridge, but I suppose in the Anglican church the orders are so confused that it might be easier than elsewhere. His theological views at least must have been very odd, at least as far as one can judge them from what Galer says. At first he went back to the East End, but he was an ill man by then—not simply in his body; I rather think from a couple of hints that Galer has dropped that the experience on the Commission broke his heart as well as his health—and after a couple of years he was sent back to a country parish in the Cotswolds, back to near his beginnings. He died there in 1956, when Galer was twenty-four, Harry twenty-three, Jessica twenty, Mary ten and Sarah eight. Galer was staying with me just before his father died; I remember that well.

The next year, when Harry qualified, he emigrated to Canada, and Mrs Detheridge went with him, taking Mary and Sarah; Jessica stayed in England, married to a clergyman who lives in the wilds of Yorkshire; Galer visits them every Christmas, and Mrs Detheridge has been back once or twice to visit her daughter and her daughter's children, but I gather that she is getting a little ga-ga now, and can't travel. Certainly she didn't come back for Galer's wedding, though Harry and the two girls did.

In the end though, what do the facts matter? I may have got half of them wrong, or Galer may have mythologised about part of his father's life. That doesn't matter. What matters is what Galer sees now, these years after his father's death, the years before, although that massive body is now small dust in the dust of the Cotswolds; and I can't know what Galer knows, not simply because he won't tell me, but because it's all deep down there in the other parts of his mind. Oh, I can see signs; I can look at a photograph of John Detheridge and can see his son there, in every bone and hair and inch and sinew; and I can hear Galer turn on a small-minded colleague in the common room and say, "You are despicable", and I see old Detheridge rushing out into the street waving his pickaxe handle around his head and driving the louts down the street; and I can see Galer brooding over a history of modern Europe and I see not him but his father staring gravely at the bodies in a Gestapo grave, or at the clawed concrete ceiling of a gas chamber. But to know what happens, down there, where fathers are no longer men with biographies and habits and opinions and feelings, but are like great shadowy trees with roots that stretch up from light into yet more light . . . Galer's terms, those, not mine, because how can I, of all people, know that? Even if my own father had survived, could I have translated that sapling sufficiently to be able to say, "Home is a forest"? Yet I love Galer because he is a tree himself, massive, sheltering, deeply rooted; I stand in his shadow, and in the shadow of the forest of farmer, soldier, teacher and priest. Dead men too, the faces of those people I have seen in documentaries of the concentration camps; they became part of John Detheridge, broke his heart perhaps, and so they became part of his son, as I am a part of his son. Dead men, the SS and Gestapo, the clerks and the railway porters, everyone, God knows, because there they are part of his dream too.

And yet I was fool enough to send Nigel Westcott to him. Oh fool, foolish Jenkyns. It was a game we played with each other, Galer and I: we used to send boys–usually those we were bored or annoyed with–from one classroom to the other, carrying little notes to say things like: "In olden times the bearers of ill tidings or insults were executed for their temerity. This boy bears evil tidings . . ." Once we kept some loathsome boy whom I was meant to be teaching Latin to–gardening was more his line–busy for nearly three periods in a row, sending him backwards and forwards with the various stages of an argument in syllogisms. Poor boy, if he read the notes he must have been very worried about the state of his teachers, for the series began, "All schoolmasters are fools", and ended "Therefore most sheep walk backwards". Of course, I was allowed to cheat; Galer stuck to the rules. But you could never rely on Galer's mood; sometimes I would send a note across and the boy carrying it would bring it back to me to say, "Mr Detheridge is not in the mood, he says, Mr Jenkyns." So that was that, and for a week I would keep away from him, and then a note would come from him to say, "Will you please explain to the bearer of this note what the difference between threw and through is? Sincerely, Galer."

Because I would not make out that Galer was a ponderous humourless man; he was capable of a wild and manic humour, oh usually of the black variety, savage, satirical, cruel even. If he hadn't been that sometimes, God knows he would not have been able to take me, because I am that almost every day. But mine I know is defence, his is just fun. He thinks he needs no defences.

But still I sent Nigel to him. With an extract from the *Golden Bough* as my joke:

Unable to discriminate clearly between words and things, the savage commonly fancies that the link between a name and the person as a thing denominated by it is not a mere arbitrary and ideal association, but a real and substantial bond which unites the two in such a way that magic may be wrought on a man just as easily through his name as through his hair, his nails, or any other material part of his person. In fact, primitive man regards his name as a vital portion of himself and takes care of it accordingly.

Galer as primitive man, you see; which he is. And Nigel's father a great anthropologist. Hence a marvellous joke, with a pleasantly sharp edge. I know how holy Galer's name is to him, and I had met Nigel's father, the wild old wicked old Adamson Westcott, and I had been teaching Nigel most of the year. I had already recognised in him a kind of perverted version of what existed between Galer and his dead father. Yet when I sent him, I did it because I thought it might be amusing to confront those two and that quotation, and indeed there were times when it was, when Galer would come puzzling into the common room to repeat to me some outrageous remark that Nigel had made about Napoleon or Hitler or the present state of Africa or whatever. But I should have seen that there was something of myself in Nigel too, I should have seen that he was nothing more or less than another version of Jim/John Jenkyns as he had been when that wall reached across the road and smashed at my face and legs. But a long time ago, before I met Galer even, I made a decision to ignore what happens to me outside the area I have designated as my self; even if I have to make it smaller and smaller every year, it is an area which I know I can control, and the acreage outside my direct ownership can crop whatever it wishes, trees, weeds, grass, bramble, thorn, whatever. I don't care for it, that's all. Of course, it must affect my area of supervision, but I have decided to pretend that it doesn't. Control or despair. Or is it control and still despair? The psychologists can go stuff themselves, for all I care. Galer isn't like me; what happens down there is holy for him. But for people like Nigel and me, what happens there cannot be allowed to exist, because the moment it does, woe betide the watcher ... a different version of the sons of men, perhaps.

Anyway, I sent him to Galer as much for a joke as anything; and it became as serious as life itself to Galer. He took the boy under his capacious wing, and the boy watched and waited. Have you seen boys standing on a river bank watching swans? They look at all that power and beauty, and you can see them thinking, "Ah, what power, what beauty." But if a nasty man like Jim/John Jenkyns says to one of them, choosing the right one of course, "Here, lad, is a lovely big heavy knobbly rock; power and beauty too in this, and how well it fits your hand", and within ten seconds the rock will sail across the water and, if the swan isn't hit, you'll see it trying to fly, great wings beating at the water, head thrusting forward in strain, and the pathetic ugly little legs threshing at the surface of the water. If he isn't hit ...

But Skarfe too. Never forget the absurd beautiful Skarfe ...

One night, as I was walking back from the staff car-park—

CALL

I had been in the shining pub in Burston most of the evening – I saw that the light in Galer's classroom was still on. So I went in to see him and perhaps to take him away from his work to give me a cup of coffee. I didn't bother to knock – why should one knock at a classroom door? – but Galer looked at me as if I had walked into his bedroom. He was sitting in there with Nigel Westcott, talking. Oh, carefully I say that: talking. It's so easy in these days of consenting adults to think that a friendship between two men, or between a master and his pupil, is sexual; and perhaps it is, in the strict sense, but there is a mile gap between liking and laying. It was their talking that was sacred, to Galer at least. Soul talking to soul, he would have thought it, if he needed words. With a desk between them, and a pile of books that they had obviously abandoned an hour or two before, and a feeling of personal intimacies so strong in the room that for a moment I could almost imagine them as clouds of smoke around their heads. Galer's earnest head – and a look in Nigel's eyes when I came in that said, "Mine, old Jenkyns, mine: no longer yours – you bugger off, old man; I've got him now..."

I couldn't stay there, of course; Galer with Nigel was complete, and I was an unwelcome temporary stranger. So I went upstairs to the flat, to see Skarfe. She was sitting in their lounge, with a newspaper on the floor next to her, a pile of mending on the floor on the other side of her, and a book closed on her lap. She didn't get up when I came in.

"If you want Galer," she said, "he's downstairs, with a boy – Nigel Westcott." She held back some word at the end of her sentence; I guess that it was "again".

"I know," said sympathetic Jim/John Jenkyns. "But I've come to have coffee with you."

She jumped up from her chair. Almost kissed me, I guess. A very little wealth and some ill-health, but Jenny jumping from her chair. "Good," she said, "good." And smiled.

71

When I first met Skarfe, when Galer brought her proudly to my rooms at the beginning of one term three, no, four years ago to tell me that this was the girl he was going to marry, I thought that she was ugly. By the middle of that first evening with her I had decided that she was almost beautiful, and by the end of the evening I had fixed her as ugly again. She told me once, in a flash of confidence, that her nickname at school had been Giraffe. Skarfe/Giraffe: the rhyme of course. But it was more apt than most nicknames: long thin legs, a heavy body – big-breasted, wide-hipped – long thin arms ('arms both long and small', I remember), a most elegant lovely neck, curving, shining, shadowy secret below the chin and where the long fair hair fell on her neck and shoulders; but again the head a little too small for the body and the neck, and the mouth too big for the nose, but the eyes Egyptian, dark. Dark and fair she, all lack of proportion. Yet when she began to move, she had the same absurd, clumsy, graceless gracefulness that a giraffe running has; and somehow all the lack of proportion became harmonious. She should have been absurdly ugly, yet moving she was absurdly lovely. Harmonious, especially when she moved.

She was much younger than Galer; she had only just left her provincial university when he married her. She was very much the youngest of a big family, three brothers, two sisters, the children of a country solicitor from near Lancaster, old friends of the Detheridge family since before the war. She had taken a degree in – of all things – Botany, and for her first two years as Galer's wife had acted as part-time lab. assistant in the school Biology labs. But she had no real interest in her subject and soon gave up the job to concentrate on the wifely arts. She had known Galer's father when she was a young girl and perhaps she thought that Galer would love her as well as his father had loved everyone. Or as he seems to have loved everyone. For a year or two of the marriage, I suppose that she must have been one of the happiest people in England; she adored her husband, he was old enough to seem wise and kind, young enough to be her lover, and he adored his ugly/beautiful wife. On his own terms, of course. They both seemed to live in a haze of sensuality, those years; oh, not at all publicly, because Galer was the kind of man who wouldn't even hold hands in public – a thoroughly private sensuality, as if their marriage bed had been a perfect temple. Perhaps she thought that it would go on like that forever; perhaps she didn't want to have children too soon, in case the temple was violated; perhaps she didn't realise that what Galer loved was not Skarfe, the absurd and beautiful individual Skarfe, but 'his wife'. "My wife," he used to say, proudly. Not Skarfe, never Skarfe. Worshipped her with his body, yes, oh yes, because she was his wife and was going to be the mother of his children. But Skarfe as self wasn't important to him. In that way I don't suppose that she was as important to him as I was; she was adjunct, she was mate – Mrs Galer Detheridge, the other necessary half. Herself gathered into the larger self, the Detheridge self.

She must have had clues before Nigel; she must have begun to feel that Galer seldom talked to her, that he almost never told her about his teaching unless she asked, and then haltingly and briefly, that he never told her anything about the school, either of importance – what money was going where, how the school was going to react to legislation, and how the various parts of the school were functioning – or even gossip – who was having a baby, whose son had failed Common Entrance, whose wife had been over-spending, who had had a row with the Headmaster's wife, and who was not on speaking terms with whom. Skarfe relied on me for those things, the two of us gabbling trivialities to each other while Galer brooded over . . . whatever it is that Galer broods over. And perhaps I should have tried to do more than I did; perhaps I should not have waited so long before I acted, because when I did act it was only to protect, to comfort, to show her that she was still her own person... one way of putting it... because I could by then prevent nothing. Should I have told Galer what he was doing to... his wife? HIS wife? "MY wife," I can almost hear him say. No, that would have been impossible; that would have been, in Galer's terms, disloyal, and she loved him always enough to accept his terms. We could talk around the subject, we could even joke around the subject, but neither Skarfe nor I would have dared to talk about what we both knew.

"Coffee," Skarfe announced, coming back into the lounge with a tray. "Coffee for my visitor, Mr Jenkyns. Black, no sugar, you vain man," she said, pouring it out for me and then pouring her own and adding three large spoons of sugar. Absurd Skarfe, figure like a giraffe, name of a bird, water-bird, air and water bird, dark bird, never know where it will come next through the water.

"Tell me, Jim—I mean, Please, Mr Jenkyns, Please, can you advise me? I have this problem with Daddy, I mean My Father, Please, sir." Our boys have long since lost the habit of punctuating their sentences to the staff with "please" and "sir", but she must have been remembering her own schooldays.

"Well, young man," I joked back in a gruff schoolmasterish voice, "most young men of your age have problems of one kind or the other with their fathers..."

"But mine is a special problem, because it's mine," she piped back at me; she had the voice of that age wrong, but she was trying.

"Well, yes, young man," I said. "Freud. He has the answer. Read Freud. Here's my copy of *The Oedipus Complex and Other Stories of Love and Revenge*. My name's in the front, so make sure that you return it." That was cruel, I knew; but she probably wouldn't realise. I watched her eyes carefully, but she thought I was still in the arena of joke.

"Oooh, I can't read Freud. He's dirty, my Daddy says; my Daddy says he'll castrate me if he catches me reading Freud."

I was beginning to laugh. She was so clever in her absurdity. But the joke could go a stage further and I said, "Well, yes, young man. You must treat it as a source book. Read it critically; don't take the ideas as sacred. And if you have any trouble with your father, tell him to get in touch with me first."

Skarfe abandoned her schoolboy's voice and tried to put on Galer's. Deep in her chest she growled, "And I'd like to see that old man lay a finger on my . . ." and she blushed the word instead of saying it and began to laugh. We were still laughing minutes later, for she had so perfectly caught Galer's pretended anger, and looking across the room at her I realised, for the first time, that I could, if I cared to, get up from my chair, cross the room, take her hand, lift her from her chair, turn up her face to me and . . . whatever she, or I, had wanted. There it was, ready for the taking. For comfort, protection, whatever.

But we were still in our chairs, giggling at each other, when Galer came in a few moments later. He stood in the doorway of the lounge, enormous man, brooding, dark, angry in his desire and love. Oh yes, love; don't get me wrong, love for his wife, love for his friend, love for his pupil. But love in his terms, Detheridge love, larger than any one man, no matter how largely he could love.

"What are you two giggling about? Jim being salacious, I suppose," he said. He did not ask, he said, not needing an answer. He could not have dreamt for a moment that it was him that we laughed at. If it had been me coming into that room, I would have known for certain that it was me the people there laughed about, even if it hadn't been. "Is there any more coffee, darling?" he asked Skarfe and when she said that she would make more, he let himself drop into a chair and said, "God, I'm tired. Sorry to have been so long, but that boy is in a mess and I had to talk to him."

"What did you say?" Skarfe called from the kitchen.

"I said sorry that I am so late," he called back.

"It's all right," she answered through the door. "Jim and I have been gossiping." I wondered what she would have done if Galer had responded to her unspoken invitation to ask what the gossip had been. But she probably knew quite well by then that he never responded; gossip was out of his range.

So I in my turn asked what was wrong with Nigel. Did I say "now"? I don't remember, but I expect so.

"Oh, it's that bloody father of his: he's a menace, the old man. Oh, I suppose that we shouldn't blame him really; he's just too old and preoccupied to understand what he is doing to the boy." Galer got up from his chair as he finished speaking and walked over to the high window to look out through the curtains; he may have been looking to see if Nigel was still standing outside the Studies Centre, or he may have simply been looking out into the darkness.

"What kind of a mess?" I asked; I knew pretty well, because there was always talk in the common room about Nigel Westcott and his bloody father, though thank God, I was no longer trying to teach the boy. Oh, the trouble was trivial enough, thoroughly dependent on the fact that St Michaels was a fairly traditional English public school, but pile up enough trivia and you have a mountain, and even if Nigel had been in a heavenly school run democratically by a whole committee of A. S. Neills and Kurt Hahns he would have been in trouble. He wanted to be in trouble, you see.

So, Nigel would come to school dressed in jeans and sweater instead of the bloody silly be-suited or be-blazered uniform our boys are supposed to wear, and would say, when the duty master asked what the devil he thought he was, "My father told me to come like this; the fields are so muddy this morning that I wasn't to come in my suit, he said." So the master on duty would see the Headmaster and he would phone Nigel's father, who would say, "Of course I didn't tell that fool boy anything of the kind–but don't expect me to enforce your ridiculous rules about uniform..." and slam down the phone. The Headmaster would call Nigel from his classroom, and Nigel would swear blind that his father had forbidden him to wear his suit, and while the Headmaster was explaining to Nigel that whatever he or his father felt, the school did have certain rules about uniform, and if he wasn't prepared to honour them, he would have to... lo! a phone-call would come from Adamson Westcott to say that he had now remembered that he had said something the evening before to the boy, but had meant it as a joke, and would the Headmaster please punish the boy for having no sense of humour. So the Headmaster would tell Nigel what his father had said, and Nigel would storm and rage that it hadn't been a joke, and that it was grossly unfair for the school to get at him for obeying his father, and so on. He would not be punished.

And next morning he would appear, properly be-suited, but having made damn sure that on his way to school over the fields he had slipped in the mud at least twice... I remember that once I saw Nigel walking across the lawns in front of the main building, sauntering along, anxious to be noticed; he was wearing a light and splendid purple shirt–I mean distinctly purple. Then I saw the Headmaster, deep in conversation with the Bursar, come out of the school offices, look up, see Nigel there in all his purple glory, and I'll swear that the Headmaster turned tail and fled back again into the offices rather than have to deal with Nigel and his father again. He must have known exactly what would happen; he would ask Nigel what on earth he was doing dressed like that, and Nigel would say that he had had a choice of coming to school in a purple shirt or without a shirt at all because his mother had been too busy to do the washing that week. He would then phone Mrs Westcott to remonstrate, and would get the old man himself, for he answered all calls himself, unless one needed him urgently, when he would not talk at all on the phone; and if you ask him for Mrs Westcott, he says, high-pitched old liar, "She's in the fields; but I'll deal with it if you will tell me who you are." And there would be no point sending Nigel home, because that would mean a visit from the old man and two hours of futile argument. I know: I've taught Nigel, I've tried to phone Mrs Westcott, I've had Adamson Westcott call on me, and I know.

Of course, we should have sacked him. We should have sent him off to cause chaos at a place like Dornford's or Dartington or somewhere; but St Michaels is trying to establish a liberal reputation and so doesn't sack difficult boys, not unless they actually assault a staff member or molest a small boy or smoke pot in break or rape a local schoolgirl, or whatever. St Michaels is also trying to build up an academic reputation, and to sack the boy who is undoubtedly the brightest we have had while I have been here would be silly; for Nigel's mind is formidable; I taught him and I know. For eight months I could not get him to write a single essay or read a single set-work (though he read enough on his own to satisfy a polymath), despite every punishment I knew or could invent; then, a fortnight before the external exams, he came casually to me at the end of a lesson and asked for a list of all the set-works and the various other reading that I had recommended. I gave him the list, about twenty books in all, laying it on thick to show him what he had missed and that he hadn't a hope of catching up now. But, God help the righteous, he must have read a good many of them, either in a fortnight or before when my back was turned, because he was the only boy in the school who got a Grade 1 in both Language and Literature papers, and even a Nigel Westcott can't do that unless he has read the set-works. I gather from other staff that he did just the same to them. The unfairness is gross, but then we are making the unfairness of intelligence our guiding light in meritocratic Europe. Damn Nigel for having the supreme merit? Not bloody likely, cry the mongers of reputations, where Oxford and Cambridge scholarships are added up like the prices of cattle in a market. Jenkyns knows after all; wasn't he the only scholar of his year from Ely Grammar School? Wasn't that lauded by the staff? Wasn't Jenkyns delighted with his own merit?

But Nigel put the fear of God into me: there was a kind of sardonic look about him, as if he had looked clearly at the world and found it wanting. As if he had looked clearly at Jim/John Jenkyns and his larger friend, Galer Detheridge, and had found them wanting too. Bred on his father's largeness of mind, largeness of spirit, largeness of adventure? Hating them, fighting them, yet relying on them? Mocking, yet not the way I mock? Writhing, yet standing back from the writhing to enjoy it? I have a little classification scheme for human beings; it's as fallible as all schemes but it gives me my own kind of pleasure sometimes.

You know how you sometimes in a wood or beside a hedgerow find fledglings fallen out of nests; they hop and bleat under the trees or at the side of the road. Well, there are four or five kinds of people: those who stop to say, "Oh, look at the poor little thing; it's lost its mother. Oh dear, what shall we do?" Hundreds of them I know. Then there are those who pick it up and put it high on a branch of a tree and then go away quickly before it falls off again. I am one of them. Then there are those who pick it up and take it home and feed it and buy books on wild birds and keep it in the warmth of the kitchen – and ninety-nine times out of a hundred bury it in the garden. Skarfe is like that. And there are those who pick it up, say "Damn. Any sign of a nest?" and when the answer is "No", which it nearly always is, they turn their backs on the others and very quickly and cleanly wring the bird's neck, and drop it in the ditch. Galer is one of those. Thoughtful, often, in a strange way, and not callous at all. Nigel is another, though he might, in certain conditions, torture the bird, which really makes him into my fifth kind.

But Galer doesn't believe in that fifth kind. Because the really terrifying distinction between the fourth kind and the fifth is that there may not be a distinction at all; perhaps they are the same and we don't see the sameness. At least, I know that's what people like Galer think. I told him my classification scheme once, when I still believed in the difference between the fourth and fifth kind, and it was he who said that there wasn't a fifth kind at all. When he wrings that fledgling's neck, he says that he knows that inside him there is a little squeak of primitive excitement, the hunter minimised but still there, and so he thinks that he and Nigel are the same – in fact, he thinks that there is only a fourth kind, or is it the fifth?

So when I asked him what kind of mess Nigel was in this time, he said, "Oh, you know, Jim; you've dealt with him and his father – you know what they are like together. Exactly the same, except that Nigel is a kind of cock-eyed version of his father." He paused to look at me as if his remark explained everything. I shook my head to show him that he hadn't made sense; he's a strange man, Galer, because when he has thought things out, he can be brilliantly articulate, but when he is in a muddle, he becomes an almost gibbering idiot. I know that the clarity of the way people use words is meant to reflect the clarity of their thoughts; but most of us learn to dress up vagueness and silliness very finely – Galer can't. If there is confusion in his mind, confusion invades his speech. There's no pretending; and so he is used to my shaken head.

"All right," he said. "It doesn't make sense. But I'll tell you what he said tonight. We were talking about . . . oh, the whole Freudian business – he's been reading a bit of Freud – " I nearly giggled: Skarfe and I had got our version more accurate than we could have guessed. "Anyway," Galer went on, "he came out with a story that his father had tried to kill him when he was a kid . . ."

"Oh God," I said; this was a new one, and I thought I had heard all Nigel's lies.

"Of course it's a lot of bloody nonsense, a fantasy of some kind – I suppose the Freudian answer is that he is transferring his own guilt on to his father."

"Sucks to Daddy," I tried to joke; I did not like the conversation, and I was on the way to laughter.

"No," said Galer fiercely. "Don't start being funny, Jim. This is bloody serious. I tried to explain to Nigel the whole fantasy business, you know the idea of the displacement of the father; but he can't see it at all. Christ, I know about these things – I've lived them and I know."

I haven't lived them and I know too; perhaps Nigel did want to slaughter his father and was fantasising the desire into the opposite. Perhaps. I suspected something very different. But I love Galer, even his blindness, and so I played his game. "What were the circumstances?" I asked therefore. "When did old Westcott try to kill the boy?"

"Oh, what does it matter?" Galer burst out. "Nigel says that it happened when his father was drunk . . ." It was common gossip that the old man did have bursts of boozing every three months or so; he had elevated it into a principle, a sort of alcoholic catharsis. "Well, Nigel insists that in one of the drunk spells his father came at him with one of the tribal axes that he apparently keeps in his study, swearing that he was going to kill Nigel."

"Fantasy or not," I said, "I wouldn't fancy having that

old devil after me with an axe, even if only in imagination."

"Of course, it's fantasy," Galer asserted. "Everyone has it about his father . . ." Not me, I thought, not me; but Galer has forgotten me—he was talking about his kind, Nigel and him and Harry and all the rest of them. "No, but if they do, they at least either shove it away again or they try to understand it. Nigel doesn't; he refuses to admit that it's a fantasy . . ."

Skarfe came in, then, thank God, bearing coffee; and Galer did not go on with the conversation, and next time I tried to make him speak about it, he pretended that he didn't know what I meant. He had probably decided by then it wasn't a subject I really comprehended. Nor would he discuss it in front of Skarfe; fantasies of the killing of fathers are not, in Galer's mind, things that are discussed with women, even if the woman is your wife. Another aspect of Galer, that: reticence before his wife. Like making love, which is too important to talk about.

But I thought then that Galer had it all wrong; I thought that Nigel was teasing him. I thought that Nigel had taken the Freud home with him, had devoured it in an evening, had thought, "What nonsense! But what fun—I bet I can make old Galer believe that I have a fantasy about my father having tried to kill me; good idea to make it with one of those tribal axes, Fraser and Freud pleasantly mixed. And then he'll try to persuade me that it's really me trying to kill my father metaphorically—and by God there are times when I would like to take an axe to the old man—and I'll pretend that I don't understand." Thus Nigel: I had taught him and I knew his mind. Oh, devious, I realise, but that's Nigel. I know, because I can follow him twist for twist and turn for turn; the difference is that I love Galer, you see. Because if Galer is right to think that he and Nigel are of the same kind, then I am also right to suppose that Nigel is of my kind—and perhaps

I am of the fifth kind after all, the kind who enjoys the writhing and squeaking. But Galer is so gullible that if Nigel had wanted to fool him, he could have done so without even trying. I know that I can fool Galer in the same way. Mention the word "father" to Galer and he's lost – oh, splendidly lost, but lost still.

Poor gullible Galer. So much love and so much foolishness. Why, if you took Galer on a tour of Hades and told him that it was Paradise, he would go up to Satan himself to say, deeply in his chest, "Tell me, God, have you seen my father anywhere here? He's been waiting for me for years." And if Satan laughed and laid a fiery hand on his shoulder, Galer would shrug it off and look that little man in the eyes, as much as to say, "Hands off, God, or whoever you are, or I'll strike you down." Then he would march off, through the dark flames, nodding every time he passed an acquaintance, but he would stop for none of them. He might stop for me, though, for a few moments to say sternly, "Come along with me, Jim, and we'll see if we can find your father somewhere." What is it that Dante says that they do to adulterers in hell? I forget now, but I'll be there, self-conscious man suffering from adultery. Poor Gullible Galer. Too much love and damn near all of it wrong.

6

It did not take Galer long to realise that Jim was right about Nigel Westcott's intelligence; within a fortnight of his joining Galer's Sixth Form class he had produced a piece of work on Ruskin that was outstanding, as even the senior

English master, D'Arcy, acknowledged. "Of course," said D'Arcy when Galer showed him the folder of notes, illustrations, quotations and text that Nigel had presented to him the day before, "the boy has natural advantages: how many boys have fathers who can lend them a complete works of Ruskin? Or even discuss the nineteenth century intelligently?" But that Nigel had been helped by his father did not alter the quality of the work; and Galer found it delightful that Adamson Westcott should take the trouble to write him a note to say that he was most impressed by Galer's approach to teaching his son. "You're quite right," the note said, "to realise that what my son needs is total independence; give him the books, suggest the interesting topics, and then let him sweat away on his own. You won't, I assume, worry if I give him a hand occasionally."

No, Galer wrote in reply, he would be delighted if Mr Westcott would encourage Nigel with his work, though he pointed out that he used the method of independent exploration with all his pupils, not simply with Nigel. But the old man was right; Nigel had the kind of mind that responded to Galer's method. You could never be sure how boys were going to respond; sometimes very intelligent boys would collapse when faced with making up their own minds about the work that they should be doing, and sometimes apparently stupid boys would respond strikingly and individually. The response did not necessarily mean all that much about the intrinsic quality of a boy's intelligence; it meant more about the independence of his judgement. For Galer the second was of course much more important than the first; you were more or less born with your intelligence, but you were not born with intellectual independence. To Galer it did not matter how long a boy took to work out a problem or understand a situation, as long as he did it for himself, without the teacher telling him what he should think, though of course it was delightful when the two qualities of intrinsic ability and nurtured independence coincided, as they so obviously did in Nigel Westcott.

But the delight grew perplexed as the term went on and Nigel produced no more work; he would spend his time in class paging through Galer's books, reading half a chapter in one, a paragraph in another, never settling to examine one topic through a series of views and interpretations. Galer let the boy be for a time, then suggested gently that he should settle down to one topic for a substantial time. No, replied Nigel, he was getting some background work done; he would keep on browsing until he found a situation or personality that intrigued him, and then he would be ready to work at depth – Ruskin had been a special case, he insisted, because he had been interested in him and his work for a long time. Galer therefore wrote out a long and careful list of various topics which he thought might interest Nigel; but Nigel looked through it and handed it straight back to Galer, saying simply, "Nothing there that interests me, I'm afraid." There were a couple of other boys in the class, who, seeing the brilliant Nigel browsing, decided that it was an easier way of passing the time than the protracted study that Galer insisted they do; and soon most of the boys in the class were not working properly.

So Galer interfered; they would take a topic as a class, he announced, so that he could demonstrate the techniques that he expected them to use. Because there were a couple of relatively stupid boys in the class, he decided to choose as topic a personality rather than a situation or a problem and, since one of the examination requirements was a knowledge of Napoleonic France, he decided to choose Napoleon for a joint project by everyone in the class. One boy he set to read a short biography; one (the son of a local solicitor) he set to study the Code Napoleon, another to study the reasons for Napoleon's emergence as a man of power; one (the son of a naval officer) he set to look at the effects of blockades generally, another to study the Russian campaign; one boy was to write an account of the Hundred Days, and the two stupid boys were to make a model of Waterloo, with coloured counters for the various armies and troops; and Nigel was set to write an extended analysis of the effects of Napoleon's period of power on the political climate of England.

At first his remedial efforts seemed to be working, for especially the two stupid boys were very excited by the work he had set them to do. They went off to the carpentry workshop and came back with a hardboard frame, they cycled into Burston to buy plaster of Paris for their relief map, they got the mathematicians to advise them about scale and the geographers to advise them about contours and map-reading. The naval officer's son turned out to have a flair for finding good first-hand sources, and Spencer, who was working on the Hundred Days, read more in a week than he had done all term. Then, two weeks later, on a Monday morning, just as the other boys were settling down to work, Nigel announced loudly that he thought the whole scheme a waste of time, since he had realised over the weekend that Napoleon had not existed at all.

"What on earth do you mean?" Galer asked, cautiously.

"I mean simply that he didn't exist; he is an invention by bourgeois historians to cover up their lack of understanding of the economic infrastructure." Nigel flourished the last words.

"But I've spent all weekend reading about Napoleon," said the boy working on the biography.

"Pure fabrication," Nigel asserted. "A very clever trick, I can tell you, but lies, all lies." Even the two stupid boys, who had arrived for the class early that morning so that they could get on with their model, were drawn away by this; it was obviously a new game which Nigel had devised and it looked like being amusing, because Mr Detheridge was looking lost.

"All right," said Galer. He knew that the period was probably a write-off already, because even if he shut Nigel up, the boys had lost their concentration. Another teacher would have told Nigel that he was being silly and that he should get on with his work; but Galer did not work that way, because it was the easy way. He would take Nigel on in his own terms. "All right," he said again. "Let's hear your case."

"Oh no," said Nigel. "Be fair. I assert that Napoleon is a fiction. Surely it is up to you to prove his reality?"

"No," Galer said. "Challenger must move first."

"No. You see, I think that you are part of the conspiracy too. After all, you're being paid to teach us history. And so you have a stake in the fiction that Napoleon was a real person, not an invented concept."

"Of course, everyone in history is to some extent an invented concept . . ." Galer began.

"You mean that all this stuff about Napoleon is a lot of lies," Dickson interrupted fiercely; he was always ready to suspect his teachers of lying, whether about the past or about his performance in exams.

"No, of course not," Galer said. "But the image we have of the past is always from a mass of views, which we have to sort out and evaluate. I mean, people in England thought Napoleon was an early version of Hitler, but elsewhere he was worshipped."

"You are making assumptions, sir," Nigel butted in. "You keep saying 'he' and 'him', not 'it'."

When you settle down to it, to prove anything about the existence of the past is difficult, and once conspiracy is mentioned, all the evidence that you adduce may be said to be part of the conspiracy. Nor was it the kind of argument Galer enjoyed, partly because it was one of tricks and counter-tricks, debating points and politician's bluster, a form of superior game—oh, it was quite fun with someone like Jim Jenkyns, because with him the argument was all, the subject merely a joke—and partly because Nigel had already managed to divide the class into teacher and taught. So now Galer argued and explained and, at the very end of every argument and every demonstration, there was Nigel, with a grin on his face, to say slyly, "Conspiracy", or "Fiction; interesting fiction, but then so is Jane Austen interesting."

When the bell went at the end of the period, and the boys stood up to leave, Galer knew that he had lost. Of course, everyone believed that Napoleon had existed as a person as well as a concept, but Nigel had won the argument, and Galer had been able to find no actual reason to demonstrate his view. Nigel had turned the argument into a game between him and his teacher, and that was hateful. The past was too important to turn into light-hearted amusement. So when Nigel came up to his desk to say, "That was a jolly good lesson; thanks very much—it was terrifically exciting and interesting," he was astonished and angry.

"No," he said. "It was bloody stupid and pointless. Now for God's sake, go away and don't be such a fool." As he spoke, he felt his anger grow; this boy was a menace, he felt, and had to be told. But Nigel, who had been so delighted in his own cleverness, looked as if Galer had hit him, and Galer had to turn away. He knew that he was wrong to get angry over such a triviality, but Nigel's impertinence—in the proper sense—had hurt him. He looked through the windows across the park to the massive bulk of the old mansion, waiting for Nigel to take his books to leave; but when after a minute or two he realised that the boy hadn't gone, he turned, ready to continue his show of anger. Nigel was standing there at his desk, a tall sixteen-year-old, and he was crying, chin wobbling like a child's and tears on his high cheek-bones.

"Oh, for goodness sake, Nigel, don't be silly; it's only one period wasted, and perhaps it was quite fun really."

"It was only a game," Nigel cried.

How do you deal with a sixteen-year-old's tears? Ignore them and keep talking? Put a fatherly arm round his shoulders and say, "Come on, old man, don't be silly"? Offer him your handkerchief? Keep quiet until he is recovered? Galer felt helpless and yet in a strange way exultant; that the boy was crying did at least mean that he was not corrupt, that he had provoked the argument out of misery, not spite, that he cared what Galer thought. "All right," Galer said, almost to himself and sat down at his desk, waiting for the tears to end. At last he said again. "All right now, Nigel?"

"Yes," said Nigel. "Sorry, very childish of me. I'm in a bit of a state, I'm afraid."

"What's wrong?"

"Just the usual things at home."

"Want to talk about them?"

The boy shook his head, but Galer knew that the shaken head meant little at that stage.

"Why don't you come and see me?" he asked. "Come in tonight and we can talk about historiography."

"What's that?" Nigel looked up now.

"Oh, it's the study of how history is written, a sort of history of history. What we are arguing about in class, in some ways."

"What time?" Nigel asked.

"Oh, come after supper—about eight. I'll be in here; I've got some marking to do. Is that all right?"

"Yes, I'd like to," Nigel said, picked up his books, and went to the door. As he got there, he half-turned, saw Galer looking after him, and smiled brilliantly. It was a kind of triumph for him too.

*   *   *

Nigel was not, Galer realised, simply a brilliant individual; in some ways he was a brilliant example, for he took many of the ideas of his contemporaries to a logical extreme. Adolescence combined with a fashionable anarchism to over-simplify the world: authority was wrong, the individual – as long as he was true to his own moods and impulses – always right. Control or create, reason or imagine. Yet, though Nigel's reason was rapid and his judgement individual, he wanted to triumph in other terms. Create, not control. Most of the time Nigel and his friends did not see that it was control and create, imagine and reason, judge individually and respect the authorities. There was for Galer nothing exclusive in the concepts of reason and imagination. To impose order on chaos. To discover order in chaos. Nigel wanted to destroy order, and he was clever enough to triumph; he had a mind good enough at the business of creating order to be able to disorder at will. He took the evidence of a pattern and re-deployed the evidence to make chaos, and then asserted that chaos had existed before the attempt to find a pattern; and because knowledge was limitless, chaos was limitless. Every time Galer tried to show that the inverse might be true, that because knowledge was limitless, the chances of finding a pattern were limitless too, Nigel would answer Galer in his own terms: the assumption was of chaos, therefore you had to start there before you began to seek out a pattern. To impose patterns on fertile chaos; not discover in.

Galer was too honest with himself to pretend that he believed that a pattern had existed before the chaos – patterns were imposed on, not discovered in – or that the patterns were not made by the limited mind of man. Yet it was the best mind there was, the mind of man, and therefore you had to be content with the inadequate. Otherwise, there had to be a God, and Galer would not or could not believe in a God who had existed before chaos began, not even in a God of Doubting, a God above the God.

*   *   *

Nigel's brief and triumphant tears did not signal a capitulation, emphatically not, and what had started as a game became, gradually, a point of passionate difference. But at least Nigel no longer disturbed the work of the other boys in his class, because he leapt so far ahead of them that he began to deny all past, not simply the past of Galer's history books. Tell an ordinary boy of sixteen that Napoleon had not existed but had been invented, and he will join in the game with delight, because it means that he does not have to think about Napoleon, nor even to think, because there is usually a Nigel around to do the thinking for him; but tell him that his memory of yesterday is a false invention of his unconscious mind, and he will begin to squirm. Thus, Spencer tried to use one of Nigel's arguments to avoid doing some work for Galer; and before Galer could show him that his was a silly version of the argument, Nigel did the job for him. He swung round in his chair to say, "All right, Spencer. What did you do yesterday evening?"

"Oh, I worked on the Hundred Days for an hour, and then watched the box . . ." he began.

"Oh no, you didn't," Nigel flashed at him. "You went to bed at eight, saying you were tired, and you masturbated . . ." Nigel rolled the word round his mouth delightedly, "and because you are guilty about it, your unconscious has invented this story—oh, not deliberately," he said loftily, "you can't help your unconscious being like that."

"That's nonsense," Spencer said fiercely.

"Prove it," Nigel grinned happily.

"Well . . ." Spencer hesitated, and the other boys began to

giggle. Spencer blushed and tried to look angry, but he was too intelligent not to realise that Nigel had trapped him perfectly. So to maintain grace with his fellows he capitulated, and nobody in the class, not even Nigel himself, said another word—in class at least—about the falsity of the past.

But that victory too contained its own failure, for Nigel now tried to re-divide the class, this time Galer and him against the stupid masses. Galer was too experienced a teacher to let that happen and he managed to make sure that no one thought that he took either a special interest in Nigel nor had any kind of exclusive delight in his mind. But because Nigel had turned against them intellectually, the rest of the boys reverted to the kind of intellectual Toryism of their parents—and that was in some ways as worrying to Galer as their half-baked anarchism had been. Still, he was used to that problem and could cope with it, as well as with Nigel, provided that he had time enough to see Nigel alone after classes for the day were over.

* * *

He tried, once, partly out of guilt that he seemed to be spending so little time with her, to explain to Skarfe why it was important for him to help Nigel. But either he could not explain adequately or else she was not interested, though she made less and less effort to hide her resentment that evening after evening when Nigel appeared to discuss this or that or the other with Galer, she would be excluded from their talk. So she said that she disliked Nigel; she distrusted him, she said, with those charming eyes and fluent tongue and that mop of black hair—"like a scavenger bird he looks", she told Galer once, and after that he stopped talking to her about Nigel. He loved her very much, but there were some things that she did not understand.

* * *

CALL

When Galer was first at university, one of his tutors had explained to him that when you were faced with a person who believed that there was a tiger outside the door there was almost no way in which to prove that there wasn't. You could say that there were no tigers in England, except in zoos and circuses; but the tiger had, of course, escaped from a zoo or circus. You could go to the door and throw it open and say, "Look, no tiger"; but the tiger would have slipped round the corner, ready to come back as soon as the door closed. You could say that you would go outside the door yourself and show that there was no tiger by returning unharmed, but you were in league with the tiger. You could even say that it was not important whether there was a tiger outside the door or not; but the terror of the person who waited would not change.

The story had stayed with Galer for years now; sometimes he would wonder what it would be like if he were to go to the door, open it, and find there waiting for him a baleful, steady-eyed tiger, shadowy in the shadows of the passageway; or what it would be like to be that particular tiger, raging and silent, waiting outside the door for the one particular person to pluck up enough courage to face him. Once he had even dreamed that he was both the person waiting in terror inside and the tiger waiting silently outside the door.

*   *   *

Gradually, the staff began to come to Galer when they had problems with Nigel. The master on duty would see him in the common room at break and would say, "Oh Detheridge, young Westcott arrived half an hour late for school this morning; he says that his father is ill, and that he had to be home to help his mother. Can you check up for me?" So Galer would talk to Nigel and find out whether or not the story was true. Nigel's French teacher would come to him to say, "Oh Galer, what to do with that spoilt child, Nigel Westcott?

He simply won't do his work for me. How do you get work out of him?" So Galer would explain that Nigel was in a mess and had done no work for weeks. Jim would say to him, "Galer, I thought I'd better mention it—I saw Nigel on the train to London last night. I tried to catch him on the platform to find out what he was doing, but he disappeared like a randy dog after a bitch on heat." So Galer would ask Nigel and would find out that he had been meeting his parents at Covent Garden and had not wanted to talk to a member of staff at that particular moment.

Of course, Nigel was officially not his responsibility; in fact he was in Shafter's tutorial unit and, as Galer grew more and more involved with Nigel, so Shafter seemed to resent his apparent interference more and more. In the end, Shafter protested to the Headmaster; it was pointless, he said, for Westcott to be in his care since the only person on the staff who dealt with him was Galer Detheridge. The Headmaster knew that it was not a clear case of one member of his staff interfering with the functions of another, for Detheridge was in charge of the Sixth Form Studies Centre and so had some pastoral responsibility for all the boys who worked there; but he hated unclear responsibilities and therefore called Detheridge and Shafter to a short meeting to discuss Nigel Westcott.

In the end, the three of them agreed that Nigel was to leave Shafter's tutorial unit and be treated as the special case that he obviously was; he would henceforth become Galer's official responsibility. All complaints about Nigel's behaviour, appearance, work and manners were to be made first to Galer, who would deal with them as he saw fit. Shafter, an elegant young Geography teacher, was apparently happy to lose Nigel from his tutorial unit, for, he said, "the boy's a bloody nuisance, and uses up time I want for other things". Galer scowled at that, not simply because he thought Nigel too important to be dismissed so simply, but because he knew that "time for other things" meant studying the "Situations Vacant" in the *Telegraph*. Everyone in the school knew that Shafter hated teaching and wanted to get a job in industry or commerce as soon as he could find one well-paid enough. Teaching was too important a job for people like Shafter.

* * *

When Galer told Jim Jenkyns his news in the pub that evening, Jim laughed and said, "Well, for once the school's name for something means what it says: Nigel becomes a tutorial unit all on his own." Then he looked over the top of his drink and said, seriously enough even for Galer, "Look Galer, do you know what you're doing with that boy? He's hard work, you know."

"I know already," said Galer, and only then answered the question. "Yes, I think I know what I am doing."

"I hope so," said Jim quietly, so quietly that Galer was not sure that he had heard correctly, though he did not ask Jim to repeat himself.

* * *

Galer wrote a note to Adamson Westcott explaining the decision that the school had taken and asking if he might come to visit him and Mrs Westcott some time soon to discuss Nigel's problems at school. The old man did not reply and, after a week of waiting, Galer phoned. Had Mr Westcott had his note, he wondered. Yes, he had. Well, could he come to see him? And Mrs Westcott too, of course. He would be delighted to see Mr Detheridge some time, replied Mr Westcott, but at the moment he was correcting the proofs of a long article for an American journal and so was unable to see him.

Three weeks later, Galer phoned again; it really was urgent that he see Mr or Mrs Westcott, he said. For once, it was Mrs Westcott whom he spoke to. She was chatty and pleasant;

yes, she and Adamson were worried about Nigel too, he seemed to be unhappy and, as far as she could see, the school wasn't giving him nearly enough work to do. The trouble was that her husband was engrossed in some urgent work—it was no longer the American proofs, but a review of a major new book on the pygmy tribes.

"Well, can't I come and talk to you, Mrs Westcott?" Galer asked, as patiently as he could.

"Really, Mr Detheridge—I have got the name right, haven't I?... oh good, such an interesting name, I think. Well you see, Nigel isn't really my son, he's Adamson's son by a previous marriage; you know, Catherine Easton, the actress, was his mother. And I don't like to interfere. So, if you wouldn't mind waiting until Adamson has finished his article..."

"But surely he can spare the time to talk to me just for five minutes on the phone?" Galer demanded.

But Mrs Westcott was as firm as he was. "Writers have to be ruthless, Mr Detheridge; Adamson never takes phone calls when he's busy on his writing."

You liar, thought Galer; he talked to me a week ago and he was writing then. But it was pointless going on; the Westcotts either did not want to talk to him or they did not care a damn about the boy. So, after extracting what he knew was a worthless assurance from Mrs Westcott that her husband would phone as soon as he had time, Galer rang off. They were quite impossible, the Westcott parents, and he would have to deal with Nigel on his own.

* * *

Talking to Galer one day after class, Nigel noticed the photograph of John Detheridge that stood on the mantelpiece. He got up from his chair, walked over to the mantelpiece, and took the photograph down. He looked at it carefully for a moment, before turning to Galer to ask, "Is that your father?"

"Yes."

"Is he dead?"

"Yes."

"You're lucky," laughed Nigel; and Galer did not dare answer.

* * *

He gave Nigel an *Introduction to Freud* to read; twenty-four hours later the boy returned the book.

"I got the impression that you were a Jungian," he said to Galer.

"Have you even read this?" Galer asked him, pointing at the little paperback on the table.

"I started it," the boy said, "but I wasn't enjoying it. The whole business frightens me," he added, carefully – as carefully as if he had rehearsed the remark. "But you are a Jungian, aren't you? My father says he's the only one of them who had any understanding of anthropology or history."

Galer shook his head. "I'm nothing," he said. "I've read quite a lot of Jung and I accept some of what I've read and don't understand some, but really I don't classify myself that way."

"Doesn't all that business frighten you?" Nigel asked. Galer could see that he was not being completely serious, because he had a strange little smile at the corners of his eyes and mouth.

Again Galer shook his head. "No," he said seriously. "No, it doesn't frighten me at all. Why does it you?"

"No, you don't," said Nigel, smiling broadly now. "I'm not going to have you psycho-analyse my fear of the unconscious."

"I wouldn't dare to," Galer smiled back. "I'm a teacher, not a psychiatrist." He meant it too, and Nigel and he talked of other things.

But the distinction was both clear and important to Galer; he was not qualified to deal with abnormal psychology and not qualified to psycho-analyse. He wasn't sure that he believed in psycho-analysis either, because he was afraid that disturbing the unconscious might do more damage than it could help anyone, unless of course that person was incapable of living with other people and needed help from doctors. True, his method of teaching depended on a view of the nature of the mind but he was dealing with basically healthy minds. If Nigel was ill – and he didn't believe that he was – he should be in the care of a doctor; otherwise he needed someone who was able to help him sort out his intellectual and emotional confusion. The intellectual confusion was Galer's professional concern; the emotional confusion was both a professional and a private one, and you could not really separate the responsibilities. After all, he had become a teacher because of his father's example and so he did have special qualifications for dealing with Nigel. Some time it might emerge that Nigel needed psychiatric care; then Galer would willingly hand over responsibility. Until then, he would care for Nigel as well as he could; and it was not arrogance that made him think that he was specially equipped to help Nigel – it was love.

*　*　*

Sometimes it seemed to Galer that he had been a teacher all his life; certainly he could not remember a time when he had not wanted to be one. Nor was teacher quite the right word; he had wanted to be a schoolmaster, concerned with more than the academic part of education, concerned with every part of a boy's growth. Perhaps the desire had begun even before conscious thought was possible? Perhaps he had learned it from his father long before he could speak? How could anyone possibly say when a man began? Certainly he existed before he thought, if existence meant breathing. Perhaps he existed even before he breathed, perhaps even before he was conceived, as his own father must have dreamed of his son long before he was born, as Galer himself dreamed of the son that he would have before long, and as Galer's son would in his turn dream of his son. The generations came and went, yet persisted in their generations; there were changes, there would be changes, but nothing would disappear for good. One man would have something special about him, about his face say, wide-set eyes or a cleft chin; his children might not inherit that specialness of the body, and someone on the outside might think that it had disappeared for ever. But it would come back again; some old woman, looking at a grandchild, would exclaim, "Why, he's got his grandfather's eyes exactly," or "Good heavens, look at that Detheridge chin."

It went further than that too; suddenly, in a dream, you would become a hunter again, standing behind a barricade of thick bushes and thorn trees at the end of a narrowing gully. There would be fire up in front and you would hear the animals coming down the gully in front of the fire and you would wait for them, holding a bow or a spear or a club even, and you would hear the animals' hard breathing as they came down the gully towards the trap, and you would not know whether the breathing was yours or theirs. Or the dreaming would take you even further back, and you would become one of the hunted ones yourself, who ran carefully and breathed heavily and who knew that there was a trap in front but who could not avoid it because there was a worse terror behind. Every man was a part of his own past and his own future; there was only one real terror, that the young might not realise their memories.

The terror meant that teaching the young was work that might break a man's heart if he were not careful; Galer knew this already: that was why he needed to be alone sometimes, to be assured of aloneness, because he felt that he had demands made on him the whole time, someone asking him a question or demanding an answer or testing a new-found will against his authority, every moment of every day of every year, and no one had enough love to cope with that, not all the time.

* * *

"For God's sake," Galer burst out, "don't you see that if you don't believe in the past, you can't believe in the future either?"

"I don't know that I do," said Nigel. He was being very careful this evening, keeping his voice level and his eyes steady.

"But if you can't believe in the past, and don't believe in the future, what point is there? I mean, why go on living at all? There's got to be some point, some direction, even if it's only downwards."

"Not necessarily," Nigel replied carefully. "You see, I don't believe that there is any point at all, not in the long run."

Galer could not hold back his terror any longer. "But if you think that when you're sixteen," he said, "what on earth are you going to believe when you are thirty? And when you are my age?" The boy smiled at him across the desk, an infinitely mocking smile that said, 'You foolish man, you know what I mean. I don't believe in history, any more than I believe in your ancestors; I don't believe time, and I hardly believe space. At the moment I am sitting in your classroom, with my senses more or less in order, and I impose on the chaos around me some limited form of order. I could, on the other hand, be dreaming; I could be in hallucination; I could be mad, and all these things mad too, wood under my hands, wood under my feet, the grey smell of books in my nose, the slow sound of your voice, your voice, the sight of you across the desk, poor foolish man who believes . . .'

But Galer did not believe what Nigel's smile said. He could not believe it.

*   *   *

He must have been very young when he first dreamed the dream. It would have been when they were still in the north, before they moved back to London, because the builders had been in the house, building an extra bedroom for Harry and Jessica, and they had left a pile of sand in the front garden. It was in his dream, the sand. Four or five, he must have been. In the dream, he was standing on top of the pile of sand, singing some nursery rhyme . . . what was it? "I'm the King of the Castle,/And you're the Dirty Rascal." And then the Dirty Rascal had appeared, a terrible man, gaunt, grey-faced, tattered, like the men who must have been in and out of the house during the strikes and hunger-marches, drinking mugs of tea and gobbling meals, talking fiercely, having no time for the small child who crawled at their feet, trying to find his father in the crowded room. He had stood silent, looking down at the terrible man, hoping that the man would not notice him, when suddenly he was on the ground and the man was on the sand-pile, looking at him from a grey face and with steady eyes, and then he was running desperately up the long path of the garden to the front door, and he was beating at the door, hammering at it, trying to make someone let him inside. And all the time the terrible man was coming slowly up the path after him, and he hammered and hammered at the door, but no one came. Then suddenly the hands that beat at the door were not his hands any more, but the hands of an old man, wizened, scarred, crooked hands, that still scratched and beat at the door that could not be opened. The terrible man had gone away then, or perhaps his hands were those at the door, but there was still no one in the house, no one at all to let him in.

That was all; but he had gone on dreaming the dream for years, or perhaps when he had been dreaming other dreams and woke up, the only dream that he could remember was that one.

Once – it could not have been the first time, but once – when he had woken in terror from the dream, his father had come in to comfort him. What was your dream, he had asked, and Galer had told him. Yes, his father had said, yes, I know that dream. It's from the old days, you see, when we were all hunters and were sometimes hunted. And the old man's hands? Well, they are your hands too, like mine, because you are dreaming of what you will be one day. But you mustn't worry; there will always be someone in the house for you. You just have to let them know, and they'll be there; even when your mother and I are dead, you'll have sons and daughters of your own. Go to sleep now; I'll be next door if you dream again.

7

That Sunday, three days before they were to leave Cornwall for St Michaels and the start of the summer term, Galer took Skarfe walking. He did not really like walking with her, because she wandered rather than walked, a tall girl, easy-limbed, but liking to stop to look at plants, mosses, nests, stones, and other stillnesses. Galer, on the other hand, liked to cover ground, wanted always to keep moving, resented stopping for longer than was necessary to steady his breathing after a long climb. So though they might start walking together, as often as not Galer would get bored and angry with Skarfe's leisurely pottering and would march ahead for half a mile, then turn round and march back to where Skarfe would be sitting smiling at her husband from the side of the path. Sometimes Galer would accept the smile and would sit down beside her and they would talk a little, until Galer grew impatient again and she would be forced to walk on with him; but more often than not he would refuse to sit down and would stand in front of her, impatiently waiting until she had gathered herself together and had gathered together her collection of flowers, plants, leaves and stones; then they would set off again, Galer adjusting himself to her pace until he could bear it no longer and would march ahead of her again. She was almost worse than Jim, Galer thought; he had once and once only taken Jim walking, on what was meant to be an easy ramble over the weald, and Jim had complained of exhaustion after two miles, had been limping after three, and after four was hitch-hiking his way back to where they had left his car. Never again, Galer had said to Jim in the pub that night; and now, walking with Skarfe, he thought again of Jim, spending his holiday in Ely, reading two books a day, visiting the cathedral and looking for someone to argue with, seeking out his women, "or whatever", and he smiled as Jim's own phrase slipped into his mind.

"What are you smiling at?" Skarfe asked him.

"Oh, I was thinking about Jim."

"Why?"

"I don't know; I wonder how he's enjoying his holiday."

She did not answer and Galer looked at her in some puzzlement; she was usually always ready to talk, and now she was silent.

"Am I walking too fast for you?" he asked.

She shook her head. "No," she said. "I'm just enjoying having you to myself."

Galer reached out a hand to her shoulder and stopped her, then turned her to face him. "Sorry," he said.

"Don't be," she answered. "I do understand some things about you; and you mustn't worry when I want you to be things that you aren't, because really I want you to be what you are."

It did not mean much, but he understood; and he was glad that he had decided to make this day separate for Skarfe. He would walk with her, slowly, easily, pottering along, stopping when she stopped, waiting for her, helping her with the useless collection of odds and ends that he knew perfectly well would sit for a week or two on her dressing table and then be thrown away. Today was for her; and later he would tell her why he had brought her on this particular walk.

The Detheridge family had discovered Lerryn during the war; his mother had brought him, Harry and Jessica down to Cornwall for a holiday—they had stayed on a farm near Lostwithiel, with a friend of his mother's called . . . what was it now? Johnson . . . Jackson, was it? Something ordinary anyway. Mrs Jackson it must have been. Her husband had been killed in France very early on and she had gone on running the farm herself, with a few Land Army girls to help her and one old man. He couldn't remember her now and he couldn't even remember where the farm was exactly. But for one marvellous weekend his father had managed to get away from his War Office job in London and the whole family had been there together. Harry, his mother and he had walked into Lostwithiel from the farm to meet his father off the train, and they had stood there on the platform waiting for him; and then the train came in and he walked towards them, a tall man in uniform, taller by far than any other man on the platform, a big tired man who picked up both his sons, one in each arm, and still holding them managed somehow to hug his wife too.

Out of the haze of bright images Galer selected one and allowed it to invade his mind. It was Mrs Jackson who had told them to visit Lerryn, a small village about a mile and a half away from the farm, on one of the tributaries of the Fowey; she packed them a picnic lunch – sandwiches, hard-boiled eggs, cold potatoes in their skins, a thermos of tea for Mr and Mrs Detheridge and a bottle of milk for the children – eggs and milk, oh what luxury they had been then. The family had walked to Lerryn along the high-hedged narrow lanes, Mrs Detheridge carrying Jessica, Mr Detheridge carrying Harry when he got tired, and Galer walking proudly next to his father, and they had eaten their lunch sitting on the side of a stone bridge. Afterwards Mrs Detheridge put Jess to sleep in the shade of the trees at the river bank, and his father, Harry and he had gone off to explore. They had found a footpath past the old granary and had followed it right along the tributary until they reached the Fowey itself, and then they had followed the Fowey upstream, for a mile or so through thick woods, until they came to a church that perched on the eastern bank of the river. They had stopped there and his father had showed them an epitaph carved just inside the porch. The words had gone now from Galer's mind, but the image remained of his father running his fingers over the carved words as he read them to his sons.

They must have met their mother on the way back; perhaps they were away longer than they had said they would be, and she had brought Jess a little way along the footpath to meet them. What else had they done that day? He searched but could not find any clear memory, except that it had been evening when they got back to the farm, because he remembered his father carrying him upstairs to the bedroom that he shared with Harry, and he had been very tired but gravely happy, because it must have seemed to him that his father would never go away again.

* * *

He had never been back to Lerryn, although the family had stayed in Cornwall again after the war, and although he had been coming there at Easter time almost every year since he had moved to St Michaels. But now he was taking Skarfe there; he wouldn't tell her why, not yet, but he was taking her back to that place of the immortal past, and they would walk along that footpath down the bank of the river until they found that same church, and he would show her the epitaph that his father had shown him, and this time he would never forget the words again.

Galer had looked at his ordnance map and knew that the walk was still there, the clear line of the footpath running along the edge of the river to the church of St Winnock, an easy walk that ordinarily he would manage in an hour at the most if he were on his own. But with Skarfe it would take longer. So they had taken a bus from the coast into Lostwithiel, and from there they had walked across the fields into Lerryn. Skarfe wanted to explore the village but Galer would not let her; he wanted to look for the footpath of thirty-odd years before, he did not want to walk through a village that had grown so much since he was last there, or to look at cottages that it would be pleasant to own if he were not a schoolmaster on schoolmaster's pay. So they walked down the river, past the old granary that had now become some rich man's retreat, for there were new stone walls around it and bright curtains at the windows. But just past the old granary Galer found the footpath; it was still in use, though the old leaves of the last autumn were thick underfoot and though someone had put gates across the path. They followed the path steadily for a few hundred yards, walking along ten or twelve feet above the river and then swung inland to cross one of the bigger streams that run from the hillside down to the deeply cut river.

Skarfe stopped there for a long time, sitting on the little

wooden bridge over the stream, swinging her bare feet in the water and laughing at the cold and tug of it. Galer stood patiently on the bridge with her, looking up the valley; there seemed to be a house up there—he thought he could see a roof through the trees and there was a smell of woodsmoke that seemed to come floating down with the stream.

Two hundred yards on, the footpath swung them upwards to join a timber track that had been built since the war; Galer could see the old path running a little way below them, but it was too thickly overgrown now for walking. So he and Skarfe stuck to the timber track, walking side by side, quicker now, because the foresters had sprayed the land above the track with weed- and tree-killer, and Skarfe said that she hated the silence and the deathly look of the dead old trees that stood above the closely-packed sharp-headed new pine trees that grew hideously functional where the old wood had been. "Bred for the axe," Skarfe said angrily, "like broiler chickens in those ghastly little houses," as she looked away from the dead trees to the river that was now at least fifty feet below them down the untouched steep banks.

The timber track ended a little way after the tributary met the main river, and then they were in a thick wood, where the trees had not been cut for years so that the old ones fell clumsily across the new and the footpath, now no more than a track, was heavily shadowed. They walked until they could no longer see the land cleared for the pine trees, and then sat down in a small clearing where the sun fell shadowy through the trees above them and ate the lunch that Skarfe had prepared carefully that morning.

When they had finished eating, Skarfe lay back on the short grass and smiled up at Galer; tall girl, long-legged, in dark blue jeans and fawn sweater, big-breasted, dark-eyed, bright hair against the dull green of the grass. "I suppose that you want to walk again—you won't even allow me time to digest my sandwiches," she said, laughing at him because she knew that he wanted to start again.

"Well," said Galer seriously, looking at his watch, "I'll do whatever you want, but if we are going to see that church and then walk back to Lostwithiel in time to catch a bus . . ."

"Please can I have just a few minutes?" she said, still laughing.

"Of course, if you want them – but we'll have to hurry later."

"I don't care," Skarfe said. Then she sat up quickly, looking at him, stretching out a hand to his arm. "Oh, blast you, you impatient man. Don't you see that I want you to make love to me?"

Galer looked round them into the green shadows of the trees. "But, darling . . ." he began.

"But nothing . . . the local people will be having their dinners in their houses, it's too early in the year for picnickers, there aren't any tourists but us, we haven't seen anyone for hours, and it looks as if no one has been in this wood for a hundred years anyway." She was very sure of herself in her desire. "Or don't you want me?"

Of course he wanted her; there were no words for the wanting, there was only a knowledge of warmth and shining darkness in her body. So he turned to her and, first gently and then almost in rage, made love to her, the two of them half-naked on the ground under the old trees where no one had walked for a hundred years.

Afterwards, when they lay side by side on the ground and the trees above them turned back into trees, and grass into grass, and sky into sky, Skarfe said quietly to her husband, lying next to her with an arm stretched out as a pillow for her head and his eyes half-closed against the cloudy glare, "I wasn't going to tell you this, Galer, until I was sure, but it is a good time, isn't it?" Galer sat up at that and looked at her, gravely at his wife lying on the grass next to him. "Oh dear, it's so difficult to say without sounding silly, like every other person in the world has sounded," Skarfe went on, turning away from him, lying there still but turned away from him.

He took her shoulder gently and turned her back to him. "Tell me," he said. "It's a marvellous time for telling things", and all the time he felt growing inside him like a great flowering tree the certainty of what she would tell him. "Tell me," he said again, fiercely this time.

"I'm going to have a baby," she said, then giggled. "I don't mean from just now, but . . . well, my period is nearly three weeks late, and it's never late usually; and . . . well, I didn't actually feel sick this morning, but I've felt very wobbly for the last three or four mornings . . ." Her hesitating voice trailed away as she looked at Galer, leaning above her, dark eyes looking down at her, Galer unable to move, unable to speak, unable even to smile at her for fear of disturbing one leaf or petal of the great tree that grew and grew inside his mind.

"Oh, Galer, you are pleased, aren't you?" Skarfe said, looking at his quiet unmoving face.

Pleased? he thought. Pleased? What had pleasure to do with this? If there were no words for that other thing, how could there be words for this? If you took one tiny leaf off that tree and held it out to the light, and named it, that might be pleasure, and one flower named from the tree might be joy, but the tree itself was unnameable, immortal unnameable. He put his hand across her eyes as if he could not bear to have her see his face, then ran his fingers down her cheeks and across her mouth, forcing it open, pushing the lower lip down and then bending to kiss her. He lay down next to her again, but she sat up and leaned over him so that she could look at him.

"No," she said, "don't close your eyes. I want to see you."

They looked at each other, Galer almost afraid to look for fear that she would see too much. "It was a good time to tell you then, wasn't it?" Skarfe asked. Galer nodded but would not speak. "I hope I'm right, about the baby I mean," she said.

He could answer that. "My mother always says that most women know long before doctors can tell."

"Good: then I know," and she kissed him now, bending over him so that her hair became a bright tent around his face. "Isn't it strange," she went on, "to think that there is a baby growing inside me? Give me your hand," and she made him rest his hand against her stomach, pushing up the jersey and thick blouse so that he could feel her skin. "You can't feel anything now," she whispered, "but you will, Galer, you'll feel him move soon, in just a few months."

He could still find no words, so now, half-teasing, half-serious, she put her hands on his shoulders and pushed him hard against the ground, pushing against his bulk as if he had been trying to fight her. "Oh, wordless man, my husband," she teased him, "nothing to say still? You won't talk about making love, you won't talk about babies growing, you won't talk about love in the abstract, nothing like that. You just do them, don't you, make love, make babies, all the rest . . ." She leaned closer to him, her face just above his, the two of them staring at each other in the tent of her hair while she whispered, "Well, I'll do the talking for you; I'll tell you things. I'll tell you that sometimes when you push me over on to my back, and then put that big hand of yours down there and open my legs for me, and then open me for you to . . . and then you come on top of me, big, heavy man, and you are ready for me, and you push yourself into me, big too, wanting you, open for you . . ." all this in a low whisper that even he could hardly hear, her breath on his face and her hands hard on his shoulders; then she knelt up, away from him, and said, not whispering now, "No, you're right, words won't do.

You know," she laughed, "I feel so strange now; I feel as if I owned everything, the ground here, the trees, the sky, everything—" she scrambled up on to her feet, saying as she did so, "I know what I'll do. I own this place, don't I, so I can do what I want to here," and before he would say anything, she began to undress, jersey pulled over her head and thrown down, jeans already undone slipped down and stepped out of, the buttons undone of her blouse and that thrown on the jersey, hands behind her back and the bra off so that her heavy pointed breasts swung free, and then pants slipped down and stepped out of, and she stood there, absurd Skarfe naked, too thin and too big, beautiful Skarfe naked, bright-haired and long-limbed, graceless, big-bodied, beautiful naked Skarfe. She turned away from Galer and for one moment he thought that she might be walking right away from him into the trees, but after a few steps she turned back to him. "Look," she said, as if he could have done anything else. She raised her hands above her head so that her breasts moved and flattened.

"Come here," Galer said; he was ready for her again and he wanted her.

"No," she said. "Wait. Look now," and she turned sideways on to him and thrust her belly out. "It's very small still, but it's growing," and she brought her hands under her breasts, cupping them upwards. "These will be enough to feed my baby, won't they? Won't they, Galer?"

"Come here," he said again, laughing now at the way he wanted her.

"No," she said again, "you just wait. I own this place. You wait," she faced him now, close to him, still standing there naked, and her face was very serious, cloudy with her own wanting. "Look," she said, and she put her hands down between her thighs and spread her legs for him, and spread herself wide for him to see. "Look," she said, voice shaking.

DEATH OF FATHERS

"You look at flowers, don't you, you look right into them. Well, look at me now, big man without words. I don't need words for that either."

She came now to kneel next to him, but when he reached out to touch her breasts and to pull her down to him, she pushed his hands away. "No," she said. "This is my place. You wait for me," and first with her hands and then with her mouth she fondled him until he could bear to wait no longer and pulled her over backwards so that he could enter her. But she said again, "No, please, Galer, please wait for me." He lay back again, groaning and laughing at her slowness, and let her do with her hands and mouth whatever she wanted, what he wanted her to do, until, when his whole body seemed to be bursting apart, she slowly put her legs across his body and, pushing down and thrusting and twisting so that her breasts shook and her hair moved like the branches of the tree above them, and lifting her body high and hammering it down again, she brought him the whole way through, herself the same way through, way upon way, wave upon wave, tide upon tide, sea upon sea, until there was nothing but that shining darkness.

Afterwards, when he had time to recall all that had happened, all that she had done for him and he for her, he was astonished at her sensuality. Oh, he had known that she was passionate, but up until then there had always seemed a reticence in their love-making that had now disappeared into complete abandon. She knew that too, because lying there afterwards, still on top of him, he still inside her, her head down, cradled on his shoulder, she said quietly to him, "You didn't mind, did you?"

"No," he laughed at her. "It was . . . oh, wonderful, if that's the right word."

"I wanted to show you, you see," she said. "And I do feel strange, knowing that there is a baby there inside me; what I said about my thing, you know, being like a flower, well, that's what I feel."

"I feel too still," he teased her now.

"Mm," she said. "Me too. Oh, I'm sleepy now."

"And cold too, I bet," Galer said, laughing.

"Are you cold?" she asked, half-asleep.

"No," he said, "but I've still got some clothes on." Gently he pushed her off his body and made her sit up, saying, "Come on, you had better get dressed now, my wife—you mustn't catch cold," and he helped her to dress again and dressed himself. But Skarfe was still half-asleep and lay down on the grass, head cradled in her arms, eyes closed, weary from her own excitement, and in a moment or two Galer could see that she was asleep. He stood up quietly, pulled off his heavy blue sweater and carefully so that he would not wake her tucked it over her shoulders; while he stood there watching her, she cradled herself deeper into her arms, elbow under her head, hands in the bright hair, and he knew that she was sound asleep. Quickly he turned away from her and moved on through the wood; it was only half a mile or so before it ended and then only a field or two to cross before St Winnock, the church perched on the banks of the Fowey, and just inside the porch an epitaph, the words of which he could not remember any more.

Yet when he got to the edge of the wood and looked across the fields to where the church was, he did not want to go any further; it was enough to have come that far—the rest of the journey was no longer needed. It was there already, the journey; he held it safely in his mind, and he would never forget. He stood there for a long time, looking across the fields to St Winnock, then turned and quickly walked back to where his wife was lying.

"Where've you been?" she asked sleepily as he sat down next to her.

He replied before he had time to think. "Oh," he said, "I've just been down to the river . . ." and, as soon as he had said it, he knew that he would never tell Skarfe that he had been here before. He would let her go on thinking that he had seen a walk marked on his ordnance map that looked pleasant, and that he had brought her here simply because of this. He would let her go on thinking that this day was entirely her own, hers to share with him, yes, but hers. She would be right; she would own this place for good, and he would never tell her that he had owned a part of it long before he had ever brought here here.

"Don't worry, Galer, I'll wake up soon," Skarfe murmured through her half-sleep. But within a minute she was sound asleep again, and he sat there quietly under the trees of the old wood next to his sleeping wife for a long time thinking of what had happened and of what was coming.

8

At first everyone at school thought that Nigel must be ill, but after he had been away for three days and still no note or call of explanation came from his father or stepmother, Galer mentioned his absence to the Headmaster, and the Headmaster got his secretary to phone the Westcotts to find out what was wrong with the boy. Within half an hour the Headmaster sent a senior boy to the Studies Centre to ask Galer to call on him in his study as soon as possible; Galer, although he was meant to be teaching, left his class and went straight away. After all, it was Nigel who mattered.

"He's gone," the Headmaster told him. "Run away–three

days ago. I spoke to Westcott myself in the end. He was almost incoherent, but I managed to gather that the boy walked out after a row of some kind and hasn't come back."

"Why on earth didn't the old man tell us?" Galer burst out.

The Headmaster shrugged. "I asked him," he said. "He wasn't even apologetic about not telling us. The assumption was that it was none of our business if his child didn't come to school."

"But didn't he think we could help? My God, he is impossible, the old fool."

"I didn't say that," the Headmaster smiled at Galer. But Galer would not return the smile: if Nigel had been gone three days, there must be something badly wrong. There were no friends that he would have gone to, no friendly neighbours who would conspire with him against his father. What had happened, Galer wondered; what had his father said to him that drove him out of the house? What new pain was there, striking down at the boy?

"Didn't the old man give you any idea of the cause?" he asked.

"No. I pressed him, but he just mumbled and murmured, and I couldn't get anything like a sensible reply."

"And they have no idea where he is?" Even as he asked the question, the knowledge of where Nigel had gone to came flooding up like a tide into his mind. Galer knew where the boy was; he knew as certainly as he knew that he was standing in the Headmaster's study looking out of the window to where a gardener was carefully pruning the rose bushes.

"No. Have you?"

Instinctively, Galer answered, "No." He had promised the boy not to tell anyone and promises–especially to those over whom one had power–were not to be lightly broken. "No," he repeated, and the Headmaster, either taking the repetition to signify doubt or hesitation, or perhaps seeing the truth in

Galer's eyes, asked carefully, "Are you sure? Westcott says that his son has been spending a lot of time with you, and I got the feeling that he thought that you might know where the boy is likely to have gone."

Galer needed to avoid the question. His first lie had been instinctive and so was, in his terms, forgivable; but his second, he knew, would be deliberate. "Most boys," he avoided the question, "go to places like Bromley when they run away. There are a couple of teenage communes there, and it's very much part of the drug business."

The Headmaster scribbled a note down on his pad, then looked up at Galer. "I thought you'd told me once that young Westcott had got past that kind of trouble, that he had moved on to higher things, so to speak. Is he still attracted to that kind of thing, the 'drug scene', whatever that may be?"

"No," said Galer. "No, he's not at all. I just said that most boys seem to run away to places like that."

"All right. What friends has he got that he might have gone to?"

"He hasn't."

"But, Detheridge, he's always surrounded by dozens of boys. I've seen him."

"But they change; it's never the same crowd – he moves from group to group. He's thoroughly a loner."

"You mean he bores the other boys?"

Galer shrugged; what was the point in answering? How could you possibly explain to this man that Nigel was special, that he didn't fit any of the patterns which headmasters and their hangers-on made up.

The Headmaster ignored the lack of answer. "He must have gone somewhere. You say he wouldn't have gone to London or somewhere like that. You say he hasn't any friends he'd go to. What about girls?"

"None he could go to," Galer was curt.

"Why?"

"Because they're local girls, and they live at home, and anyway, he's Nigel Westcott..." His voice trailed away; he knew already. What was the point in concealment? What good would it do Nigel?

The Headmaster carefully drew a line through his note, put his pencil down on the pad, leaned back in his tall-backed chair and said, "Come, Detheridge, you do know where the boy has gone, don't you?"

"No," Galer said. "No, I don't know. Not in fact. But I think–*think*–I may be able to guess..." He hesitated; he had already begun to break his promise. He was no good at lying.

"But you don't want to say?" the Headmaster pressed him.

"I made a promise to the boy," Galer said firmly. He was not going to be bullied.

The Headmaster sighed and rubbed a hand across his forehead. "Yes," he said, "yes. That's so often the way with us, isn't it? We get caught between the two sides. But I think here you have a duty to tell someone. You see, the boy may be in real trouble of some kind. I made the boy's father promise that if he hasn't turned up by four o'clock this afternoon he will phone the police. Any normal parent would have done that already; but sometimes I think that Westcott is so keen to keep only his hands on his children that he won't let other people even breathe on them." He had made his little speech without looking at Galer once, almost as if he were repeating something that he had learned by rote; but now he looked up. "If you like," he said, "you can tell me what you know about where the boy is, and I'll pretend that I found out somewhere else, and won't mention your name..." But even before he had finished his sentence, he knew that he had chosen the wrong man and he went smoothly on to deny his own suggestion. "No, that wouldn't do, would it?"

Galer shook his head; the anger he had started to feel at the man's willingness to involve himself and others in such duplicity had been as quickly dowsed by the recognition of the mistake. Still, although he wanted to tell the Headmaster what he knew, he did not trust himself to speak immediately. He wanted so much to tell someone. The Headmaster was right: Nigel might be in real trouble now; he might have injured himself, or be ill, or have fallen down some stony cliff . . . But he forced himself to shake his head.

"All right," said the Headmaster. "All right; but you see that I shall have to tell the old man something, and you can't now expect me to say to him, 'No, no one here, not even Mr Detheridge, had any idea where your son has gone'."

"Where he might have gone," Galer corrected him.

"All right. But you see my problem." He smiled as he leaned back again. "I'm caught just as much as you are, you see." Galer nodded. "I'll tell you what," the Headmaster went on. "I won't phone his father again until lunch-time." He looked at his watch. "That'll give you two hours nearly to think about it. You come back here at one o'clock and we'll decide what to say to Westcott. That all right?"

Galer nodded. It would give him time to think, at least.

*   *   *

In fact, he did not need time. Once he was out of the Headmaster's study, he was able to see immediately what a position his inability to lie, and his acceptance of the Headmaster's idea of a conflict of loyalty, had now put him in. Before he got back to his classroom and his waiting pupils he had decided what to do. He was going to find Nigel himself. He was sure that he knew where he had gone to.

He stopped off in his classroom, wrote two notes, one to the Headmaster asking him to delay phoning Westcott as he was going immediately on his own to the place that he thought

Nigel might have gone to, and another to Skarfe to tell her that he would probably—he meant 'certainly', but wrote 'probably'—not be in for lunch that day, as he had got involved in a crisis over one of the boys—he didn't mention Nigel's name in the note. He told his class that he was cancelling the rest of the lesson and that they should go to the library to work on their own, and chose two reliable boys from the delighted troop to deliver the notes for him. He knew that he should go upstairs to see Skarfe himself; but telling her would mean that he would have to explain more than he needed to in a note, and at the moment he did not want to explain.

He phoned from the boys' phone in the basement for a taxi; for once he regretted that he couldn't drive a car—the taxi would cost him a packet, though he could probably persuade the Bursar to refund him the fare, since this was school business, or partly school business, at least. He couldn't of course ask Jim to drive him, not only because Jim would be teaching, but for the same reason that he had not been up to see Skarfe—he did not at that moment want to discuss his errand with anyone.

When the taxi arrived, ten minutes later, he directed the driver and then settled down in the back seat to remember exactly what Nigel had told him one evening three weeks or so before.

*   *   *

Galer had been talking about Cornwall and the way he used his holidays as a way of recovering from the exhaustion of the perpetual testing of his will and authority by the boys in his care. Suddenly Nigel interrupted him. "I've got a place like that, too. A lot closer than Cornwall, though." He laughed. "I use it as an escape hole when I can't stand home any more. I suppose other people know about it too, but I've never seen anyone there."

"Where is it?" Galer asked idly. He had been enjoying talking about Cornwall and the sensations of cliff-top walking and he hadn't wanted to stop. But every time Nigel proffered information about himself, it was a kind of victory for him, and so he listened carefully.

"I can't tell you that," Nigel said. "It wouldn't be an escape hole any more, if a schoolmaster knew about it."

"Oh, nonsense," said Galer. Damn the boy, he thought; every time I think that I am getting him to understand that I am on the same side as him, that we do not, in this kind of situation—though we may in others—represent Authority and the Governed, he comes out with one of these statements about the nature of schoolmasters that shows he doesn't really see me as a person at all, only as Authority capitalised. "I'm not going to spy on you in your hidey-hole."

"Nonsense back to you, Galer," Nigel smiled at him; he had slipped naturally into a habit of calling Galer by his first name when they were alone together and Galer would not have dreamed of making him call him anything more formal. "You are a schoolmaster, aren't you, even if you aren't quite as wooden as the rest of them; in the end you are bound to be on the side of the gods." Partly he was joking, Galer knew; if he had been wholly serious, he would neither have been there nor would he have mentioned the possibility at all.

"Yes," Galer joked back therefore. "I can't separate one function of me from another; I am a schoolmaster and have obligations to the school, if only because it pays me a salary— I also have friendships inside and outside school which I have obligations to." It was an argument which they had had often enough before; now they were simply reminding each other of the grounds of the argument.

Nigel looked carefully at Galer, then said suddenly, "All right. I'll tell you. But you must promise that you won't go there yourself . . ."

"That's easy enough; I like walking, not lying low in hiding places."

Nigel ignored the interruption and went straight on... "And you must promise not to tell anyone."

"All right," smiled Galer.

"No, you must promise."

How young he seems sometimes, thought Galer; most of the time an adult, with sophisticated problems and sophisticated attitudes, and then suddenly he will use the phrase of a ten-year-old. "All right," he said. "All right, I promise."

Nigel nodded in acknowledgement, looked long and carefully at Galer behind his desk, then said, "You know Farlane's Pool?"

"Yes." It was more a lake than a pool, about seven miles away from Burston, on the road to Wilehurst, a very popular picnic place, because it was close to the main road and yet far enough away from it to seem silent, on the edge of the ridge of the weald, wooded and protected from the winds by the hills that ran behind it.

"Well, you know just where you turn off the main road to the pool, how the other side of the road there is almost a cliff?"

"Yes."

"Well, nobody goes there now, because they are all too concerned with getting to the pool, but there is an old track, probably the original road before they cut the main road through the ridge, up the side there. It's almost completely overgrown now, but I went up there one day when the rest of the family were having a picnic at the pool, and I walked right up to the top of the ridge—it's jolly steep too, there—and then over a little valley, all overgrown with brambles and things, and up the other side; and right at the top, just on the edge of the fir plantations—you know them...?"

"Yes," Galer said. They ran back nearly a mile from the

top of the ridge; you saw them when you took the turning to Colley from the main road, and there was a good walk through them along the top of the ridge.

"Well, it's all Forestry Commission land, that," Nigel went on, "and you know those great big fences along the road, and so no one actually goes down into them. I suppose that they haven't fenced the other side, because the ridge will naturally keep most people out."

Galer nodded. "It sounds marvellous," he said. He meant it sincerely; the south-east was so crowded that anywhere where no one else went sounded marvellous, and he had often wondered how to get into those quiet plantations himself.

"I haven't finished yet," Nigel said insistently. "You see, the plantations don't actually run up to the very edge of the ridge. There's about . . . oh, about fifty yards, a hundred in some places, where the land is pretty rough, hollowed and torn—you know how it gets in some places—and they haven't planted just there. Actually, I think that patch may not belong to the Forestry Commission . . ."

"Is it National Trust? There are patches of National Trust land all along the ridge."

"Well, there aren't any signs up, so I don't know. But it may be private land. You see, there's an old ruined house up there; it looks like an old shepherd's cottage that was converted some time quite recently, I mean twenty or thirty years ago, but nobody can have lived there for years, and it looks as though there was a fire some time; the walls are all blackened and the roof is burnt. But because it's built on a slope, there is a basement, a sort of half-cellar basement with a door in the front, though the back wall is actually in the hillside. And it's perfectly habitable. I spent a night there once, during the holidays just for the hell of it, made a little fire and slept in a sleeping-bag."

"You have to be very careful about open fires indoors,"

Galer said. "They can be poisonous, you know, sometimes; in the old days before proper ventilation lots of people died that way."

"I know," the boy said impatiently; "I made the fire just under the window so that there would be proper ventilation. I'm not a fool."

"Sorry," Galer said.

"Oh, for goodness sake – you are just like parents are; tell them something exciting and all they say is, 'Do be careful!'"

Galer had replied of course; but what he said no longer mattered. The important thing, the map, was in his head, carefully there, almost as if Nigel had deliberately drawn it for him.

*   *   *

He made the taxi driver drop him on the main road just before the turning to Farlane's Pool; the man was obviously a little worried about what Galer was doing, so Galer told him that he was looking for a boy who had run away from school. The driver said something about the nature of the modern young and then, to show that he did not really mean it, offered to wait for Galer – without payment. But Galer did not know how long the walk would take him and besides if Nigel were up there he would have to stay to try to persuade him to come back again. "No," he told the taxi driver, "I'll hitch back – it's easy on the main road. But thanks all the same." He paid the man his fare and waited until he had turned the car round and had roared off up the hill again. Then he crossed the main road and walked along a few yards, looking for the old track that Nigel had told him of.

When you were looking for it, it was easy to see, a bramble- and weed-thick cart track leading steeply upwards. He pushed his way through the tangle of undergrowth at the side of the road and began the steep climb; but it was as not as difficult as it looked from below and the footing was still good—whoever had made the track had done it well enough for it to survive years of neglect. Within a few yards he settled into the long-striding, slightly stooping, loose-from-the-hip walk that he used so effectively. It could take him miles even over rough country when he was walking and had become habitual enough to use even on a steep hillside.

It was colder at the top of the cliff where he was no longer protected from the wind; the climb had not been long enough for him to be properly warmed by it, and he wished now that he had gone up to the flat to get a coat. He could not see anything that looked like a ruined house and he could not remember from what Nigel had said where to go now. In the end he decided to go straight ahead across the slight dip in the ground above the cliff and so on to higher ground from which he might be able to see better. He was beginning to wonder whether Nigel might not have invented the story of the house—perhaps he had seen the overgrown track once, had decided that it would be exciting to walk up it and so had imagined finding shelter up there.

But once he was on the other side of the dip he saw it; it was even more dilapidated than he had realised from Nigel's description, a few blackened beams over broken stone walls, two hundred yards down the line of timber, again in a slight dip, which was why he had not been able to see it sooner. He walked quickly down, keeping just inside the edge of the timber where the ground was almost clear of the thick grass, weed and bramble of the open.

It must once have been a marvellous cottage; the ground curved away in front of it and you could see for miles over the hazy weald—the kind of place that schoolmasters dream of buying for fifty pounds and converting into a habitable retreat, though Galer realised that if this place had been for sale at all it would have been bought long ago, probably by some wealthy businessman. Galer came out of the trees and stepped quickly down the remnants of the terracing in what must have been the garden, round a fallen stone wall, and to the front of the house. Yes, Nigel had been telling the truth, he saw; the basement, built to fit the steep fall of the land, was still habitable – it even had a door. He knocked on it and, when there was no reply, stepped quickly inside.

No one was there but, as his eyes grew accustomed to the dark, he saw that Nigel must be living there: there was a sleeping-bag rolled neatly in the far corner on some dry branches and grass and, on the other side of the room, just under the small window, the ashes of a fire carefully raked into a pyramid; and on the table made of a piece of slate balanced on two coarse cut stones stood Nigel's store of provisions and equipment – a bag of sugar, a tin of instant coffee, a plastic mug, teaspoon, various tins of soup, meat, vegetables, a small saucepan, another spoon, a fork, a knife, a tin-opener and so on, all meticulously arranged. Galer noted everything carefully; this expedition had obviously been carefully planned and Nigel was looking after himself properly. For a sudden moment he was tempted to go away immediately; Nigel must be around somewhere – perhaps he had walked into Colley to buy more food or had simply gone off exploring and if he went away, quickly, Nigel need never know that anyone had disturbed his sanctuary. He could go back to the school and tell the Headmaster that he had been mistaken and, in a few days, when he grew tired of sleeping rough and eating slender, Nigel would come back to his family and would still have a real sense of something achieved, entirely on his own.

Yet Galer knew that it would not do; he would not lie, even for Nigel, and he did not really believe that Nigel was achieving anything – for this was escape, not discovery; what Nigel needed to do was to challenge his environment from inside it, not escape into some romantic dream that would sooner or later disintegrate. Nigel was not establishing his independence, because this was only the independence of reaction; he was not breaking out of society, he was parasitic—if only because the money he used now must come from his parents—and he had to learn that you could not have the advantages both ways. So he would wait and take the chance that he was disturbing a temporary paradise.

He went outside again and settled himself down to wait; the wind was behind him now, the fallen walls protected him, and the sun was still warm, though it was late autumn. Soon he fell into a light doze in which sun and wind became a dream of new senses...

Nigel woke him as he came clattering round on the stones of the fallen garden wall. Galer looked up at the boy who stood there smiling at him.

"Hullo," said Nigel. "So you've come. I was expecting you to arrive yesterday."

"Were you so sure that I would come?"

"Why do you think that I told you about this place?" Nigel stopped smiling and looked at Galer seriously. "You haven't told my father yet, have you?"

"I haven't even seen your father. We only found out that you had gone this morning—he didn't bother to tell the school."

"He's probably ashamed."

"Why should he be?"

"Did he tell you why I walked out?"

"The Headmaster spoke to him, not me; no, I don't think that he did say."

Nigel shook his head. "He thinks that you teachers interfere too much. He says that you spend too much time doing things you aren't paid to do and too little teaching us the things that we must know."

"Do you think that?"

"I don't know. Isn't the sun marvellous?"

"Yes," said Galer, yawning and standing up. "I went to sleep. You were right; this is a magnificent place."

"Yes," the boy said. "The only trouble is that there is no water. I found an old well down below there—" he pointed down the hillside, "but it stinks a bit, so I have to get water from a stream up in the woods. About half a mile away—but marvellous water. Look!" He lifted the billy-can that he had put down at his feet when he found Galer asleep in the sun. "I'm just going to make some coffee; would you like some?"

"Yes," said Galer, "I missed my lunch coming out here."

"Oh," said Nigel. "Would you like some food? I can open a tin quite easily—I'll even heat it up for you. Or you can have some bread and cheese—it's a bit stale now, the bread, but you can toast it over the fire." He led Galer into the basement. "Home," he said, "look. Isn't it marvellous? Perfectly dry, and the fire keeps it quite warm, really."

"I came inside when I got here," Galer explained.

"Just to check up that I wasn't lying unconscious in there, half-starved, groaning for my father?" The boy laughed; he was very happy, excited at his own exploits, and enjoying having an audience after three days of silence. "Look," he said. "Raking the ash up like that keeps the fire going inside—" he scraped the ash away and the red coals began to glow in the dark room. Carefully he poured some water from his billy-can into an old and carefully cleaned tin, set it on the coals, scraped them back around its base, and put some little pieces of dry wood on top of the coals. Soon they were blazing and surprisingly soon the water was bubbling. Nigel took half a loaf of stale-looking bread wrapped in newspaper from his haversack, cut a thick slice from it, stuck it on the end of a long twig of green wood, and told Galer to toast it in the flames. He cut Galer a chunk of cheese, put it on his one plastic plate, unrolled the sleeping-bag to make a place to sit, and made

Galer coffee in the one mug, and used the tin for his own cup. Carefully he wrapped his handkerchief round it so that he would not burn himself and, after looking critically at Galer's singed bread, made him sit down on the sleeping bag and handed him the plate of cheese and his mug of coffee.

"All the comforts of home," he said, watching Galer gobble his bread and cheese. "Here, I'll make it even better for you." He got up, went into the corner of the room, and from behind a pile of stones brought a half-full bottle of whisky. "I pinched this from Dad," he said. "I'll bet that he'll be angrier about that than about my going away without leave. Poor Dad; the doctor only allows him one bottle every fortnight now, and I bet he doesn't buy another one, just suffers grimly until the fortnight is up." He uncorked the bottle and slopped a little into Galer's coffee, and then a little into his own. Galer sipped it gratefully; he was cold now that he was inside, and in some obscure sense he was very frightened. He had expected to find Nigel miserable, longing for a chance to go back again to his parents and his home, and instead he found a happy, confident, apparently self-sufficient young man, who managed to treat him as the novice. Nigel was the one in control of this situation, not him; and that made it even more difficult to see how to persuade Nigel to come back home with him.

"Yes," he said, "this place is marvellous. But how long do you think you are going to go on like this? How long can you go on?"

"Oh, the whisky will probably stretch out another week or so; and I've got a bit of money still, and so I shall manage for food. And I met one of the Forestry Commission men yesterday when I was fetching water, and told him that I was a university student on holiday—they expect lunacy from students—and would they mind my staying here? But it turns out that this isn't Forestry land at all, but National Trust, though it hasn't been developed because of its position, so anyone can come here. So unless you tell my father where I am, and he tells the police, there is nothing anyone can do. The school can't do anything, can it?"

"It could, but I don't think it will, unless your father asks us to."

"And he won't."

"He promised the Headmaster that if you weren't back by this afternoon he would tell the police."

"But he won't be able to tell them where I am," Nigel said triumphantly. "I made damn sure that I never mentioned this place to my parents. You're the only person who knows about this. Unless you tell them." He looked steady-eyed across the room at Galer.

"But then why did you tell me?" Galer burst out. He put his coffee down and leaned forward on the sleeping-bag. "Can't you see the impossible situation I'm in. What happens if your father asks me if I know where you are?"

"He won't. He won't admit that anyone might know more about me than he does himself. And he won't tell the police either. His bloody tribesmen didn't need police and so he thinks we can do without them. He says that Peel was one of the worst men England has ever had."

"But that's nonsense," Galer exclaimed, "complete nonsense!"

"Explain please, sir," Nigel sneered at him.

"Oh, for God's sake, can't you forget for a moment that I'm a schoolmaster."

"No, I can't. Nor can you. You sit here and you're a private person—you go back to school, you're teacher again. You can't do it, Galer, you can't. The moment the Headmaster or my father say to you, 'Where's Nigel?' you'll remember that you are really a teacher, that they pay you, not me. You've told me that often enough, haven't you?"

"Not like that."

"Not your words, all right, but the same sense. You are a single man, and you can't separate yourself into compartments—do those words suit you?"

"No," Galer said fiercely. "No. But you're right that I can't separate myself into parts. You shouldn't have told me about this place..."

Nigel interrupted him. "But I did, you see, I did."

Galer went on as if Nigel had not spoken. "You must have known what it would mean. You said that you were expecting me yesterday, didn't you? You've been planning this for weeks now, you were already planning it when you told me how to find it."

"Yes," Nigel said triumphantly, and it was more the note of triumph than the word which made Galer look at him in horror. It was the triumph that made him realise that he had been trapped, but even now he refused to believe. "Did you tell me deliberately, so that I would have to tell your father, or someone?" he asked.

"Yes," said Nigel. "I knew what you would do. I knew you would come here and I know what you'll do when you get back. You'll go to your bloody Headmaster and you'll say, 'I know it was a promise that I made to that boy Westcott, but if you want to find him, you just go to Farlane's Pool—take a policeman with you if you want—and you take the track up the other side, and across the dip to the trees, and you look down the hill, and you'll see a ruined cottage, and that's where you'll find young Westcott! You'll have to hurry, of course, because he may not be there when you get there.' There are lots of places I can go to, you know. I can survive on my own—I've proved it now."

Galer looked at the boy in silence for a long time before he spoke. He hadn't understood anything at all, he thought, not one thing; and even now he could not entirely believe what his intellect told him. But it did seem that the boy wanted him to betray his secret; he actually wanted Galer to go back to his father and to say, 'I can tell you where you'll find your son'. He wanted to be betrayed. He wanted to force Galer to betray him. It was all a long complicated game to make Galer break his promise, to make him betray one loyalty in order to fulfil another. Then suddenly he spoke, very gently for the words which he used, "What if I make you come with me?"

"You'll have to use force, Mr Detheridge; you'll have to knock me down first and you'll have to carry me."

"I could do it if I wanted to," Galer said.

"Oh yes, no doubt you could—but I thought that you hated violence." The boy smiled across the room at him, and Galer knew that every exit had been closed except the one. And across that there hung a neat little noose of the kind poachers use to snare rabbit paths with. He stood up quickly. "All right," he said. "If that's what you want. I'll go back and tell your father where he can find you."

"Oh no, that's not what I want—I want you to go away and tell my father that you have no idea where I am; but I know what you will do. There's a difference between wanting and knowing."

"No, you're wrong, there isn't," said Galer. "I have to tell your father; you have given me no choice at all." He turned back to the boy in final appeal. "Nigel, for goodness sake, be sensible and come back with me now—you are putting me in an impossible situation. If you come back I'll do everything in my power to sort things out with your father."

"No, you don't, Mr Detheridge," Nigel sneered. "I'm not interested in your terms—always halfway. The halfway man, Galer Detheridge. You always go on about synthesis, don't you; putting things together to make a good conclusion? Well, that's not the way the world is; it's all or nothing, that's what it is. And you're on the side of all—all the headmasters, all the police, all the fathers. The great collective voice of the tribe. One or the other, and you're one, and I'm the other."

"All right," said Galer fiercely. "All right—you have won the argument, in your terms at least. Now for God's sake stop being an adolescent brat and come back with me."

"No," said Nigel. "I want to do this properly. I want you to go back there to tell them. And don't worry; I'll wait here until they come, and by the way I want my father to come to fetch me. Will you tell him that? In fact, if he doesn't come, I won't come back at all. Unless they tie me up and carry me."

"Why?" Galer said helplessly. "Why? What on earth are you trying to prove? That in the end I'm on the side of authority? But I could have told you that myself."

"You could now," Nigel said. "You see, Mr Detheridge— if I may call you that—I want you to understand that I hate you. Because you are a hypocrite. Simple you see. That I hate you. That you have stopped fooling me with your hypocrisy."

Galer looked at the boy. Was that the truth? Was it all hatred for complexities of responsibility that he did not understand, or was the boy ill? What was happening inside that mind, what terrible things had escaped their chains and were roaming about loose there, laughing and sneering and weeping and roaring? Perhaps the boy was just ill. But he looked all right, and there was a reason in all that he had done, a logic that stretched over weeks, that casual events could have made him foretell, that another man—a man like Jim, for instance— might have been able to foresee. But there was nothing to do now but act.

Nigel walked with him as far as the edge of the near-cliff above the main road; they did not speak to each other again but Nigel waited to watch Galer go down the steep track. At the bottom Galer stopped and looked up; the boy waved as he might have done to a friend who had come calling.

* * *

On his long walk back to the school, Galer refused two offers of lifts, one from the parents of one of the boys he taught and one from a local farmer. "Can't we give you a lift?" they said and "No, I want to walk," he replied each time. He needed to walk, he needed to feel the hard stones of the roadside under his feet. Deliberately he shut all thoughts away and let his long stride carry him steadily back to the school.

He went straight to the Headmaster, told him that he had found Nigel and that the boy was perfectly all right physically, but that he insisted that his father should fetch him. The Headmaster drove him to the Westcotts' farm and came in with Galer to tell the old man that Nigel was found. Galer tried hard to make Adamson Westcott phone the police – since the thing had to be done, he wanted, as Nigel did, that it be done properly – but just as Nigel had predicted, the old man gave them a lecture on the iniquities of having an organised system of crime detection and prevention. The Headmaster, although of course he regarded the lecture with benign amusement, did not want the police brought into a matter that was purely to do with the boy's parents and the school.

So the three of them drove out to the turn-off to Farlane's Pool and Galer told them where to find the boy; he refused to come with them, despite the Headmaster's obvious displeasure, but sat in the front of the car waiting for them to come down again; nor, as the four of them drove back to the Westcotts, did he once look round to the back seat where Adamson Westcott and his son sat without talking. But when they got to the Westcotts' farm the old man, with a belated show of politeness – for up to then he had treated both Headmaster and Galer as interfering buffoons – offered them tea and Galer insisted that they go inside, again despite the Headmaster's obvious embarrassment; he made it clear that he wanted nothing more than to escape back to his seat of administration.

So the fourth Mrs Westcott made tea, ignored her stepson's reappearance—not cruelly, but simply as if he made a habit of running away from home—and the four men (or three men and a boy) stood in her kitchen and drank mugs of tea, the Headmaster and Galer on one side of the room and Mr Westcott and his son on the other, the mother, cheerful, competent, chatty, bustling between. The Headmaster talked to Galer about some trivial detail of school and Mr Westcott talked quietly to his son; and all the time Galer stared across at the boy, willing him to look round, willing him to look across the gulf to him. But he would not, not until the Headmaster said firmly, "Well, Mr Detheridge, if you have finished your tea, we really must be getting back. I am sure that the Westcotts have a great deal to discuss; and we expect to see you back at school shortly, young man." Then at last Nigel looked round, nodded in reply to the Headmaster, and looked carefully at Galer. To Galer his look said plainly and simply, 'Betrayal. You see, I was right all along; you have betrayed me, and I have betrayed you. We are not so simple as these other people, you and me, but we understand now. Betrayal is all.' And out of the darkness of Galer's mind came a memory of his father's eyes saying across a room to him, 'Love,' and his voice saying, 'Loving other people is what matters, son.' But that was no good any more, it had gone wrong, it didn't satisfy. He was dead, that father, and the past was dead and the future too.

* * *

Nigel came back to school a fortnight later; he looked as though he had been very ill, and the official line that his father and the Headmaster had agreed on to cover his absence was simply that. He came into Galer's classes, sat quietly at the back, said not a word to anyone, other boys or teacher and, though he read his books and took his notes, he turned in no written work to Galer at all. After a fortnight of this, Galer could bear his silence no longer and stopped him as he was leaving class one day.

"Just hang on a moment, Nigel," he said. "I want a word with you," and when the other boys were out of the room, the last sensibly closing the door behind him, Galer said, "Look Nigel, I know that you are probably not going to forgive me for what happened, but it's no reason to stop working; there are still things I can teach you, or show you where to find them, though of course if you want I'll get you transferred to another class."

Nigel shook his head. "I'll stay, if I may. There's nothing to forgive, you know," and added, as an afterthought, "Galer." He smiled steadily. "In fact, it's probably the other way round, isn't it?"

"I don't know," said Galer; nor did he – it was all confusion, a thought this way, a thought that, anger, bitterness, love, friendship, loathing, despair, all like flames of different colours in his head, all burning and mocking each other and weeping for each other.

"You know that I'm going to a psychiatrist these days – twice a week, Tuesday and Friday afternoons; instead of playing rugger. The Headmaster arranged it. Did you know?" Galer nodded; it had been he who had suggested the need to the Headmaster. "My old man says it's a lot of bloody nonsense, expensive too. 'Now in the tribes . . .'," he threw his voice high in imitation of his father's hectoring manner. "But he's quite a nice man, the doctor, really; he doesn't say anything, won't say anything, just asks awkward questions. The only thing he's said directly so far is that I have to admit to myself that I am in a disturbed state – he's said that once I do that I'm on the way to adjustment, whatever that is." He smiled satirically. "He's a specialist in adolescent problems. But it's hard work admitting that you are nuts, much harder than anything you make me do. So don't worry if I don't do much work for you."

"All right; I won't," said Galer and for a moment he allowed himself the luxury of thinking that perhaps it was going to be all right after all; perhaps the boy was simply ill and would, with care and guidance, learn to cope with the world again. And perhaps one day they might even become friends again, when Nigel was no longer a pupil and could see more clearly what being a schoolmaster meant. But it was only a moment that he felt that; looking at Nigel again he knew that he still did not understand what was happening behind those steady eyes and careful mouth.

* * *

Just after Christmas, one Friday afternoon when he was meant to be in London at the clinic, Nigel hanged himself in his father's garage. He acted as intelligently as always, for at the inquest a police sergeant gave evidence of having found a book on forensic medicine at Nigel's bedside; he had borrowed it from the local library and had left a careful marker at the chapter on death by hanging. As the book said that hanging by wire was more effective than by rope, since wire could not be as easily removed, Nigel had used a thin bit of flex from his own table lamp. He must have knotted this round one of the beams of the garage, said the police sergeant, and must have then stood on a chair from the kitchen and made a noose in the flex, at just the right height, and put it round his neck, with the knot immediately below the occiput—the police sergeant called it the 'lump of backbone at the back of the neck', and the coroner corrected him with the formal name—and then must have kicked the chair away.

The police doctor told the coroner that the boy must have died quickly, though by strangulation rather than a broken neck.

CALL

The psychiatrist from the clinic in London said that he had been seeing the boy and that it was clear to him, for various technical reasons, that he had been in an early stage of paranoic schizophrenia.

The coroner said that he did not think it was necessary to call the boy's father, the anthropologist and author Mr Adamson Westcott, since it would only cause more pain in an already painful case. Nor did he call on the Headmaster of St Michaels College. He expressed his sympathy to the parents of Nigel Westcott, who had clearly taken his own life while of unsound mind.

*   *   *

For reasons that no one at St Michaels understood, Adamson Westcott managed to persuade the Anglican bishop of the diocese to give the necessary dispensation for a suicide to be buried in consecrated ground – or rather for his ashes to be scattered on consecrated ground, for old Westcott insisted that his son be cremated. The school was represented at the service by the Headmaster and his wife, three members of staff – Messrs Tremone, Jenkyns, and Detheridge – the head boy of the school, and three of Nigel's classmates, who were given permission to miss classes for the day. There was an unfortunate scene at the graveyard after the priest had scattered the ashes and said his slightly abbreviated prayers, for when the Headmaster tried to approach Adamson Westcott to offer his condolences, the old man, supported by his wife, deliberately turned his back on the man and walked away.

*   *   *

For Galer, the real funeral was later that day. He made Jim drive him out to Farlane's Pool, and telling him that he would not be gone longer than half an hour, he walked up the old track, across the shallow valley at the top, and went into the basement of the burnt-down cottage. He went like a man looking for something and, sure enough, he found it—Nigel had left the half-full bottle of whisky that he had stolen from his father behind the little pile of stones in the corner. Galer took the bottle carefully outside, stood in the mid-winter cold, looked down over the miles of the weald, opened the bottle, drank half of it, and recorked it carefully. Then he threw it as hard and as far as he could down the hillside. He didn't see it break, but he saw its wheeling curve through the air, heard it fall, and knew that his libation was made. He stood for a moment or two longer, then turned away and went back down the near-cliff to where Jim was waiting in the car. For the time being there was nothing to think; he had completed what he saw somehow as a necessary action and now he must be still again, waiting for the thoughts to come slowly, a great flood-tide of thoughts that were both triumph and misery to come darkening in.

9

Pastoral care, ho ho. What do they think parents are for, anyway? Conception, pregnancy, parturition, a bit of food, and then . . . why, the teachers can take over! In the old days the priests would have had the care of their souls. Or godparents. Now godparents are for giving them a couple of fivers a couple of times and, if they live long enough, getting them a job if they don't make university. Now it's teachers who guard their blessed souls as well as their minds. Bodies too, maybe. Or are we only substitute nannies? I suppose that's why we are thought so much more important than we were a hundred years ago; then we were ushers and we whipped their minds with grammar and their backsides with tawses. Oversimplification, I realise, but we do a deal more than we used to; and the trouble is that people like Galer think it's our inherent duty. Who sorts out the bed-wetter and the sadist? Teacher. Who protects the soul of Nigel Westcott? Galer Detheridge. And, dammit, he believes it; he believes that he could have done things that the Father of the Tribe of One could not. Even the 'boy' (I fall into Galer's term, the boy, the boy, never Nigel) thinks that Galer may be able to help him; so he goes to Galer, and Daddy stays at home. A bit of the big world, that's what he should have had. Pack him off to the wide world. Become Daddy himself. That's what we should have done pastorally, bloody sheep. Arrange a mating, forbid contraception, and give Nigel a son to grow up to hate him. Let Galer have his own son too, and we would have seen then what Nigel could have done to him. False-Father becoming Archetype. False-Bastard becoming Big Daddy. Make a marvellous story, that would.

But in life it happens different, see; and if you don't like my life, bloody reader, you can go story yourself. Nigel runs away; Galer knows where he's gone; torment of tractions – who do I love best, my father (his father, Headmaster, St Michaels, God) or my son (briefly named Nigel, deathmonger)? Oh my son, my son! Choice without choice, Daddy wins every time. You betrayed me, cries son. And the terror of it is that Galer really believes that he did betray him. Told me that himself. "Betrayal," he said.

It doesn't follow, of course it doesn't follow. But you try to persuade Galer of that. I joked, I argued, I listened, I explained. Could anyone have been a better friend than I, quoth lyrical Jim. Querieth John. Smileth Jenkyns. The basis of epistemology is nothing to do with knowledge but a certain blank look in the listener's eye. Wednesday's aphorism. Means little, doubt I. But how can you make a man like Galer see what a man like Galer can't see?

I made my efforts more formal. I told Skarfe that I wanted to talk to Galer alone, and I took him off to a restaurant in town. Habit from the days before his marriage. Fed and drank mightily, talked much—at least I did. Galer survives the evening with a certain stony eye in his head, while I, poor I, get so tight that he has to get a taxi to take me home and has to put me to bed. Next, I thought I might shock him out of himself; I told Skarfe that I was taking Galer to a theatre in London and, instead, I took him to a certain flat where a couple do a performance of a rather different kind. Made me so excited that I would have made love with a Quaker; until, on the way home in the train, Galer got to discussing—mark you, discussing—the performance. "I must remember to ask my wife...", he said, though I happen to know that he never did; because all that the performance excited in him was a certain curiosity about the psychology of the participants. When I suggested that the psychology of the audience might be more interesting, since the participants' motives were likely to be economic—profitless evenings cost me a great deal—he looked at me as if I were mad. Did he even wonder why I had taken him? He must have, but he must also have decided that it was simply an error of judgement or taste on my part, and so he would not discuss that. No shock value, even. Poor old Satan. Satan satanised.

Anyway, I gave up trying to break the cycle of misery that Galer fell into after Nigel killed himself. Misery? Is that the right word? I don't know, to tell the truth. His mood seemed to be a strange compound, misery predominating of course, but there were elements of something else there too. But when I come to explain what else, I am in trouble. For instance, when he made me drive him out to Farlane's Pool after that ghastly funeral and the ghastly Headmaster's display of diplomatic insensitivity, he came down that cliff looking almost as if he had discovered that Nigel had been bluffing the lot of us and had been sitting up there on the mountain-side. And he stank of whisky – I mean stank. I had to have several drinks myself when we got back before I got the smell of him out of my nostrils – and the smell of meat burning in the crematorium. Oh, people say that you can't smell a thing; but I can. Twice I've smelt that smell, and so when I die I want to be buried decently in the ground, where only moles and worms can smell my death. Who wants to go out in a smell like the school dining-room over-cooking Thursday's chops?

I asked Galer about the stink of whisky; never a one for keeping silent at moments of crisis, is Jim/John Jenkyns. He likes to talk more and more as things get worse and worse. No decent reticence there, nor awkward reverence for that matter. Awkward irreverence, maybe. Not like Galer; face like a stone all through the service and through the 'ashes to ashes' bit, not even a giggle when the priest said, "Ashes to ashes", and scattered the little bits of burnt Nigel to the wind, which unfortunately did not let him rest respectably on the grass till the next rain came, but swooped him up into the air and the trees and, God being willing, and though I'm not much of a hand at natural history, the trees were ashes. Final joke, that. Nigel's final hilarious joke, ho, ho.

Back to whisky. Galer growled something that I couldn't properly hear. Was he thinking of starting a pub up there, I asked, and was perhaps testing whether whisky tasted as good on top of a cliff as it did anywhere else. Oh shut up, Jim, he growls, I'm not in the mood. Very seldom is either. But I left off, and fell to puzzling out, like any hero of a thriller, how the chief suspect could possibly smell of whisky after taking a walk up a cliff-face. After the suicide of the protagonist too, mark you. I had certain clues to ponder. One, Nigel had holed out in these parts – at any rate, I had heard Farlane's Pool mentioned, though I had thought that meant Nigel had chosen the most celebrated picnicking spot in the county for his retreat from civilisation, which, to tell the truth, just about fitted my picture of his all-round exhibitionism. Beating Big Daddy at his own game, you know. But perhaps Nigel had gone up that cliff—well, not quite a cliff. I knew that Galer had known that he was there, and had arranged for him to be fetched down. So this return trip could be in the nature of a pilgrimage, Galer being the kind of man who might go in for those kind of things.

But where did the whisky fit in? In-spiration! Nigel probably nicked it from his old man before he took off for the wilds of deepest Kent, and he must have left it hidden up there, possibly for returning to later. Galer had gone up there to check if there might be some left in the bottle and had been in luck. But it sure was a long way to come for a swig of whisky; I'd have given him some in my rooms if he had asked. So why come back here to finish off Nigel's stolen whisky? Whisky . . . whisky . . . spiritual equivalent, ho, ho. Perhaps therefore some kind of rite of identification. 'I am still your brother, dead Nigel.' That sort of thing. But it doesn't fit Galer and Nigel; nothing very much brotherly there, more fatherly perhaps. Ah, exclaimed the great detective, that's it; it's some kind of assumption of the role of father.

Oh, no, my dear Poirot/Maigret/Marlow/Appleby/Heat. It won't do. It simply doesn't stand up. Not enough fact old chap. I mean, I couldn't very well have turned to Galer to say, "I Know Why You Drank the Whisky. You've just become Adamson Westcott. May I congratulate you on your elevation, old chap?" It was there, nevertheless, hunch, futile maybe, but there; I did at least recognise that what was happening to Galer in those hours—and days and weeks afterwards, for that matter—was happening somewhere deep down inside him. And it gave me a moment of terror, that hunch—yes, even a jokester can have moments of terror—which is, in my sad case, more or less the same as an apprehension of death. I gave up being a materialist years ago, I think from the moment that steering wheel twisted in my hands and drove me straight at the high brick wall on the road into Henley, and I don't see why one shouldn't smell death metaphorically if one may smell it literally. And the smell of whisky in the car turned into the smell of death, more potent for the creation of fear than the smell of burning Nigel or burning mother had been. Galer was away from himself, and probably there are not all that many people in the world who can recognise those who have gone away there for a spell. So I had to do something. Hence my attempts to divert him.

You remember, don't you? Jim/John Jenkyns went mad once. Too much brooding on what happened down here (tapping the base of his skull). Decided that it wasn't going to happen again, so would concentrate only on what happened up here (tapping the top of his head). It's strange, think I, that a man who wants to show that another man is mad should tap his forehead with a finger, thus. He should really tap his finger thus, or cross both hands over his heart and sweep them out to the audience, like a ballet dancer who wants to mime love. The bewilderment of excess. That's it exactly. Someone else's voice, as always. The other is the snow. But that's Galer, slow-voiced, snow-voiced.

What about Skarfe in all this? What about absurd and lovely Skarfe? She's a strange one, that girl, strength there that is hard to realise. She was very good with that man after Nigel died, but she was near breaking point too. What's it like to watch someone that you love turn to stone? I know, I suppose, because I love Galer too. It's a little less bad for me, though, because when he suddenly abandons the world and goes far away from himself, as if he were talking to dead people or were dead himself, I can always go away, go to sit over whisky in the pub or in front of the bloody box, or just get in the Green Monster and drive over the green fields of nether-England. Skarfe has to stay with him, looking at those steady eyes and that wordless mouth, as he holds himself very still in his chair. Perhaps it's not so much Galer needs succouring, but Skarfe; perhaps I should protect her from that silence rather than wasting words in the air around Galer's head. Damn dead Nigel; I hope Satan has found a nice sharp fork to toast him on. But probably all he's doing at the moment is holding Nigel in readiness (in the deep freeze maybe) for the imminent arrival of the great Adamson Westcott–and what fun he'll have then, good old Satan: perhaps he'll join them together like Siamese twins and they can talk to each other until Judgement Day. Oh blissful torment, while I watch my friend, and my unhappy Skarfe watches him too, eyes always on that too much love.

But they go to Cornwall this Easter as usual; and Galer will be able to walk there, walk himself into being animal again rather than stone; and Skarfe will be able to love him properly again, dark bird of the air, beautiful air-named Skarfe. I rather thought that I might be invited to go to Cornwall with them, but nothing has been said, so I shall keep my mouth shut and shall arrange to go to Ely to see my blessed dead mother's blessed friends and walk round that cathedral and find some pompous clergyman to argue with about the building of the octagon and sit outside the cathedral and look at the pretty mums wheeling their brats in chrome and dark blue prams. And, if God is kind, dear dead mother's dear friends will try to introduce me to some eligible young things with unfortunate legs and stringy hair–and I can be charmingly unavailable. Unless of course there happens to be another one of those... what was her name? Mrs Pamela O'Brien, O'Bryan, O'Breighan, whatever? "So sad," said mama's oldest friend, whispering and signalling with her eyes towards the slim-legged young matron talking to some dreary housewife near the door of the sitting-room. "Such a nice young woman, and her husband, an Irishman you know, left her last year, and she's got two such pretty children," and I looked over the assembled tea-drinking fiends and saw Mrs Pamela Whatever looking at me, and both of us knew whose pretty slim legs I would be lying between that night, and whose firm matronly backside would be bumping steadily up at me. Strange how it is that one knows when one does know; and I was quite right of course—the casual meeting, the casual conversation, the casual invitation "to come in some evening for a drink after I've put the children to bed", and heigh ho! Very experimental young matron, Mrs Pamela Whatever, and that's the kind of holiday I really enjoy. The nice thing about the Mrs Whatevers of the world is that they enjoy their safe little reputations for being hard done by as much as they enjoy being done hard; and when you meet them next day, they say politely to the people who introduce you, "Oh yes, Mr Jenkyns and I met yesterday, at Mrs Simpson's, wasn't it, Mr Jenkyns?" Call me Jim, I say, or John. Polite day, and oh so impolite night! So pleased to have met you, pretty hard-done-by Mrs Whatever! Heigh ho!

O Gaiety thy name is Jenkyns! But He Weeps, old chap, He Weeps Bitter Tears beneath the Gay Exterior. When I was at university, I had for a couple of terms a girl-friend who used to say, "Don't talk about that—or this—it gives me the 'morbs'": the morbidities, I suppose. Don't talk about mothers, they give me the morbs; don't talk about finals, it gives me the morbs; and so on. She was a lovely big-breasted girl, poor girl; after I threw her over she took up rowing for her college and got an oar or a paddle or whatever the thing is, but it increased her bust even further and, by the time I went down, I heard talk that she had had to give up rowing, because there was not enough room in the boat for her, her breasts, and eight other people, even though the cox was flat-chested. But 'morbs' was a good expression. At the moment I have the morbs badly; there's hardly room in the boat for anyone else, my morbs are so large. Ho, ho.

To cheer myself therefore, I have made a belated New Year resolution: that I, Jim/John Jenkyns, shall pay more attention to the things about me. I shall use my senses fully. I shall pay tribute to things. I am going to make a start on the statue of old *Abraham Crouch, Visionary and Builder, 1821*–blank. I have already told the Headmaster that Crouch should be cleaned and that the school should find out when he died and pay to have that missing date filled in. Unless it turns out that the poor old bankrupt is alive somewhere, a Victorian immortal, living frugally on the Welfare State. After all, he deserves his immortality, railways magnate nurtured on Young England and Ruskin, who built the magnificent Victorian Gothic mansion that still serves us as the main school building, with its thirty bedrooms (not counting servants' quarters, naturally) and dozen reception rooms, its false parapets and ornate porticos, heraldic devices and leering gargoyles. He must have been very sure of his dream, old Crouch, because he had his monument built long before ideals swamped even money, and now the portly builder in bronze dreams and watches over all we do.

I have therefore devised a new school song, which begins:

> *Oh Crouch, who stands erect*
> *Upon our beauteous lawns . . .*

One day I am going to sing it, God help me, to the assembled staff. Let the cheap Burgundy flow and the Spanish Sauternes be served, and uninvited I shall rise and sing my song:

> *Be with us through the day*
> *And when the night is long.*

CALL

> *And when the dawn comes up again,*
> *O Crouch, we rise to thee,*
> *And think of higher heavenlier things*
> *And distant lands beyond the sea.*

Oh magnates of England, where are you now? I can imagine no experience more holy than to build a Utopia and then watch it crumble, saying as it fell wise words on the nature of men and angels. Galer would weep for fallen men and I ... well, I would weep for Galer, perhaps.

10

The wind on the headland was so strong that it seemed that he might almost be toppled over and crash down the side of the hill to the steep cliffs above the sea; it tore and tugged at his thick jersey, snatched at his hair, caught at his face, but his footing was firm and he exulted both in the strength of the wind and in his own rootedness. Out there in the sea three trawlers were struggling through the waves that the wind had blown up, one after the other disappearing in a tangle of mist and broken water and then reappearing before the next wave hurried against them; on the headland below him the grass and red heather flattened and raced as the wind swooped, and above him the sea-gulls dipped and wheeled and struggled upwards only to be forced back, seeming to skid back on a gust and then strain against the air to regain their distances.

Yes, Nigel was dead and, yes, his father was dead, but he, Galer Detheridge, man without words, man in the wind, man firmly rooted against the wind, he was alive; and in his strength and in the quick strong movements that had carried him around the bay and on to this headland he carried the generations. His father was dead, yes, but he survived; he too would have exulted in this wind and cold, the fine mist of the sea spreading on the grass around him, the stones piled high behind him, the three trawlers struggling to a safe harbour, the yellow flowers on the hurling and straining gorse, the burnt bracken, all that existed, alive in the wind. His son was not born, but he existed, image in his mind, child growing month by month, small boy gravely walking, and man who would carry Galer inside him long after he was dead. His father survived in him, son existed in him; father in son, son in father – what other truth did a man need? Even if he died, even if he allowed this wind to topple him, his son would go on, and his father would never die, son would never die, he would never die. He had allowed his body to drive him these miles, cliff-top, beach, fallen rocks, sheep-tracks, hill-side, gully, across streams, inland for a small river, and then the last steep climb through waist-high gorse and heather that caught at his legs, and now he stood there, high on the headland, facing into the strong wind that came roaring up from the sea, like the sea itself, and he would never die. There was no such thing as death, no man's death, every man part of the generations, stone, sand, earth, sea, the wind off the sea, and a man in the wind on the headland, certain that he would never die.

Part Two

Response

'We usually speak as if death pursued us, and we fled from him; but that is only so in rare instances. Ordinarily he masks himself – makes himself beautiful – all-glorious; not like the King's daughter, all-glorious within, but outwardly: his clothing of wrought gold. We pursue him frantically all our days, he flying or hiding from us. Our crowning success at three-score and ten is utterly and perfectly to seize, and hold him in his eternal integrity – robes, ashes, and sting.'

Ruskin, *Unto This Last*

11

The world prospered.

*   *   *

"Early November," the doctor said, "late autumn," and standing up, smiled at her. "You're a strong healthy woman, Mrs Detheridge, and I'm sure you'll have a perfect baby." He said this to everyone he saw, a busy G.P. who did not have time to make up new speeches, but because her delight was so apparent he added, "and a beautiful one too, if mother is anything to go by. Now you come to see me in a week's time, and we'll do a proper examination, blood and so on, and I'll tell you all that you have to do." Skarfe smiled goodbye to him, stopped in the waiting-room to make an appointment for the next week, and went home to Galer.

He was sitting reading in his classroom. She looked round the door, saw that he was alone, and walked in. "Hullo, husband," she said, kissing him and then sitting on the edge of his desk.

"Hullo, wife."

"Dr Rankin says that I am pregnant definitely."

"I don't know why you even bothered to go to him," he laughed at her. "We knew, didn't we? We don't need doctors to tell us things like that."

"But he needed to do tests and things . . ."

"Forget all that; forget doctors – I'm your husband and I'll look after you." He grabbed her hands and pulled her off the desk, saying as he did so, "Here, stand up and let me look at you." He turned her sideways and then ran his hand over the slight outward curve of her stomach.

"It's beginning to show, isn't it?" she asked. "I mean, if I tell people now, they'll have to believe me. They won't just think I'm making it up."

"Yes," he said, "you can tell people," running his hand over and over the place where inside his child was growing.

"Do you remember . . .?" she began but he stopped her with a hand over her mouth.

"No words," he said. "Leave it without words."

That was Galer's creed: don't speak, don't find the words, allow the feelings to exist before the words. Words placed the feelings too exactly, or they made them too small, or they made them vague. Respond to the world, yes, notice everything around you, pay tribute to everything that was born and died and re-born, but without words, and without thought too. Open the shuttered doors, yes, and peer down there where the dance of flame in the shining darkness leapt and twisted and where the pulse of the immortals beat slower than the pulse of the body, but without thinking about what you saw, allowing it to dance and flame and continue its slow pulsing. The only prayer that mattered was "world without end"; the rest was hazy, incomplete, fragmented.

* * *

Harry wrote from Canada:
We are all delighted with your news. Even my young Peter, who does not seem to realise that your son will usurp his temporary position as male heir of the family. But Ruth and I are delighted to let you take over the burden. I wish only that Dad was alive to see his grandsons increase and prosper; how he would have exulted in them. I expect that he would have taken two-year-old

RESPONSE

Peter on hundred-mile walks through the country. It was so good to hear that Lerryn still survives—of course I remember that day. Did you get as far as the church, or did Skarfe collapse at the Detheridge stride?

Mother is very frail, poor old girl; I read your letter to her but I don't think that she comprehends much. She's taken to calling me John and regularly addresses Peter as Galer; he's much confused by his other name, because of course he knows all about his Uncle Galer in England. Mother has a collection of equally doddery old friends around her, who re-create England every day at tea time; but she is very rude to them sometimes, and her deafness makes her muddle whispers and shouts. One old dear from "the old country" came to call yesterday, and Mother called loudly down the passage, "Drat that Mrs Perkins; another boring Tory", but then of course smiled sweetly and gave her "good tea", thinking Mrs Perkins hadn't heard her whispered shout. Mother is thoroughly back into the Socialism of forty years ago, and makes the most fiery political statements that I have heard in Canada for years—including those half-baked nationalists. But her friends, all very respectable, seem to regard her socialism as another kind of deafness: you know, "she doesn't mean to be rude, poor dear".

The girls continue their teaching happily, though I think that Sally's latest man is the marrying kind, because he plays with Peter and then looks meaningfully at Sally. Sometimes the two teachers make me feel a little odd, what with you at St Michaels and Sally married to her clergyman, as if I had deserted the family somehow. But my job goes well, and the work I'm doing at the moment may be important one day; I won't try to explain it, though—it becomes more and more abstruse every day. If I remember, I'll send you an article from the office tomorrow; it's a kind of summary of what the Institute is concerned with these days.

Best wishes to Skarfe and the mad Jenkyns; I remember him with great affection. He remains unmarried, I suppose, and still continues the long search for a girl like his mother. Ruth sends her love, and Peter too . . .

* * *

The world outside him existed again without a flaw, no dead things arching and heaving in the waves, no stone speaking its utter and silent truthfulness. He would stand for hours, marvelling at the perfection of the flight of a kestrel, the hover, swoop and dive through the clear air, or he would watch a spring plant pushing its way up through a trapdoor of earth, seeing it as if his eye had been a camera slowed down to take in its whole growing, or, walking through Burston or London with his wife looking for the things his son would need, a cot, a pram, a bath, a playpen, clothes, toys, he would stop suddenly, leaving Skarfe to walk on alone, while he stared across the street at some mother wheeling her child down the pavements, and Skarfe would realise that he had stopped and would hurry back for him, laughing at him, and would take him by the arm and bring him back to pavements and shopping.

* * *

Galer decided that the spare room of their flat was not good enough for his son, so he set about redecorating it. He painted the walls and ceiling a brilliant white, and all the woodwork a brilliant yellow; but he was not satisfied and so went specially to London and found, after hours of searching, a wallpaper designed specially for a nursery, flying horses and dancing elephants and strange wide-winged birds, in yellows and oranges and light browns. He searched through the villages round about St Michaels for an old-fashioned rocking-cot and, in the end, found one, filthy with old varnish and peeling paint, in an outhouse behind one of the cottages in Colley. An old woman who had heard him asking in an antique shop

RESPONSE

where he might find such a cot had told him that he could have hers for nothing, though it was old and dirty. He spent evening after evening sandpapering away the old paint and varnish, and then painted it carefully with a colourless varnish that did not obscure the fine old grain of the wood. He built huge open shelves for the child's toys, shelves wide and long enough to hold toys for ten children, Skarfe told him, laughing at his pride.

*   *   *

So the summer term passed, the baby growing inside Skarfe, Skarfe walking with grace, and Galer watching her, wordlessly. World without end, it was.

12

Skarfe grew. Galer flourished. Big man, Galer, doubled in size now. Firmly believed that his wife—not by name, merely by rank—would in about six or seven months forward in time from that moment in time, make all timeless. World without end, and don't bother to say Amen. He told me once that was the only prayer he believed in, and that mark you, in these short-lived days. Jenkyns continued finitely, half-hearted. Half-hearted, see. Oh, you wit, Jenkyns, you wit. Applause, ladies and gentlemen, if you please, for Jenkyns the Witty Welsh Exile. I puke on my own wit. I weep for my own wit. Double-named Jenkyns, maker of death, Jenkyns artificer of the most ornate coffins in Western Europe.

What was it that RLS said on that island? I can't remember,

says Jenkyns. Look it up, cries Galer, look it up. All right, sir. I've looked it up:

> *The embers of the day are red*
> *Behind the murky hill.*
> *The kitchen smokes: the bed*
> *In the darkling house is spread:*
> *The great sky darkens overhead,*
> *And the great woods are shrill.*
> *So far have I been led,*
> *Lord, by Thy will:*
> *So far I have followed, Lord, and wondered still.*
>
> *The breeze from the embalmed land*
> *Blows sudden toward the shore,*
> *And claps my cottage door.*
> *I hear the signal, Lord – I understand.*
> *The night at Thy command*
> *Comes. I will eat and sleep and will not question more.*

Good effening, Jenkyns the Death. But on second thoughts I'll misread the signal, Lord; I think I'll just sit here and admire the sunset. To hell with you, old man.

You see, ladies and gentlemen, I know the end of the story. Unfair, yes, but my time is time past. Jenkyns does not live, but he re-lives. JENKYNUS COMMENTATUS. Skarfe Detheridge, you see, suffered from a condition called *placenta praevia*; that's when the placenta lies below the embryo, not above it, so that when the baby starts to be born, pressing down on the uterus, he tears the placenta away from its moorings, and bleeds to death before he's out of the womb. Technically, of course, he doesn't bleed; his mother bleeds and he dies of a lack of oxygen. Nowadays the doctors usually manage to do a rush Caesarean section ('untimely ripped') and get the baby out in time, and then sew the mother up quick; thirty years ago mother and child died, sure as one day they'd die anyway, and I expect that where babies aren't born in hospitals, they die still—press down, tear away, bleed, die shortly thereafter. *Anoxia*, more properly *hypoxia*. With Skarfe's baby the doctors failed—or call it Galer's son, because the poor old bugger was right the whole time about that, at any rate. Skarfe survived; they sewed her up quick and filled her up with blood again, and she survived. Mother survived, baby died, father... well, can you imagine Galer with his son dead before he had breathed? End of story.

Beginning of story too, because why did that particular baby die? I'm not asking why any baby died, I'm asking why that one baby died? Why did Galer Detheridge's beloved first-born son die before he even breathed? Undoubtedly, the doctors have the right answer: he died because his mother suffered from *placenta praevia*. Its incidence in the population is about 0·5 per cent, and the perinatal loss is 3·6 times greater than the normal average of perinatal losses. Various other factors, such as the age of the mother, the prematurity of the birth, the health of mother and embryo, are contributory causes; since Skarfe was young and healthy, and the embryo apparently so, the chances were reduced to probably about one to three hundred; and perinatal loss reduced to about one in two thousand. In other words, Skarfe and her baby were unlucky. Or Skarfe was lucky and her baby was not. This had nothing to do with the fact that the child's putative father was a man called Galer Detheridge, whose father was called John Detheridge, and whose son was to have been Unwen Detheridge; and whose friend was a double-named dealer in death.

Modern theologians, damn them, would probably agree. Since God's mercy is infinite, his ways are mysterious. I mean, they can afford to be mysterious, can't they, because he (He, I mean) can forgive anything, even his (His) own mysteries.

Mediaeval theologians would presume that someone had sinned and that the baby's death was a punishment on the living for their sins—though it was a bit rough if the baby wasn't baptised, since he wouldn't get eternal life, unless God managed to squeeze out a bit of extra mercy. Since they are damned already, there's not much point, but damn them too for good measure. Alternatively, let us say that the statistics picked Galer and Skarfe to suffer and their child to bleed to death *in utero*. Up yours, unsubtle statistics; could you not have chosen better? Again, up yours, Wittgenstein: how can you say that the baby died when it did not live, for life we define as breathing? I say it was conceived—in at least two senses of the word—and therefore it lived.

No answers. All I can tell you from my refuge in Hades is what I saw and what I and a couple of other people did. Don't ask me to imagine, because I have exiled that part of me. Jenkyns the Self, remember. I can't tell you why that baby died, because I don't know. Ignorant Jenkyns too, imperfect story-teller. Nor can I tell you why Galer believes that his son's death is something to do with him, nor why Skarfe believes that too; I don't even know that he does believe that. Perhaps he believes that it is a punishment for pride, the gods frowning on his monumental *hubris*. I have often suspected Galer of being an adept of the old gods; I am sure that the business of the whisky-drinking after burnt Nigel's scattering to the winds was a libation to the angry gods, or whatever. Perhaps he believes that it is a punishment for some sin, for loving his father wrong, for loving his wife wrong, for loving his son wrong, perhaps even for loving me wrong. Perhaps he believes that old Adamson Westcott came back from Africa with a great ju-ju, which he used to curse Galer's unborn son in the womb, to revenge himself on—or for—Nigel. God help me, I don't even understand why Nigel died. Oh, I could give you a list of possible reasons, though the list may be incomplete, and though you'll need to evaluate the reasons yourselves. That was a person choosing death, and even then I can't tell you his reason. Galer's son didn't choose anything, he just died before he had time to be alive. God help me again, I don't even know why I tried to kill myself, those years ago; I put the blame on the steering wheel, just as the doctors put the blame on a medical condition.

If I don't know what's going on in my own head, how the hell, O fellow-inhabitants of Hell, O ladies and gentlemen, O rapt reader, can I tell you what is going on inside the heads of Galer and Skarfe? I know about a tiny bit of my own head, and I call that my self; I can tell you a world about that, but nothing else about me. I know an acre or two about Galer and Skarfe, and I can tell you about that, what they did, what they may have seen, even what they may have felt; make up your own reasons when I've told you my story, but for God's sake don't pretend that you know. You don't know. You guess. I don't know. I guess. Even I guess, and I love them...

Returning then, from Cornwall; Skarfe grew weekly – and Galer doubled in size. As if he were the first man in the world whose wife expected a baby. The strange thing was that he could almost have been that – certainly there was more smiling in the environs of St Michaels than I had ever seen. Of course, in a smallish school, especially in the country, one man's mood – if that man is a Galer Detheridge – can affect nearly everyone. I noticed that people in the common room were very gentle with him; and inevitably one heard talk like, "Old Galer will be all right now that he's going to have a brat of his own," and "He'll get over that ghastly Westcott business now," and "Just what he needed, a bellyful of his own." It surprised me, because I had not realised how many of our apparently unaware colleagues had understood what Nigel's suicide had done to Galer, and I had not understood either how much affection there was for him. Oh, I had known about the boys, but I hadn't known about the staff. It's strange, because he isn't a particularly pleasant man, or gracious, or kind, or even polite; but I suppose that people recognise in the man a weird kind of integrity to his own feelings, and respect him for it, almost as if he were the image of what they would like to be if they had enough courage.

I myself, Jenkyns the Self, stood back from all this joy: oh, I am not saying that I didn't find a little enjoyment in my detachment, nor that I didn't respond to Galer's delight, as he walked around the school looking at small boys playing their small boy games and older boys in their serious discussions of Art and Literature, the Conservative Party and Anarchism; in his actual dealings with boys I could see that he was, as it were, practising for his own son. Perhaps that was the whole reason for his being a teacher, I realised now for the first time.

Of course, being a Detheridge, he was sure that it would be a son; he was ponderously certain about it: "You see," he explained to anyone who asked, "for eleven generations—which is as far as we know back—the first child of any of the branches of the Detheridge family has been a son, so I am not simply wanting a son, I know that I am going to have a son." I kept on meaning to ask the statisticians what the chances were; doctors of course say that the chances are roughly 50-50, but I don't really see why they should know, about that kind of thing anyway.

But, you see, the irony of ironies was that Galer assumed that because Skarfe was his wife, the child was his. Of course it's a pretty valid assumption, one that most men make, though sometimes I wonder what the statistical evidence is. Because I knew that the child wasn't necessarily going to be Galer's. I knew for a very simple reason; you see, for the last three months, since shortly after Nigel died, I had been sleeping regularly—and irregularly—with Mrs Galer Detheridge, wife of my closest and oldest friend, the absurdly beautiful/beautifully absurd Mrs Detheridge, giraffe-like Skarfe. And neither of us were in the habit of practising birth control; after all, Skarfe had been sleeping with Galer for three and a half years and hadn't conceived, so why should she conceive because her partner changed? We didn't think, of course, but it remains true that her pregnancy opened up various possibilities. Ironically, of course.

You are shocked, ladies and gentlemen, and you angels who hide your faces behind your bright airy wings. Of course you are bound to be, though you must remember that I am in august company. When I finally arrive in that portion of the Underworld known as Adulterers' Corner, a row of semi-detached houses I expect it will be, where no one will sleep in the same house more than a single night and where monogamous boredom will seem heaven, I shall have good company – Nelson, Parnell, Dickens, Dante Gabriel Rossetti, not to speak of hundreds of bishops, dukes and kings. Though there it will not be one's worldly status that counts, but the quality of one's adultery, and I feel certain that to have slept with one's best friend's wife secretly will confer on me a certain immortality – oh, irony upon irony!

So, ladies and gentlemen, to the details: what's that you say, madam in the front row with the face of my mother? Spare us the ghastly details? Sorry, ma'am, this is my speech, and I am going to tell as much as I want. If you don't like it, you may leave – and you can listen from behind the swing doors at the back of the hall. Or close your ears. Or talk loudly to your neighbour, who doesn't want to hear either. Nevertheless I speak . . .

Galer was away that first day; he had taken a couple of teams away to Hurlingham, I think it is, to play in some Seven-a-Side rugger competition. It was in February, about a fortnight after Nigel had been scattered to the winds. I never take games myself, of course; instead I administer the school library. That afternoon, after lunch, I looked in for a moment on the library but there didn't seem anything urgent to be done, so I went for a stroll through the school grounds. But I couldn't find anyone to talk to and it wasn't much of a day for strolling, being beastly cold and blustery, so I went up to the Detheridges' flat and scrounged a cup of coffee from Skarfe. I used to do that quite often, of course, whenever I felt that I wanted to talk; and Skarfe and I often used to sit talking and drinking coffee while Galer was away, taking games, or seeing boys, or reading in his classroom, or walking great distances in the country, or whatever it was that kept him away from Skarfe at that particular moment. Moreover, I can promise you that at that moment I had not one idea in my head of any kind of adventure with Skarfe; I was going to see her because I liked her and because she made good coffee—as simple as that.

I knocked at the door of the flat, but there was no answer; I thought Skarfe must be out, but tried the door to see if it were open—at least I could leave a note. It was open, I went in, calling out, "Skarfe, it's Jim: are you in?" and she replied. She was upstairs in the bedroom, she said, dress-making. "Come up," she shouted. Their bedroom is up a narrow flight of stairs, because it is built almost into the roof of the house. Instead of windows it has enormous skylights, a sort of studio bedroom, and would be marvellous for a painter, because the light is clear and soft up there.

Skarfe was kneeling on the bed, with a dress-pattern spread out on the bedspread, and she was carefully cutting round the pattern, unpinning as she went. She half-turned as I came in and mumbled through her lipful of pins, "Sit down—I won't be long now." The only chair in the room was piled high with clothes, so I had to sit on the bed; and because there were no windows to look out of, I had to look at Skarfe.

Now, I shall be one of the first to regret the passing of the mini-skirt; all those flashing thighs and delicate knees delight me. But most women don't seem to realise that the mini-skirt can become, in certain postures, even less than mini. Take kneeling and bending forward. Perhaps one of the young ladies in the audience would be kind enough to demonstrate. You, perhaps, miss in the ... let's see, three, four, five ... eighth row. Perhaps you would be prepared to come up here to the platform with the speaker and would be good enough to kneel down on the table. With your back to the audience, miss, delightful though your front is. Now will you bend forward ... right forward, miss; don't worry, I shall hold your hands to stop your falling. Just a little more, as if you were stretching forward to cut out a piece of material four feet in front of you. That's it, miss. Thank you very much. Very kind I'm sure. Perhaps if you see the manager after the show, he can manage some kind of contract for you ...

The demonstration has, I hope, ladies and gentlemen, made my point clear. In certain postures, that is, a mini-skirt conceals nothing. So knelt Skarfe on the bed and, as I have said before, there were no windows to look out of. Not that I wanted to, actually; because, gentlemen, which of you surveying the view presented by that pretty young thing who carried out the demonstration for us, did not feel ... well, shall we use a cliché? ... a certain quickening of the pulses. If you see what I mean, ho, ho. You did? I assumed that you would. So can you imagine me, in that situation, looking away?

Anyway, Skarfe finished her cutting out and returned to some kind of decency by kneeling upright and looking round. She took the pins carefully out of her mouth and put them in a little box on the bed, gathered up the pattern and the carefully cut material – a flowery green it was, I remember – and then turned again, still kneeling, and then leant right forward on the bed, so that the fair view was fairly exposed once more. For a moment or two I didn't realise what she was doing, because I did not think that she had understood what I had been seeing, but she turned her head and smiled cloudily at me. Of course, she knew perfectly well what she had been doing; and even if she hadn't, she must have seen from my face when she was gathering up her material what had been happening to me. So she invited me to complete in fact what my imagination had already begun.

Spare us the details, shocked sir, now you say? You agree with the former objection now that you realise? Well, I'm afraid not. I want to say them coldly so that you will hear them. You dare not escape the cold detail, I fear.

Anyway, I made love to Skarfe there and then, she kneeling fairly on the bed, I half-kneeling, half-standing behind her; of course, there were some clothes to come off first, tights pulled down to her knees, pants following, and while she pulled her skirt higher up over her backside and hips, I got my trousers and underpants halfway down and my shirt out of the way. We were both ready for each other and that first time didn't take long, though I had to help her on her way a little with my hand.

Afterwards, we got undressed properly, and lay in the Detheridge bed naked and shaking in one another's arms. We didn't say anything to each other then, though once I thought that she was crying—if she had been, I think that it would have been a one-time adventure only for us; but when I felt her cheeks they were dry, and when I looked I found that she was not crying but giggling.

Later, when we were dressed and drinking coffee in the kitchen decently, I asked her what she had been giggling about. "Oh, just you," she giggled again. "Sorry, Jim, but I was laughing at you, about you. You see, lots of people have told me that you're a queer. I was sure that you weren't, and I know now. But I won't ever be able to explain why I know."

"Do lots of people think I'm queer?" I asked. It had honestly not occurred to me that people might think that.

"Well, you know," she said. "A schoolmaster, and you don't seem to like many women, and there's your mother too, of course."

"Of course," said I. "Does Galer think I'm queer?"

"No, he doesn't think so," she said seriously. "He doesn't think about things like that." She giggled again. "It's so strange really; you see, Galer is a terribly passionate man, more passionate than you maybe–" and 'maybe' made the remark easier for me to take–"but he's very straightforward about sex too. You know, he never asked me if I was a virgin when we were going to get married, but the first time he made love to me, he was a bit rough, and I was nervous, and what with one thing and another, there was some blood, and so he assumed that I was a virgin. I wasn't. I'd slept with lots of men, but he's never once asked me about them. Galer would never make love to me like you did, never. Perhaps he might think about it, but he would never do it."

I did not want to talk about Galer just then; so instead I said, "Well, actually, you must be careful. You see, if you offer yourself to the wrong man in that posture, you may find yourself getting it from a different angle than the usual."

"You mean . . ." she began.

"Yes," said the randy adulterer.

"Oh," said the wide-eyed wife. "I don't know that I fancy that much."

"No," said Jenkyns. "Well, you're safe enough with me, because I don't either." That wasn't quite true either. Years before, a girl had offered herself to me in that posture and I, then a novice, had plunged wildly in and hadn't realised, until I was going well, that I had hit the other target in those parts. I had naturally made to change, but the girl had prevented me. "No," she said, "keep going–I'm enjoying it; it's different but quite exciting." Well, once you get going, it's quite exciting for the giver too, and there is not much difference in the long run, so I kept going, and that particular girl and I used that procedure regularly after that. And I may as well go on with my truth-telling now; so I tell you that Skarfe learned to experiment too, and that was an additional excitement. I'm sure that the psychologists will go mad over the foregoing; what revelations, they will cry, what joyful revelations. But, as I see it, heterosexual is heterosexual, whatever modes you happen to adopt. So think what you like about my predilections, they remain mine and mine only, as far as I and my partners are concerned. I like heterosexual experiment.

Even with other men's wives. Even with the wife of my dearest friend, Galer. Skarfe. You see, my having had Galer's wife doesn't make the slightest difference to what I feel for Galer, or what Skarfe feels for him. At that particular moment she needed someone besides her husband, because he was not really there for her at all; he was living in another part of the world, in another part of his mind, where there were no wives and husbands, only fathers and sons. I don't mean that he didn't make love to her; Skarfe made it quite clear to me that I was an additional excitement, not her husband, and I know that she went on sleeping with him all through the time she was fucking me. He came back to her totally, of course, after the trip to Cornwall and the pregnancy; I don't know what happened between them there, but the moment I saw Skarfe when she came back I knew that she was no longer available to me. Because she had become part of the dream of sons and fathers. Before then I had been protecting her from the smell of death that hung around Galer for those months after Nigel killed himself. I was protecting her and comforting her in a way that Galer would never have understood. Love? Love? What the hell had love to do with it? Pleasurable comforting, comforting the only way we knew how. The offer made and accepted, the giving and taking, the taking and giving. No, I don't feel guilt. I might if Galer had found out. of course, because he might not have been able to take it; but Skarfe wouldn't have told him, then particularly. So he won't ever find out. I feel only what I feel; I bloody well won't feel anything else.

I suppose that's what fascinates in Camus. I feel only what I feel, don't give a damn for what I am supposed to feel. Shot an Arab on the beach the other day, ho, ho. Mother died, bang, bang. Galer came with me to her funeral, last rites of friendship. Afterwards had a meal, driving back to St Michaels; various things in French, which, being translated, were: mushroom soup, veal and tomatoes in a white wine sauce, green peas, green salad dressed in oil and vinegar for me, nothing for Galer, cheese (argued with the waiter to let me have cheese before pud), then skipped pud while Galer had a sort of blancmange thing to appease the waiter. "What did you have to eat, Galer?" said I, five minutes later. "Food," he replied. Brightness falls from the air. Very little in my head then.

But perhaps altogether inadequate to think, 'Sorry, but I don't feel that.' ('Shot four hundred Jews yesterday; didn't feel a thing, I didn't. Sorry not to feel, but you surely wouldn't want me to be hypocritical about it.') Hypocrisy may be all; I'd rather have been the prisoner of a hypocritical SS man than an honest and sincere one. The great objection to the moderns, that; Galer calls it adolescent anarchism: the reduction of everything to the personal, 'Yes, I feel . . .' or 'I don't feel'. D. H. Lawrence with his hands on his gut, Alfred Lord Tennyson reducing Vastness to 'I have felt'. Ho, ho, felt whom though? Not good enough, O Splendid Presences. Though a good case for the prosecution, before those final lines. Similarly with Lancelot and Guinevere; only Arthur should have been tormented, the others should have banged away happily, even on the gravestone.

Did I hear someone? Ah, yes, madam with the soft eyes, you. Love, you say? As long as I loved her, all will be forgiven? Good for you, ma'am. But I thought I'd answered that already; love isn't good enough. I love Galer too; and he was my friend long before he married Skarfe. And I had no desire to marry Skarfe. I didn't want to marry anyone, but especially I didn't want to marry Skarfe, sincerely I didn't want to marry her. I wanted to fuck her; and to go on fucking her. I didn't want to stop for anything, for love, friendship, loyalty, duty or babies. I couldn't wait until the next time she lay naked on a bed below me, her legs spread and her hair spread over the bedspread. There's only one thing that would have made me stop, and that was her regretting our spontaneous little adultery. If she had once wept for Galer's lost honour I would have been off like a travelling salesman.

Because you mustn't get me wrong. Skarfe loves Galer, even now; she used to laugh at him sometimes, yes, but so did I. And she's been unfaithful to him–that's the phrase, isn't it? Oh, untrue, untrue, as a leper cries unclean. She did certain sexual things with me, true; but they were not meant as adultery, as infidelity–they were meant as . . .

God, how difficult it is to explain! But pursue the theological image and perhaps I can. Angels are supposed to be hermaphrodites, aren't they? Isn't that one of the scholastic dogma? From somewhere in my memory it appears. Well, assume that Skarfe and I were angels–therefore her fucking with me was no more than my masturbating, or her for that matter. We are two of a kind, Skarfe and I; we both love Galer and at that moment in time we needed to do certain things to each other, in some way as an expression of our love for the other one, the different one.

It doesn't convince you, ladies and gentlemen? You frown and shake your heads? What's that, madam? Adultery is adultery, you say, dress it up as you will. Should be undress it as you will. And you, dog-collared sir, wonder what theology had to do with it, do you? Well, if I were speaking on the Day of Judgement, theology would have a deal to do with it. A politician's answers, those, you say, shrewd sir in your horn-rims. And now you ask what Galer would have done if he had found out. I expect that he would have hit me. And I'd make bloody sure that one punch would be enough, because I'd fold up and lie down, even if he had hardly touched me; and though I'd keep one eye open, just in case he were sad enough to put the boot in, or whatever that awful kicking thing is called, I'd make bloody sure that I didn't stand up again until he was gone. Then he would forgive Skarfe, would write me a note to say sorry for having hit me, and would take her away from St Michaels, and after a while they would live happily enough somewhere else, breeding madly. Because the gates are open now. And perhaps if the child had been born with the Jenkyns nose instead of the Detheridge chin, it would have hurt him once in a while, but he would love the child equally as he had loved me, and perhaps one day he would forgive me too. But I could not bear that; I cannot bear not having that enormous brooding man to stand between me and despair.

Still, I worked out the dates as best I could, and I knew that the child might have been mine, *de jure* not *de facto* in one sense, and the opposite in another. At least, there's a chance that it was mine. Of course, I didn't make love to Skarfe once she and Galer came back from Cornwall. I had the opportunity, and for all I know she might have been willing enough; but she seemed to have decided that the child was Galer's, and it might have been as if nothing had happened between us at all. Indeed, there were times that I wondered whether it had happened at all. We have been alone often enough since then, and we haven't said a word to each other about it. As if it had never happened at all. We have even talked about the baby, and not a word has been said about my possible role in its conception. Perhaps she's decided to treat conception as the Trobriand Islanders used to; making love doesn't cause babies, it just opens the passage through which the gods can act to plant the necessary seed. Breathe the necessary spirit. A much more comfortable idea of conception than our present one. Let the gods and angels do the real work, and men and women simply have the pleasure of it. Though Skarfe said that she dreaded the pain of the birth. I would too, though I did not have to bear it.

No, I will not believe that the child died as a punishment for our sin. I will not believe it. There is too much pain already to bear that . . .

But then we were still in the pleasant days of the summer before the bleeding started. Therefore, Heigh Ho! long summer evenings, three deck chairs in the garden of the Studies Centre, the light gathering around the three people sitting there; marvellous to live in a school when the boys have gone home or are locked up safely in their boarding houses with their house-masters, and most of the staff are away playing yokel cricket in a near-by village. Galer sits looking at the sky as if he had won it in a raffle, Skarfe–dear bulging Skarfe–sits and gossips to me, and I, witty Jenkyns, think of ways to amuse her. *Ménage à trois*, heigh ho, ho, ho!

Have I told you the one about the three Welshmen who went to a brothel in Cardiff, one wanting a girl, one wanting a boy, and the third wanting a mirror . . . ? Perhaps it wouldn't be suitable, not on this evening. Beauteous, quoth the Bard. Wouldn't it have been splendid if Willie Wordsworth had been a lisping Welshman? "It ith a beauteth effening, calm and three/Dear God, the very housteh theem athleep." Or am I getting the poems muddled up? That's the Thonnet on Wethtminther Bridgth, ithn't it? Galer, old chap, you are the one who knows these things. Humph, he growls, there's a

RESPONSE

De Selincourt in the third shelf of the left-hand bookshelf in my classroom. Skarfe giggles. Jenkyns the Wild Welsh Wit continues: there's a marvellous story I heard once about the funeral of Dylan Thomas. You know of course that he died in America and they transported him back to Wales in a slow cargo boat, in some great ornate coffin that they kept in the refrigerator. Landed at Swansea or whateffer. Various poetic friends came down to meet him off the ship, and Jenkyns the Death came down from Llareggub in his hearse that was a vegetable lorry when it wasn't a hearse, and the coffin was too big for it, so that they had to rope it in, and the back of it stuck out a good yard. On the way home Jenkyns the Death got lost, and the cortège stopped in a pub or two for sustenance, and by the time they got to the funeral, various friends and others were so distraught with grief that they fell into the grave.

I heard that one years ago in some pub in London, when people still went in for stories about Dylan Thomas, and before that young pup of a poplet stole his name; but Skarfe, god bless her, thought that it was very funny – and Galer wasn't listening. God knows what was going on between them in those early days of her pregnancy. Galer never seemed to listen to a word that she said, but let her even move in her chair and he was on his feet to help her. After all, she was carrying his child – there was no mistaking that she was carrying someone's at any rate. But she was as happy as I have ever seen her, as happy as she had been in the first days of being a wife; and she was Galer's wife and she was carrying his unborn son, and that was the first kind of perfection.

13

So the summer came, flourished, and went; the boys sat their external exams, the First XI went on a short tour of the West Country, and the staff ate their end of term dinner, during which Jim Jenkyns told the Headmaster a very dirty story about three Welshmen in a Cardiff brothel, though the Headmaster fortunately did not understand the point of the story. The boarders went home, some fetched by their parents in sleek cars and some going by train from Burston and some breaking the school rule by hitch-hiking. The staff went off on their holidays and the decorators moved into the classrooms; Jim Jenkyns went off to Greece and the Headmaster went to Italy, the senior English master went to his cottage in the Lake District and the liberal French teacher slipped over to France and the excitements of provincial life. Skarfe was too pregnant for Galer and her to go far away, so they spent the summer holiday sunbathing in the pleasant garden of the Studies Centre, and Skarfe read magazines and novels and Galer read the whole of Gibbon. Occasionally Galer would leave Skarfe for an afternoon and go off walking, and once or twice he went to visit the Westcotts. Long letters came from Jim in Greece, funny, salacious, regretful, and wordy, and they looked up the places he mentioned in the historical atlas from Galer's classroom.

Then, in the sixth month of her pregnancy, Skarfe began to bleed. Not much, just a little, marking her clothes a little. At first she did not worry, thinking that this was just another one of the changes that were taking place in her body, her nipples distending, her breasts hardening inside into small tight knots, her skin stretching over her child. Nor was Galer worried; birth was all so mysterious that blood seemed part of the mystery. But the bleeding grew worse, and the specialist whom Dr Rankin sent her to told Skarfe that he was afraid there might be complications and that she should rest as much as possible. If the bleeding were not controlled, the baby might suffer; she must rest, she must walk carefully, she must do no heavy housework at all, and if she did not obey the instructions, she would have to go into hospital to ensure that she did. The specialist explained to Galer when he came in and while Skarfe was dressing, that she might have what he called *placenta praevia*; the placenta, he said, might be lying below the embryo instead of above and this could mean that when it began to bear down from the womb towards the uterus, the placenta would become detached and either Skarfe or the baby or both of them could bleed to death. But you could never be sure, the specialist said; often the placenta was more round to the side than the tests showed, and, he said carefully, there was no longer all that much to worry about, since if either Skarfe or the baby seemed to be in any danger, they would do a Caesarean section to get the baby out in a hurry. "You can thank your lucky stars for modern science", he went on. "Thirty years ago if your wife had been in this condition, both she and the baby would almost certainly die; but I can assure you that your wife will be safe, and, even if the worst comes to the worst, the baby should be all right. Your wife will have a scar, of course, but she'll be able to have more children."

"Even after a Caesarean?' Galer asked.

"Yes, and the next time the birth may be quite normal. But you mustn't think that she will have a Caesarean; one of the troubles with *placenta praevia* is that one can't be sure that it's there until the actual birth begins . . ."

"And then?"

"Well, of course there has to be a hurry, because the danger is of a massive haemorrhage."

"Will I be able to be there when the baby is being born?" He wanted desperately to be there to see his son born, and Skarfe had said that she wanted him there too.

"No, I'm afraid not—because if she does have to have a Caesarean, we won't have time to worry about you; and you couldn't be there for that, of course. Next time you'll be able to be there, but this time . . ." The specialist shook his head.

"Not at all?"

"No, really, I'm sorry. But you'll be right outside, and the doctors will tell you what is happening." As he spoke, Skarfe came back into the consulting room; she was looking very frightened, and the specialist got up from his desk and walked over to her to take her arm. "Are you all right, my dear?" he asked. Galer did not stir, did not even look round at his wife.

"Yes," Skarfe said. "I'm just feeling a little shaky; simply nerves, I suppose."

"Will she be all right at home?" Galer asked. "I mean, shouldn't she go into hospital now?"

"Well, she could, but you live so close to the hospital that it doesn't matter really, it doesn't seem worthwhile. Do you want to come into hospital now, Mrs Detheridge?" he asked, beginning to show his impatience with this large husband who would not be satisfied until he knew everything.

"No," Skarfe shook her head. "I want to be at home; and It's only ten minutes to the hospital, Galer. I do want to be home, Galer . . ."

So Skarfe stayed at home, and walked very carefully, and allowed Galer to help her up and down the stairs, and allowed him to get in a daily help from Burston. So she waited, and Galer waited, all through the holidays; and the bleeding seemed to get better, so much so that the specialist said that he hoped that his diagnosis had been mistaken. The long days of summer began to end, and the first winds of autumn came rushing into the garden of the Studies Centre, and Skarfe waited, and Galer waited. Skarfe tried to believe that nothing could happen to change their joy; and Galer looked through the great unshuttered doors and avoided words as if they had been the carriers of death.

*   *   *

Then the autumn term began, the staff dribbled back to school and the boys followed, everyone brown and sensual with sun, Jim joking about the manners of Greek men and German girl tourists, the English master inveighing against the tourists who were ruining the Lakes, the French master smugly silent, the Headmaster eloquent about the painting of the early Renaissance. The new boys were shepherded around the school by the officious new prefects, and the newcomers to Galer's Sixth Form were introduced rudely to the joys of reading and the excitement of writing, and listened carefully to Galer's talk in class. Skarfe hardly moved from her flat now, for the stairs were steep, and the bleeding, though it had lessened, was still regularly there.

*   *   *

He had put Nigel out of his mind these last months, but the blood seemed to bring him back; sometimes it seemed almost that he was back in the guise of his father, a messenger of death. Galer had been visiting the old man regularly, all through the Lent term and again when he came back from Cornwall. After the funeral, after his visit to the burnt-out cottage, he had never wanted to see the Westcotts again; but Mrs Westcott had phoned him a fortnight after the funeral to ask if he would mind coming to fetch some of his books that she had found among Nigel's belongings. He hadn't seen the old man that time, but the next time that his walking took him to those parts, he had, without thinking almost, gone into the farmyard and had asked after him. He had been taken up to the study and they had talked a little; and after that it seemed natural that whenever he went past the farm, he should turn up the long muddy lane and walk up to the farm and sit with the old man in his study for an hour or two, talking about everything except Nigel, talking about Africa, about the tribes, about the state of England, about the principles of anarchism, about everything except sons and fathers, wives and death. Or rather the old man talked, his mind still restless and curious, questioning, searching, cynical about the present and future, passionate about the past, and Galer sat wordlessly listening in a rocking-chair in the old man's study, letting the words spill through the air around his head, letting the old man talk, because his son was dead and because he too would die before very long.

But when the bleeding started, he grew afraid of visiting the farm and, when he went walking, he kept away from the land on that side of St Michaels. For a month he did not see Adamson Westcott. Then, one morning, the old man telephoned him.

"You haven't been here for a long time," he said immediately.

"No," said Galer. "My wife's not been well."

"Oh, sorry to hear that. Difficult time pregnancy, isn't it? I've not been well either and my blasted wife won't let me leave the house. I'm bored to death here. Come to see me, will you?"

It was more a command than a request, but that did not anger Galer. He understood what the old man must feel and he knew that he should have been to visit him. The old man was afraid of death, and Galer was alive; the old man's son was dead, and Galer's son was alive. Why, if he turned his head away from the telephone, he could see his wife, sitting there, big with his son, and so what reason had he to be afraid of death? True it was that Nigel's death remained, but it was only a part of everything that had happened, it was not a whole, and death could not enter his mind, not any more. So he promised Adamson Westcott that he would go to the farm that afternoon.

"Who was it?" Skarfe asked from her chair as he put down the phone.

"Adamson Westcott, the old man," he replied.

"What did he want?"

"He wants me to visit him."

"Are you going to?"

"I must."

"Why must you?"

"Well, the old man needs me, I suppose; he's not been well, and he's stuck out there on the farm, and I'm one of the few people that he seems to want to talk to. Because of Nigel, I suppose."

"You still think about Nigel a lot, don't you?"

"No," said Galer. "No, hardly ever. But you can't forget things like that. They stay—you know that already."

"Yes," Skarfe said. She sat quiet for a moment, then suddenly looked up to say, "I don't want you to go."

"But why? Why on earth not?"

"I don't know," she said, looking down at her knitting again. "I just don't want you to go."

Galer crossed the room to her and stood stooping over her, looking down at her bent head and the fair hair; but she would not look up at him. "Are you afraid if I'm not here?" he asked. "In case anything happens, I mean?"

"No," she said. "You know that nothing's going to happen for at least a month yet. I don't know why, but I don't want you to go."

"But the old man needs me and if you don't, surely you don't want me not to go?"

"Do you think I don't need you?"

"Of course I don't," he said helplessly. "Of course. Don't you want me to go out at all?"

"No, it's not that." She looked up now, quickly leaning back in her chair, her swollen stomach seeming to rise higher up her body as she did so. "I know that you have to get out of here sometimes; I don't mind at all when you go out walking – I do understand that you need to be alone sometimes. I just don't want you to go to the Westcotts."

"But, Skarfe –" at last he used her name, "if I'm not here, why should you worry that I am at the Westcotts? What difference does it make?"

"I'm frightened about Nigel."

"But Nigel's dead," Galer burst out. But he did understand now and so kneeled down next to her chair; he took her face between his hands and turned her to look at him. "You mustn't be afraid of Nigel," he said. "You know what the psychiatrist man said. I thought that it was somehow my fault at first, but I understand now: it was nothing to do with me, what he did. He's dead now, he can't hurt me or you any more. He's gone." It was not true and Galer knew that he was lying; but Skarfe's fear disturbed him more than any lie.

"Are you sure?" she asked again.

"Yes," he lied.

"He doesn't still . . ." she began.

"No, he doesn't anything; it's all right now."

She looked at him carefully, kneeling on the floor next to her chair, moving his hands from her face to her shoulders, and touching her stomach to feel the child inside her. "Are you really sure, Galer?" she asked again.

"Ssh," he said. "No more words now. I'm sure, but no more words. Leave it be."

"All right," she said.

"All right, what?"

"I don't mind if you go to see Nigel's father," she said, almost as if she were repeating a lesson learnt by heart.

He knelt in silence next to her chair, letting his hands rest on her stomach, feeling the fluttering there that was his son moving, and smiling at the life that already existed. "Now that Jim's back," he said, "I'll bribe him to take us out in the car every evening."

"Yes," she said. "You ask Jim." She looked carefully at Galer before saying, "You do trust Jim, don't you?" Galer looked at her in astonishment. Trust Jim? Why the need to say that? Of course he trusted Jim; they were friends, weren't they? So why did you need to use words like 'trust'? That was a word that enemies used, not friends.

"What do you mean?" he asked.

"I don't know. I just wanted to know."

"Then I do trust him. I'd trust him with my life – that's the way you say it, isn't it? That's the usual expression, isn't it?"

"Did you miss him when he was away?" she persisted.

"Yes," he said. "I suppose that I did. I was glad when he came home."

"So was I," Skarfe said very quietly.

"I know," Galer smiled at her. "I'm sorry that I don't talk more, but I can't. And Jim and you talk the whole time, don't you?"

"Yes, he is strange. Has he ever told you himself about what happened to him at Oxford?" Galer nodded. "Of course," Skarfe went on. "I forgot. He's told me everything too – lots about you too. I think that, in a way, he loves you, Galer, you know."

"Do you think that he loves you too?" Galer asked his wife.

"I think that he loves everyone who is not really available," she said quietly. "I love him too, in a way, because he loves you, and because he talks, and because . . . well, like I said, because he excites me."

"I understand," said Galer. "I do love you, you know, Skarfe, very much."

"Yes," she said. "I know; and you love this too." She took

his hand and laid it on her stomach again, where the child fluttered and kicked under the tight flesh.

"Yes," he said. "Both of you. I don't say it often, I know, but both of you."

"And no more words," she teased him.

"And no more words," he answered.

*   *   *

Once, months before Skarfe found herself pregnant, he had tried to take Jim with him to talk to Adamson Westcott. Jim had driven him as far as the entrance of the long muddy lane that led up to the farmhouse, then had changed his mind. "I'm not taking the Monster up that muddy stream," he said. "You'll have to swim for it, old chap."

"Well, park the car on the verge and we'll walk up," Galer said lightly, opening the car door.

"Well, actually Galer, if you don't mind, I'm going to chicken out; somehow I don't fancy talking to old Death Embodied this afternoon. I'll drop you here and go for a drive with the Monster, and fetch you in an hour's time."

Galer had tried to persuade him to come, but Jim had suddenly become adamant; he did not want to visit Adamson Westcott, and he would not come, even for Galer. "All right," Galer said at last, "I'll go, and you go for a drive."

"And I'll fetch you in an hour," said Jim, almost as if he were ashamed of having changed his mind about coming.

"There's no need to fetch me, if you don't want to."

"I'll fetch you," Jim said stubbornly.

"All right. Make it an hour and a half then," Galer smiled at him as he got out of the car. "You have no idea how he talks, the old man, you coward."

"I know," said Jim, looking through the window at him,

and then he looked away and drove the old green car away down the road, while Galer walked quickly up to the farm.

* * *

Now the lane was dry, and the ruts and peels of old mud lay as if permanent. The Westcott farm lay to the north-west of St Michaels, five miles if you kept to the roads, two or three across the fields and footpaths. To get there you walked a little way along the main road to Burston, then turned off along a footpath across the fields to Grayton, following the river part of the way, then along the road into Grayton itself and, just past the small post-office, turned up an unmade country lane at the end of which lay the lane to the Westcott farm. In fact, local people still called it the Turner farm, since the fourth Mrs Westcott had been a Mrs Turner before her re-marriage; when Galer first asked his way, the woman in the post-office had sniffed, corrected him, and pointed to the road without a word—old Westcott was obviously an intruder into the narrow life of those parts, and Galer could guess that he did not adapt his behaviour or opinions to suit his neighbours.

Mrs Westcott was in the farmyard, a cheerful rotund woman in dirty overalls and wellington boots; she called out when she saw Galer, and he picked his way carefully over to her. She buried her pitchfork into the muck that she was loading into a small hand-cart, turned to him, and said, "Very good of you to come. The old man gets confoundedly bored—I'm afraid that I'm not exactly intellectual company for him, what with cows and pigs and chickens to care for." She was joking, and Galer smiled at her; he had not forgiven her for her lack of concern for her stepson, but he had talked to her several times and she was, in fact, for all her appearance, a sensible and intelligent woman. "Don't be too long with the old man though, if you don't mind, even if he tries to keep you—he's been very frail all summer."

She began pitchforking again but remembering then, she turned back to him. "Oh, I forgot to ask," she said. "How's your wife?"

"Oh, very pregnant now, and she has to take life easy."

"I gather from Mrs Losden that she hasn't been at all well. Only gossip, I hope."

Galer loathed talking to anyone about Skarfe's bleeding, so now he simply nodded his head, to show both that she hadn't been well and that it was gossip too. Mrs Westcott smiled at him and said, "Oh well, I'm sure that she'll be all right; pregnancy is always rotten for women, or nearly always rotten. Now I must work and if you don't get up to Adamson quickly he'll be bawling at us from the window. Look," and she pointed up at one of the windows at which Adamson could be seen watching them talk. Galer waved and the old man signalled to him to come up.

He walked over the worn flagstones of the passage outside the kitchen and upstairs to the converted attic that was the old man's study – it was a long room, with dormer windows set into the roof, and the one end was virtually a library, for the old man had his bookcases arranged as in a stackroom, shelves back to back, and he worked in the open area at the other end of the room, at a great desk stood on the bare boards. On the walls and from the roof hung dozens of the collection of masks and weapons which he had made in Africa, scowling, grinning masks, with hair of straw and ivory teeth, and spears, bows, arrows, blowpipes, clubs and knives with carved wooden handles and coarse metal blades.

Adamson Westcott had started work again after he waved from the window, and now he kept Galer waiting while he finished writing a sentence. After a moment or two he looked up and said, "For goodness sake sit down, you're far too big for me to look up at."

"What are you writing?" Galer asked as he settled himself

into the tall rocking-chair in the window; he had been afraid to ask about the writing when he had first come in case the old man disliked talking about his work; but he had soon discovered that the writing was one of his main topics of conversation.

"I'm making notes for the autobiography which I reckon it's about time I started writing," he said. "Wasn't I doing it when you came last?"

"No," Galer shook his head. "You were writing a review of some new work; no, it wasn't new, it was a republication of something that you said would have better been left interred."

"Oh yes, I remember: bloody stupid book on the origins of voodoo—I slated it," he smiled happily across the desk. "No, this is towards an autobiography. I always said that I would write one; every man should write one before he dies, though pray God not all of them are published." The arrogance was in some way so innocent that Galer did not resent it; the old man assumed so naturally that his own autobiography would be worthwhile publishing. "No, watching you out there for some reason reminded me of my first wife, and I just wanted to note it down. You see, I want this book to be a stock-taking, not a rehash of old books and letters, not a blow-by-blow account of my life, so I'm not using old letters or articles or anything like that. I'm re-reading nothing for it, just remembering as best I can." He had put his pen down now, at last, and Galer knew that he had surrendered to his need to talk. "I can hardly remember her now, Ursula her name was, and sometimes I even forget that. You'd think that it was impossible to forget something like that. She died in Africa, you know, very young really." Galer nodded his head; the old man was into his stride now and he would probably not say a word himself for the next half-hour. He would listen, because this was Adamson Westcott, but even if he didn't it wouldn't matter, not very much. He knew enough about the old man to be sure that he would finish this autobiography before he died; he was determined enough to defy death even, and he would not die before he had finished this last work. So one day he would be able to read again what he heard now, about the Westcotts in Africa, about the tribes, about Ursula Westcott, who had died of malaria with complications. "In a way," the old man said, "it's probably a good thing that she died when she did; I would never have lived so long if she had lived – she used to make me work very hard. Strange, isn't it, how unromantically one regards one's own past?"

Galer heard the old man speak, and allowed his mind to wander again into the hazy images of his own past. Was his view unromantic, he wondered. No, but it was not romantic either, not in the unstrict sense of the word, because he tried to remember as clearly as he could and if the clarity was marvellous, he could not change it.

He selected one image then from the haze: the path led steeply downhill to the stream. He hesitated there, not sure whether to go on down or to wait for his father, who was fifty yards or so behind him. The path was very muddy and he did not want to fall; but if his father came up and found him waiting, he might ask, "Why haven't you gone down, son?" He was about to risk the steep rush down, when his father called out from behind him, "Hey, wait for me." So he waited and in the end he went down hanging on to the back of his father's coat, and his father slipped and slithered down, and near the bottom Galer slipped too and fell forward on to his father, and they had both ended up at the bottom of the path, thick with mud, laughing at each other.

"My God, what's your mother going to say when we come back like this?" his father laughed, surveying the mud on his coat and flannels and looking at Galer, standing there covered as muddily. "It's bad enough when you and Harry come home muddy, but when I come home . . . what on earth will she say then?" He parodied his wife's anger at her sons. "'Good heavens, John, you cost your father and me a fortune in laundry bills already, and then you come home like this, looking like a ragamuffin . . .'"

Laughing, they had looked up to see how they were going to get across the fierce little stream and up the other side of the steep dip. There were stones across the stream but the climb was, if anything, steeper than the one which they had just come down. They crossed the stream, splashing on the half-submerged stones, but the far bank had been too slippery to climb straightforwardly. So his father had crossed back over the stream and had run in great leaping strides, splashing wildly, to take the bank in a series of slithery leaps. Then at the top he had lain down on the grass and had reached down to give his son a hand and to hoick him up the last part of the bank.

Both of them at the top, what had his father said? Galer searched but could not remember; there was only the memory of laughter and of his father hurling himself across that stream and up the muddy bank. But he did not worry that the words did not come; some time someone would say a word and the other forgotten words would emerge from the haze, though for the moment they had disappeared.

Adamson Westcott was watching him. "I said, you aren't listening to a word I say. You weren't, were you?"

"No," Galer answered. "Something you said set my mind going in a different direction. Sorry." Any other man almost would have asked what Galer had been thinking of, but not Westcott.

"Yes," he said. "It's a habit you have. I remember Nigel mentioning it – he said that you had an ability to turn off from the present entirely, that you could sit in a crowded room and not notice anything happening around you." It was true, that, but what caught Galer's attention fully was the mention of Nigel's name. It was almost the first time since he had started visiting the old man that Nigel's name had been mentioned. "I, on the other hand," Westcott went on, "am a professional listener. There was a time when my livelihood depended on it. That's how we were trained as young anthropologists—listen to what was said, observe what was done, and note carefully what was avoided in speech and action. Damn good rules they were too."

Galer could not help grinning; what arrogance the man had. But Westcott observed the smile and smiled back. "Oh," he said, "I know that I talk more now and don't listen much—but that is a privilege of an old man, isn't it?" Galer nodded; after all, he had come here this afternoon simply because it was the privilege of an old man to have an audience.

"Tell me, Detheridge," the old man went on, "what do you think about Nigel now? I mean, how do you react to his death now? It's eight . . . no, nine months now, isn't it, and so the shock's gone—but what do you think?"

Galer said nothing for a long time, trying to find the right words before he spoke them. But they would not come. In the end he looked up, shook his head slightly, and said, "I don't know—perhaps I don't think anything, really; I suppose that's wrong really, but I've simply tried to put him out of my mind, away from me. I mean, I don't try to think why Nigel died; I know that I don't accept what that doctor person said, but . . . well, I don't think. I feel things about him still, but I don't think." He looked hard at the old man, Nigel's father, sitting across the desk from him, with his worn, grey-stubbled face, turned away from Galer to the window.

"Yes," Westcott said. "Yes." He got up from his chair shakily and walked across the bare boards to the window from which he could look down over the farmyard. "Did you know, Detheridge," he said so quietly that for a moment Galer did not realise that he was speaking, "did you know that I had **another son?**"

"No," said Galer astonished; he thought that he knew all the details of the old man's marriages and children, but Nigel had never once mentioned a brother or stepbrother.

"I'm going to put it in this book," Westcott said, gesturing to the pile of notes on his desk. "I wasn't married to his mother, in fact; his surname was Harman. Jeremy Harman. He was killed in North Africa in '42. I didn't hear about it until a year afterwards, because his mother hated me by then. Strange woman she was: divorced from her first husband to marry me, had the son before the divorce went through, and then wouldn't marry me. I never understood why." He stood still in the window, not looking at Galer, looking out into the farmyard. "I don't think I've ever told her," and Galer knew without asking that he meant the fourth Mrs Westcott. "My other children didn't know either; Nigel didn't, did he?" So that was it, thought Galer; this had been a secret from Nigel even. "The boy shouldn't have died, of course; he was only wounded slightly, a shell splinter in the groin, and if he had gone straight out to a hospital he would have been fine, just a small scar. He was a gunner, a lieutenant. But he wouldn't go, and the wound infected, the splinter moved, something like that, and he died of peritonitis a few days later. Ridiculous..." The old man stood at the window, looking down at the farmyard and his wife. His last word still hung in the air around Galer's head—ridiculous his death; ridiculous his old grief for the son who had not even borne his name. Galer did not speak, waiting for him to explain.

"I found out about how he died from one of the people who had been with him; I had to lie, of course, saying that he was the son of an old friend, and that I had known the boy from childhood—I only saw him a few times, and he didn't know who I was—and that I had promised to get the details for his mother. This friend of his—forget his name now—said that Jeremy stayed out of some kind of sense of duty; his men had been having a bad time in the desert, and he felt he couldn't go off for something so small. They gave him a DSO for that, posthumous DSO–not him, really, I suppose, but his mother. Perhaps all awards should be like that, to comfort the living; awards to the dead to comfort the living . . ." the old man came away from the window now and back to his chair; for a moment Galer thought that he would fall, because he did not sit carefully enough, and caught himself on the arm of the chair and nearly fell sideways. But Galer could not move quickly enough to help, and the old man cursed, and sat down more carefully.

"Old age," he said. "I'm losing my sense of balance. I keep on doing that–damn silly, looking as if I'm drunk." He looked across the room to Galer standing waiting to see if he was all right. "Sit down," he said. "I don't need a nurse-maid."

"Sorry."

"No. I probably do need one, because it's hard for my wife to have to nurse me. But I'd like to go out on my own. Just wait, Detheridge, I want to write something down–you don't mind, do you?"

"No," said Galer. What was he writing, he wondered. Something about being old and losing balance? Something about his dead sons? I wish that he had told Nigel about the other son, Galer thought; it might have made it easier for him. Perhaps he wouldn't have . . . The silence of his own incomplete thought held Galer totally still in his chair, as if movement would have woken a fiend to torment him. Had Jeremy chosen to die, as Nigel had done? Nobody could tell, of course; it might have been out of duty, a sense of loyalty to his men. Had he been afraid those last days, or had he waited quietly? He would like to know, but even if he could ask the old man, he wouldn't know the answers.

Westcott put down his pen again. "Tell me, Detheridge, what do you think about death? Do you believe all that stuff about immortality? You're not a Christian, are you?" Galer shook his head. He didn't know what he was, but he would not call himself a Christian, not in any definition. "But I seem to remember Nigel telling me that your father was a clergyman? Was he?"

"He became one after the war, for the last few years of his life. But he wasn't at all orthodox." Galer smiled to himself; he remembered so clearly the kind of thing that his father used to say from the pulpit and how regularly the bishop would summon him to explain some outrageous statement. His father had loathed preaching; indeed, he had loathed church services altogether, and Sundays had been a torment to him. He remembered so clearly how his father would come in from church to tell his sons the latest shocking thing he had said, almost by accident, from the pulpit: "I don't give a damn whether Jesus Christ was the Son of God or the illegitimate child of a simple-minded working girl; what difference does it make now? . . . whether he actually got up from that stone sepulchre and walked away, or whether his disciples came and stole his dead body away and said that he was alive, and went on saying it until they themselves were killed for believing in what they had done? . . . It seems to me that the First Commandment is one that will look after itself; the Second is the one to worry about . . . If we go to hell for looking at women with desire in our hearts as much as we would if we were actually adulterous, then I have already gone to hell several times this morning, because there are several women in this congregation whom I desire right now; naturally that includes my wife . . ." How his congregation had adored him, how the bishop had protested, how the vergers had scowled and resigned regularly!

"Shall I tell you what I think, Detheridge? About death? For seventy years I didn't really think about it at all; if I believed anything, it was just the kind of thing the primitives believe—the dead person becomes one with the ancestors, I suppose. But I've been thinking about it a lot, I suppose since Nigel died, really. Look," he said, got shakily up from his desk, went to the nearest bookcase and from it took two books. He held them so Galer could see them, one his own, the great second book, its cover uncompromising white with the clear black title, *Age-Groupings in Central African Tribes*, and the other with a lurid cover of a half-naked black woman being tormented by a witch-doctor, and the title in great bleeding letters, *VOODOO*. "Look," Westcott said, "one good book, one rotten sensational nonsense..."

"The one you were reviewing when I came last?" asked Galer.

"Yes. A rotten old book republished; and not even that cover could make it more rotten. Now," he laid both books down on the desk, "suppose that you and I died right now, suppose that everyone in the world were to die right now, every single person, but these two books went on sitting on my desk like that. My book would still be the better book."

"But surely not, not without people to read them."

"No, that's the point. Even without people to read them, my book remains the better. No, not the better book, perhaps, because if you reprinted mine badly, with a rotten lurid cover, and reprinted that fool's work beautifully, his actual book might be better, but his work would stay worse..."

"No," said Galer stubbornly. "You can't say one book is better than another except in relation to the people who read them."

"You can think that if you want; I don't, any more. I'm too old to believe in people any more. I think that my book is better than human beings—if you like," he smiled triumphantly, "I believe that in the mind of God my book is better than this rottenness. Of course, not a Christian God, necessarily, because this God may not be loving and personal, but a God of high standards at least."

Galer shook his head; he was growing angry. The arrogance of the old man no longer seemed innocent, but vicious. What mattered was people; small wonder it was that Nigel had been destroyed if he had had to cope with this lunacy, where it was not even beauty that became immortal, but intellectual rigour. No, what this man said would not do; it was corrupt and cruel, because no one person could survive in the shadow of such impossible pride. He was not a Christian, but at least the Christian God was personal, at least He cared for individual human beings. At least Christians cared for human beings, even if they seemed to apologise for suffering, as if it were a virtue to suffer. You might as well make your God a Napoleon or a Caesar or a Hitler . . .

Then terror held him in his chair, so still that for a moment he thought that he had died himself and was looking out at the world of old men and books and dead sons through his own dead eyes, as a man buried with open eyes might look at the rich brocade of the coffin lid over his face, knowing that he could not move, knowing that even if he could he could not shift the coffin lid, knowing that miles of earth held it down. It was always there, that memory, that image, but nearly always he managed to hold it away from himself; it was the one thing that he would never look at. What if when you looked at God's face, his father had said, and saw suddenly that God had the face of . . . no, he would not remember, he would not. He must put it away again, out of mind, back into the unremembered past again. But even as he fought the memory he knew that he had no choice. About that there could be no choice now. All he could choose was not to remember here in this room, close to Nigel's death, close to an old man who had reminded him of what he most wanted not to remember, in a bare-boarded study surrounded with dead books. He must move, he must break the terror that would not let him move, he must come out of the dead places. If he had to remember, he must be on his own ground, he must be moving so that he could deny the past with the knowledge of his own body.

He interrupted the old man who was still speaking, words upon words, spilling out into the air between him and his audience, not realising that the words were sounds that died in the air before they arrived anywhere. "I must go," he heard his own voice say, and repeated the words in case they had been spoken too quietly for the old man to hear. "I must go."

"I haven't finished explaining," he heard Westcott say, but he was already at the door.

"Sorry," he heard his own words again from a distance, "but I have to go now. I'll come again," and then, without noticing the words that came down the stairs with him, the old man astonished at Galer's flight, Mrs Westcott calling to him as he crossed the farmyard, striding out largely to reach his own ground, Galer moved. No thoughts, no memory, nothing but the body moving away from Adamson Westcott, from his dead sons, from the farm, down the lane, through the village, and then into the open fields. The body moving, away from death, into death, Galer Detheridge, knowing that he must remember, knowing that he could not escape now, still in terror but holding terror away from him by moving.

Once he was in the open, he stopped. "All right," he heard himself say aloud, almost as if he were speaking to someone else, "all right; I am ready now," and he allowed the memory to flood in, allowed the images to take shape, allowed them to take on the rhythm of his own slow steps along the footpath towards the river across the fields.

He had been staying with Jim in Ely when the telegram from Harry came. He had gone straight home, in terror that his father should die before he arrived; but when he got to the Rectory, the emergency seemed to have passed. His mother had told him that his father had been ill for several days but, on the Sunday morning, had insisted on getting up to take the services; he had managed Communion, white-faced and stumbling through the order of service, but midway through Matins, he had left his seat in the chancel and had staggered into the vestry; his wife and Harry, rushing round to help him, found him collapsed there, in apparent agony. A doctor in the congregation had summoned an ambulance but, when it arrived, John Detheridge had refused to go to hospital. In the end, they had taken him to his own bed, where he lay writhing until his own doctor, Dr George Russell, family friend, came and gave him a sedative.

John Detheridge had been an ill man for years by then; he had overworked all his life and even when he was in the semi-retirement of a country parish in the Cotswolds he had continued to drive himself like a young man in his first ambition. As far back as Galer could remember, his father had suffered bouts of pain; they would be talking in the study or standing in the passage and suddenly his father would grimace and hold his midriff, waiting for the first sharp burst to pass and would then gulp down spoonfuls of some patent medicine that a doctor-friend had once prescribed years before and which he never lost faith in, though it did nothing more than relieve temporarily what he called 'indigestion'. But after he had resigned from the War Crimes Commission and had gone to St Nicholas in Islington, Mrs Detheridge had insisted that he see a specialist, who diagnosed chronic ulcers and put him on a rigorous diet and told him, uselessly, to rest. He had pretended to follow the diet and had not rested at all, and each bout of pain would be followed by the spoonfuls of the foul purple medicine that the specialist had told him was no use at all except as narcotic. Then the pain had grown too much even for a John Detheridge to bear, and he had retired to an easier job where Mrs Detheridge found it easier to force him to eat sensibly and to drink milk instead of whisky and beer.

Of course, the immediate cause of his collapse had been his cheating on the dietary rules. Dr Russell had asked, almost immediately after he had sedated John, whether he had been disobeying the rules of the diet. "No," replied Mrs Detheridge firmly, and then Harry confessed that, the evening before, when his father was supposed to be asleep and he to be working at his books, his father had come quietly into Harry's room and had inveigled him into sneaking out of the back door to the pub.

"What did you drink?" asked the doctor.

"Well, Dad had a couple of pints, but then he said that he was too old to cope with beer any more, and the landlord started to give him whisky."

"Oh, Harry, how could you?" exclaimed Mrs Detheridge. "You know what happens then."

"I thought you were studying medicine," said the doctor.

Harry looked at the doctor carefully, then smiled. "Come on, Dr George," he said, "you can't even make him take his medicine. If Dad wants to sneak out to a pub, he goes; even Ma can't stop him."

It was true and both Mrs Detheridge and Dr Russell knew it; John Detheridge did what he wanted to. He had never been a drinking man, but he enjoyed pubs and many of the parishioners whom he most cared for were drinking people. When he was well, he went regularly to the village pub; recently, with the threat of the pain that followed any deviation from his diet, he had been drinking milk there, though he knew perfectly well that the landlord laced each glass liberally with whisky before he put it in front of the first clergyman they had known in those parts who actually talked to people in their own words and who would drink with the best—and worst—of them.

RESPONSE

By the time Galer arrived, the crisis seemed to be over. His father was still in pain but was not the agonised beast whom Harry had helped carry from the church that morning. He lay in his bed propped up on pillows, grey-faced tired big man, half-asleep from the drugs that Dr Russell had pumped into him, but he found from somewhere the force to say, "For God's sake, they didn't make you give up your holiday just because I had indigestion."

"No," said Galer as cheerfully as he could. "I was bored with Jim's neurotic mother, and anyway, it's not just indigestion."

John Detheridge tried to joke: "All right," he said, "ulcers, but you'd think from the way that your mother and George Russell behave that I was the first man with ulcers who had ever suffered from an excess of drink on a Saturday night."

"Harry told me," said Galer. "Honestly, it was bloody stupid of you."

"Well," his father said defiantly, "if an old man of sixty-six can't be stupid occasionally, who can be?"

There was still no arguing with him. On Monday he seemed better, and on Tuesday he began to complain about the food that his wife, following Dr Russell's instructions as scrupulously as always, fed him with every two hours. "Too little too often," John Detheridge said loudly every time she appeared with a tray. "Tasteless muck too; how about some beef, dear wife?"

Dr Russell spoke optimistically. "We really should have sent him to hospital–but he's happier here. We can't operate to get at the ulcers; he's just not strong enough to take a major operation now. When he's strong again, we can think again. In the meantime, make him stick to the diet– no variations, either, mind you, whatever he says–and then I think he'll be all right."

So John Detheridge stayed in bed, still grey-faced, still

apprehensive of the pain that had struck so savagely, but pretending to be cheerful. Galer sat for hours in his room, watching him sleeping, reading to him, persuading him to eat the bland food that Mrs Detheridge sent up from the kitchen, helping his mother make the bed—indeed, the only time that he left his father was when his mother came to wash him, and that only because his father refused to be naked in front of anyone but his wife.

Three days, four, five, and on the sixth John Detheridge seemed so much stronger that Harry took everyone except Galer out for the afternoon in the family car: Mrs Detheridge was tired and nearly ill herself from the strain, and the girls were finding the restriction of the always quiet house unbearable. Harry tried to persuade Galer to go himself, saying that he would stay behind, but Galer, though he was weary, would not go—he disliked car journeys unless he had to make them, it was a rainy day and they would probably have to stay in the car, and anyway he had some reading to do which he could do as well in his father's room as anywhere.

So, while the rest of the family went off in the old Morris, Galer sat in his father's bedroom reading, while his father dozed. But soon Galer too began to doze, in an armchair at the window, with a book open on his knees and his head fallen to one side, heavily against the side of the chair. When he woke up, his father was awake and looking across the room at him,

"Sorry, Dad," Galer yawned. "Have I been asleep long?"

"Not long. I've only just woken up myself."

"Are you feeling all right?"

"A bit of pain," John Detheridge said quietly. "I'm getting used to it, but I had better have one of those bloody pills again. Don't get up, I can manage," but Galer was already at his bedside, shaking one of the pain-killing pills that Dr Russell had left from the bottle at the bedside, helping his father sit up, and giving him a glass of water to help wash the pill down.

"Do you want me to phone George Russell?"

"No, you mustn't; let the poor man have a rest. I'll be all right once the pill works."

"Do you want me to read to you?"

"No, you get on with your own book and I'll just lie here. I can't really concentrate at the moment."

"Is the pain very bad? Are you sure you don't want me to get George Russell?"

"No, don't be silly. The pain always goes away after a minute or two."

So Galer reluctantly went back to his own book and his father lay there watching him carefully across the room; but Galer could not concentrate either and soon put his book down, to sit staring back across the room at his father. He looked very strange lying there, who had always been so alive, so full of movement and excitement, and who was now passive, not wanting to read, even to be read to, to talk, nothing, nothing but an old man in pain and . . . what was the other thing in his father's face? Apprehension? Fear? Terror even, but terror qualified by resignation . . . not peacefulness, for the lines of the face were too deep and the eyes too searching. After a moment or two he could not bear to have his father look at him any more, so he got up from his chair in the window recess and walked over to his father's bed, where he sat himself carefully down at its foot. He was closer there but he no longer had to look at him.

"Well," he said, "is the pain better?"

"Quieter," said his father.

"You don't want me to phone the doctor?"

"No, don't go on about it. I was thinking about something else, looking at you."

"What does looking at me make you think?" Galer was

almost teasing his father; he knew what he saw and he thought that he understood his father's love for his first-born son.

"Oh, when you were asleep before, I was watching you — and you reminded me of what you were when you were a baby, and what I was when I was your age."

"All that different?"

"No, I don't think so. I used to think that the wars had changed the world; now I just think that we didn't see clearly before them. And there was something else too."

"What?" Galer asked, but his father did not answer, so he asked again, "Or don't you want to tell me?"

"No, I want to tell you. I was just wondering how best to do it." He was quiet again, looking down the length of the bed at his son who would not look back at him. "Galer," he said abruptly, and Galer looked up quickly, because there was a new sound in his father's voice.

"Yes," he said.

"Have I ever told you about the time after the war, when I was in Austria and so on?" Galer shook his head; his father had always kept silent about those years, and the family had never dared ask him. They all knew that he had seen things bad enough to drive men mad; they knew that was why he had become a clergyman; and they knew that it was enough to know from the quality of his silence that he could not talk about those years. "No, I suppose that I haven't. There were — there are — things about that time that can't and shouldn't be spoken. I mean, there have been books written about it, but . . . well, nobody can say more than a tiny part of it. After my first month or two, I thought that I would write a book about it when I got back home; but, after a while, I realised that I couldn't. It would have been quite impossible. Perhaps a composer, a painter, or a poet one day . . . like Dante perhaps. But not in prose — I don't believe that it's possible. Perhaps one day, from the outside; but not anyone who was actually there. There was just too much of it... too much for me anyway."

"I understand," Galer said gently.

"Do you?" his father asked fiercely. "Oh, I know that you've read the books and seen the films but... you know, it was in some ways the smell that was worst. You know, digging up those graves—I hadn't realised that the body was capable of such corruption. Bad meat, really, but in bulk, and people too—oh, we all learnt soon enough what the mind was capable of, what foulness there was there. But the body too, such corruption. No, I don't think that you can understand."

"But how do you know that..." Galer began; he wanted his father to understand that he was capable of understanding too, if only in his imagination. He could not bear his father's thinking that he was incapable of sharing even those horrors.

"No, don't think that I'm criticising you," his father interrupted him. "Can't you understand that I'm glad that you can't share it? God knows I wouldn't want anyone, even someone I hated, to share that. Better not to understand."

Galer shook his head again. No, it could never be better not to understand; understanding could never harm anyone, it could only make a man better able to live, better able to understand himself.

"All right," said his father. "You don't believe me. Well I pray that you go on not believing me." He lay silent, looking down the bed at his son. "Galer," he said suddenly, "do you understand why I became a clergyman?"

"Well, it's difficult, but I've always assumed that you thought that you could do more for other people that way, more even than you used to," Galer answered.

"No," his father answered. "It hadn't got much to do with the other people; it was caused by people, by one person really, but that wasn't the reason. It wasn't anything social that brought me into the church; it was just one person . . . no, two people perhaps. You want me to tell you?"

"Yes," Galer said. "If you are sure that you aren't getting too tired."

"I'm all right. Here, help me to sit up a little," he said, and Galer took him carefully under the arms and helped pull him higher in the bed, then went to sit back at the foot of the bed. He was not sure that he wanted to hear, though he wanted his father to talk if that pleased him. Yet he knew that he must listen, that he must not allow himself to retreat from the words. He closed his eyes again and listened, as if he had been a small boy again hearing a fairy-tale.

"The first one was a Catholic priest in Germany who had been accused of working with the Gestapo; not just of keeping quiet, but of actually helping them. We didn't have time to worry about the sins of omission; it was commission that mattered then. And he had helped them; he had given them lists of Jews in his parish and so on, oh and other things, even worse in a way. There was a squabble about whose jurisdiction he fell under, ours or the Russians, and while we were sorting it out, I talked to him quite a lot. He spoke very good English, because he had been trained in an international college in Italy. He was a very bad man, I think, a very bad man; but he said something to me once that made me understand. He said . . . oh, I can't remember the words exactly, but something like this. 'I have always known how bad people are, and now you think I am specially bad, because you don't like what I did; but I'm not—I'm just the same as I have always been, just the same as other people.' Of course, he shouldn't have been—I know that, and I know that there were other people who weren't the same, even in Germany, lots of priests too. But . . ." he paused again, searching for the words, ". . . I suppose it was the recognition of his own evil that was strange. He knew that he was bad, he didn't pretend anything else, but he would not be persuaded that other people were less bad. He accepted what he had done almost peacefully, almost . . . almost as if he had done everything that he knew to be wrong, knowing that he had a choice, but wanting to make the choice that justified his own view of people as bad. He was the first one . . ."

"What happened to him?" Galer asked.

"Oh, we had to give him to the Russians; it was a clear case. They shot him, I think; probably quite right too—he had done some terrible things. There was a business with a Jewish family who were Catholic converts . . . but I don't want to remember that." John Detheridge was quiet, remembering it, because no one could choose not to remember.

"And the other one? Or are you getting tired?" Galer asked, suddenly anxious again; he wanted now so much to hear about this that he had forgotten his father's illness for a few moments.

But his father ignored the second question. "The other one," he said. "Well, he was a boy, about eighteen I suppose, or twenty perhaps; he was high enough in the Gestapo to give orders but too junior to be in on the escape routes that the others tried to use—you know that a good many of them got away—and he was captured by our troops. He'd been hiding in the forests with some of the other German troops, and the local people—oh, this was in Austria—were hunting them there, like animals almost, shooting them on sight. Well, we got some troops to go in and get the survivors out; some of the local people were very angry about that. Anyway, I saw all of them, and he was the one who was . . . well, I felt that he was genuinely . . . not good, but ordinary in a way, an ordinary young man who had been misguided. You know, when I started that job I thought that everyone there was like that, not evil, just misguided or mad. I changed soon enough once I started to look at what had happened. But I thought that this one was just a young boy, an ordinary boy, who had got caught up in something he couldn't understand the badness of. Perhaps he saw that I thought that; he looked like that, you see, he looked . . . well, almost as if he could have been my own son; big, of course, like you and Harry, but like you too in his way of talking, the way he treated me, the way he spoke to his guards, gentle almost. He didn't speak English, so I had to use an interpreter; perhaps that made it easier for him to fool me. Because at first he did." John Detheridge, ill and tired, was passionate now, and Galer turned to interrupt him, to tell him to rest. But his father would not let him. "No," he said. "I want to tell you, Galer. I must tell you. Give me some water, please."

Galer helped him to sip from a glass and then leaned him back against the pillows. "You see," his father went on, "he must have seen that I trusted him; and he fooled me completely. I was even talking about getting him released and sent home to his family—he talked a lot about them; his father was a small farmer in Bavaria somewhere, and he had sisters and a small brother . . .

"But then we started to find things out; we brought some local people into the cells to get them to identify the prisoners —you know, to fit faces to deeds, because of course they didn't know their names. Anyway, first one, then another, then another, identified my young man; I thought that they must be mistaken at first, but there were too many of them, and the stories began to connect. I won't tell you the stories, Galer; I remember them, some of them, but I won't tell you. But this man, Holze his name was, he had been . . . he was a specialist. It was one of their tricks in that area when they wanted information, that they would take a child and its parents in, and torture the child to make the parents talk. Of course, ninety times out of a hundred they didn't know anything, but their children were still being tortured and so they had to say something. Some of them confessed themselves to things that they hadn't done, or they named someone else, anyone they knew, as long as they said something. And then he killed the children . . . And later the parents. In one village they killed six families like that, and buried them in a wood, all in the same place. I remember that."

"Don't, Dad," Galer burst out. "Please stop now; you'll make yourself ill like this." He could see that his father was beginning to panic now, but it was not only that; he did not think that he could bear to hear any more.

"No, Galer. You must understand now. You see, this boy . . . we executed him; there was a trial of course, and the local people said again in public what they had already told us, and there was no doubt. I went to watch the execution; I had to, somehow. Oh, Galer," he said, pushing himself upright in the bed, an old man in pain from his body and in worse pain from his memory, "don't you understand? That boy, Holze, he could have been my own son; he could have been you or Harry, either of you. Big, you see, gentle; that was why he did the children, because anyone could see his gentleness. Oh, he didn't look like you in other ways, but still . . . do you see, Galer?"

"I see," he said, eyes closed, and sitting at the foot of his father's bed. But he did not see. He believed that his father was old and ill, in pain and remembering pain, but he would not believe what his father said.

Yet the lie quietened his father. "You see, Galer," he said, very quietly, almost as if he were talking to himself, "until then I had believed that . . . not that badness could not exist, but that it could be beaten. Something very simple, I suppose, that lies would be found out one day. What's that thing of Milton's, the one against censorship . . .?"

"You mean the *Areopagitica*?" Galer asked.

"Yes, that's it. Well, he says in that—at least I think it's there—that in the market-place truth will triumph over falsehood. I stopped believing in that; I stopped believing that man was ultimately good."

There was blood on the side of the old man's mouth. Galer stood next to him, with his hands on his shoulders, pushing him back against the pillows, trying to quieten him again. "Dad," he said, "Dad, you must be quiet now; I know all this already, you don't have to tell me, I have seen it. I understand why..."

"No, you don't," John Detheridge interrupted him fiercely, pushing his son's hands off his shoulders so that he could sit up again. "You don't at all. Don't you see, Galer? I'm afraid." He began to weep then, and to cough, and there was more blood on the side of his mouth. "Look," he said, looking up at his son, "I'm going to die, today, tomorrow, next week, soon..."

"Only if you go on being a bloody fool," Galer growled at him, trying desperately to find the tone of mock-anger that they used to tease each other with. "For God's sake lie quiet; we'll get you over this. You must lie quiet while I phone George Russell..."

"Damn doctors," his father said. "You don't understand, Galer, you don't." He pushed himself half-upright again, using his arms as props to hold him there, shaking his shoulders to keep Galer's hands from pushing him back again. "Galer, I am afraid. Do you understand that? I am dying and I am afraid."

"You're just ill, Dad; you won't be afraid when you're well."

The old man was panicking now, enraged with pain, and memory, and fear. "No, damn you, Galer. Please understand. You must understand. What happens if I die, and go to heaven—oh, I know that you don't believe that, because you think that because you look like me the Detheridges are immortal. We're not, Galer; we stink of death, all of us, me, your mother, Harry, the girls, even you, we all stink like those corpses already."

"Don't, don't," Galer cried out at last, standing away from the bed.

"What if I go to heaven, Galer, and sitting there where God should be is not God at all, but Hitler, and round him all those ghastly men, and that boy there, Holze, with the gentle little smile, and he steps forward when I get to them and says, 'Yes, this is the Englishman who betrayed me.' What then, Galer, what then?" The old man was raving now, and Galer came back to the bedside, and held him down, the old man twisting and fighting against his son's hands, swearing, raving, praying, as if he had a new gift of tongues. Then, suddenly he was quiet, and let Galer lean him back against the pillows, and wipe his sweating face with a towel that Mrs Detheridge had left in the window to dry, the old man with his father there, grey-faced, eyes closed; and then he opened his eyes again and looked at Galer. "Oh, Galer, that boy's face..." he began, and there was a great spurt of blood from his mouth and nostrils, and his face was white and his eyes distended and stayed open, and the towel in Galer's hands was not enough to hold all the blood, and it spread from the towel on to his hands and down his father's neck and on to the sheets and his clothes.

John Detheridge was dead before Galer reached the telephone; and when George Russell came there was nothing to do for him but to change the bedclothes and wash the blood from him, so that his wife and other children need not know how he had died. As they worked, George Russell told Galer that the danger with ulcers was always that if they perforated the lining of the intestines, they would also break an artery; had John been upset that afternoon, he asked, and when Galer did not answer he had looked once to see that there was no need for an answer. He sent Galer away, then, to burn the sheets and towel and bedclothes in the incinerator in the garden; and Galer went upstairs and changed his clothes and washed and then took everything down to be burnt. He was back in the house in time to break the news to the rest of the family as they came back from their afternoon in the car.

* * *

The memory was complete. Galer stopped his slow pacing and took note of the world again. He had missed the turning to St Michaels and was a mile down the footpath that followed the river through the fields. He looked at his watch and saw that it was nearly six o'clock. He had told Skarfe that he would be back before five; but that couldn't be helped now. The memory had come back, had demanded to move out into the light again, and there was no denying its urgency. It had happened, yes; there was no doubt of that. His father had died, afraid and in blood that could not be burnt. But he would not believe what his father had said; he had been ill, an old man ill and dying, afraid, in pain, but only momentarily. He had formed his father's image long before that time, and nothing that had happened that last afternoon could be allowed to change it. It was fear that had been only temporary, pain only temporary, and death nothing more than an episode; his father survived as he had been, because he existed in Galer's mind as he had been, not as he had been on that last afternoon.

Deliberately Galer tried to put the memory out of his mind again; he turned round and walked across the fields back to St Michaels, walking fast, allowing his striding to settle into the rhythm of his own pulse, but it was no good. The memory would not go away, it would not settle back into the unclear darkness. When he reached the Studies Centre and looked up at the windows of his home where his wife and unborn son were waiting for him, he could not bear to go upstairs. The memory would not leave him now and there was only one way for him to cure the past, and that was to forget it. He turned away from the building, away from his wife and his son, and walked back into the fields, where darkness was beginning to settle like a great black bird with over-reaching wings.

* * *

When he came home, it was very late; Skarfe was waiting for him. She had changed into her night clothes and was sitting in the drawing-room, pretending to read, and when he came in she pretended for a while that she had not noticed him; so he went into the kitchen and made himself something to eat and then made tea and took it in to his wife. She was weeping by then, sitting alone in her chair in the drawing-room. Galer did not try to comfort her, simply pulled a table near her and put her tea on it, then went to sit across the room where he did not have to watch her. After a while she stopped crying and they sat a while longer in silence, until finally she said, "I should really phone Jim to tell him that you're back."

"Why?" Galer asked quietly.

"When you didn't come back I went to his flat and we went off in the car to find you."

"I was walking."

"I knew; but I wanted to find you."

But Galer did not answer; he sat still in his chair, looking across the room to where the curtains fell crookedly over the windows, until Skarfe spoke again. "Don't you care about me at all?" she said.

He looked at her then. "I care," he said.

"How can you say that?" she demanded.

"I care," he repeated carefully, looking at her with level eyes.

"No," she said. "Not for me, not about me. About the child, perhaps. Because you think that he's yours. But not about me."

He did not answer her; he sat as still in his chair as he had done that afternoon before he had fled away from Adamson Westcott and his knowledge of death. Again it was almost as if he once moved he too would die. "Well," asked Skarfe, waiting for him. "That's the truth, anyway. All right then," she was pretending to be very calm, "all right. Suppose that he—it—is born dead? Suppose that there is something wrong with me? Suppose it . . ."

"He," Galer corrected her.

"Oh yes, I forgot; it's going to be your son, isn't it?" she said scornfully, and then passionately, "What right have you got to think that it's going to be a son? It—not he—it is inside me."

"But," Galer explained patiently, "in eleven generations . . ."

"Damn your generations; this is my baby, it's inside my womb."

"Of course, he's yours too; but he will be a Detheridge."

"Damn the Detheridges; damn you too, Galer. Can't you understand?" She was standing now, passionately trying to make the man she loved passionately see what he was doing by his silence and his obsessions. "This is one particular baby, not a specimen; it's inside here, growing inside here"—she spread her hands across her swollen stomach—"not some ancestral idea inside your head."

But he was still stubborn. He was incapable of conceding to her, even in her misery. "Yes," he said, "yes, of course, but that doesn't alter the facts of ancestry . . ."

"All right," she said quietly now, but still standing in front of him. "It doesn't. It will be a Detheridge. Its first name will be chosen by you in full consultation with your ancestors. But I've got the job of having him, and suppose the doctors are right, suppose the baby is born dead . . ."

"The doctor didn't say that; he said that you had to be

careful, because of the bleeding. He said the baby would be all right."

"But suppose that he is born dead? Suppose that right now the cord is round his neck, and he can't breathe from me . . ."

"No," Galer whispered. "Don't say that; don't dare say that." You will tempt the gods with that arrogance; you must not put this idea into anyone's head, for fear that the idea will triumph over the other ancestral idea. "Look," he said again, "in eleven generations . . ."

"Stuff your generations, stuff them – they're dead, every one of them. They want to kill my baby." She was hysterical now, raging against her husband and all that she feared. "They want to kill me. They don't care about me or my baby. They want to feed on it, like you want to . . ." Then she was suddenly calm again, leaping from mood to mood as she fought to find a way to make an impression on him. "Suppose it's born all deformed, with two heads, or flappers instead of arms, or blind? Will you and your bloody Detheridges love him then? Will you?"

"Yes," he said, The accusations were beginning to penetrate to the deeper hurt that he could not control. "But do calm down, Skarfe." He stood up and tried to take her by the arms but she shook herself free.

"I won't calm down; I want you to hear me." He turned away from her as she spoke and she now caught at his arm and forced him to turn round to her. "Galer, please listen to me. Will you love a monster?"

"I'll try to."

"You won't – I know you. I would love whatever came out of me, two-headed, hermaphrodite, monstrous, I would love it. But you wouldn't; you only love the things that are yours – your generations and your bloody ancestry, your father, your brother . . ." Now at last she broke down completely, crying out incomprehensibly and putting her hands behind her head to sweep the long hair forward over her face like a curtain to cut out the sight of him. "Oh, Galer," she cried, "I can't bear it, I can't."

For he was still the stronger and, even now, when Skarfe knew with some passing sense of mystery that her child was dying inside her, Galer felt a surge of pleasure at his own strength. He would not break, he thought, no misery or memory of death could break him; and she felt, not pity for the man who loved her so inadequately or guilt at having slept with his friend, but dependence on the strength that she loathed. So when he at last turned to her and took her shaking body into the protection of his own, folding it round with strength, she allowed herself to be held and then held on to him herself, holding tight to what possessed her. Love? What was love compared to this warmth? Yet she whispered into his jacket, "You don't understand still, do you?"

He comforted her. "Yes, I do," he said, "I understand everything." But later, when he had put his wife into their bed and had held her until she fell asleep, he did not get into bed himself but walked quietly downstairs to his classroom and sat there, not reading, not working, not thinking even, until the first light of early dawn made him stir stiffly from his chair.

14

This madhouse hath a pleasant seat. The cawing rooks to the ashhead go, and I sit in the fine old Victorian garden with my audience of kings and the sons of kings, also angels, and the sons of men. Ladies and gentlemen, forgive me for avoiding your titles, but brevity . . . Forbid that I should boast, ladies

and gentlemen, where ranks . . . who was then the gentleman
. . . grass below the elm and stones in circles. If there is a God, you see, he made rooks, and stones too, as well as Jenkyns.

Don't get me wrong, ladies and gentlemen. I am not mad. I am still at St Michaels, odd-job teacher, librarian, jokester of the common room, stalwart of the pub. St Michaels as madhouse; how about that for a perception? I wish that I could go mad. I wrote on a blackboard last week, 'I wish that I could go mad.' Joke to the boys. We shall analyse this clause, pupils. Main clause, 'I wish'. I wish what? That I could go etc. Therefore it is a subordinate noun clause, object of 'wish'. Is mad an adjective or an adverb, sir? Madly for adverbs, mad for adjectives. But in an adverbial position? Wrong. I wish to go what? Mad. Therefore object to go. The object of going is mad. Hence analysis with my dim-witted Upper Fourths. I know that it's out of fashion (calling boys dim-witted and analysing sentence structure) but there is something marvellously exciting about it – meaningless, but exact.

And so a discussion of the nature of tragedy with my bright Sixth. Professor Jenkyns, of the University of Whatever, situated in the sunken garden of a fine old hell, proceeds with his series of illuminations on the nature of tragedy. Illumination, dear pupils, is an unsteady metaphor as candlelight. Witness the angels' wings, insubstantial air. Allow me to adopt a new one. All right then? All right, sir. If the King dies, the King's Son lives, and the land is born again, or the sea. But if the King's Son dies, and the King knows that he will die too, what then? What will the land do then, or the sea say? Oh, I don't care what theory you have, whether the gods punish for pride or God punishes for sin, or a mighty man falls or a weak one, whether it is the coincidence of one weakness in great strength and the chance of events which show that weakness, or the cruelty of cruel nature or the manipulation of impassive fate, or mere chance, pure chance.

DEATH OF FATHERS

Dark bird of the sea, dark beast of the land, and a certain look in the listener's eye that means silence; sea-voice silent; stone out of water silent, stony man in his silence. No, not hearing is not silence.

You see, what is terrible depends on where it comes from. If from God, then perhaps inexplicable but not terrible, unless God is evil. If from the cruel Gods, then explicable though terrible, because they are cruel as humans are. Gods or history, chance or necessity, they too start somewhere, which may of course be nowhere. If it is nowhere, then Nigel was right; and perhaps he was right, and dancing there in the air he was perfected. Because if death is perfection, we should welcome it like a friend. So I in my stone chair, Jenkyns, wonder. Self-wonder.

Look, ladies and gentlemen, it's like this: the question is like this, I mean. Why did Galer Detheridge's son die before he had breathed? I don't know, you see, therefore I ask the question. No point in asking questions if you can't answer them? As far as I see it, no point in asking questions if you can answer them. Wittgenstein on his head. Because, says Professor De-dum, you invest this question with an ontological status, which it cannot. I cannot, but bear this question. Therefore I say to you, Professor De-dum, get stuffed up your chair of philosophy. (This damsel hath a pleasant seat, ho, ho.) I know Galer. I know his wife. Why did their child die? My child die, if mine? Though not mine. I bugger Mrs Pamela O'ntology up her status, and hence answer, I do not know. I, double-named Jenkyns, knowing myself do not know. Floating. It's pointless asking such questions; by asking them you usurp the role of God. True, cries wise Jenkyns. Fool Jenkyns replies, Say it's because of 'I' that I don't know. Because it's me that doesn't know. The limitation may not be of knowledge but of self. Maybe Galer knows. Maybe Professor De-dum knows. Maybe Mrs Pamela O'ntology knows. Jenkyns alone may not

RESPONSE

know. Certainly Jenkyns doesn't know. Jenkyns, playing a game with the air, cries like a sea-bird, Don't Know, Don't Know, Don't Know. But still I cry, Lord. Why did that child die? Answer (self answering self) I don't know.

Of course, I don't think I'm a particularly cowardly man—oh, cautious, very cautious, not so much in what I do but in what I allow myself to be. I'm the limited company of thought, memories and sensations which I have named Jenkyns; I'm not an adventurer into depth or distance, because I know what happens when I get there. So perhaps I don't know because I am afraid to know. Perhaps I was cowardly not to say to Galer, "Look, old friend, I was fucking Skarfe for two or three months last term, and that bump which died may have been a Jenkyns bump, not a Detheridge at all." Then, watching the blankness in his eyes, I could have hurried Skarfe away.

But it had changed by then: what was it she said to me that evening Galer didn't come home and she made me take her out in the Green Monster looking for him? "We must help him, Jim, we must." And then she had turned to me to say, "Sorry, Jim." I suppose she meant sorry that he had to come first now, or perhaps she just meant sorry that she was wrecking my evening. But I understood the first, because I wanted to believe that. I wasn't being brave, you see; I missed what I had lost when Skarfe went back to being Galer's alone. But I was more afraid by then of losing Galer than I missed Skarfe.

It hadn't been like that always: I remember one afternoon I pretended to let Galer persuade me to go with him to visit Adamson Westcott, but, as soon as I had delivered Galer there, I pretended to get cold feet. Then I roared back to Skarfe, elegantly naked in the flat; and an hour and a half later I returned to fetch Galer from the farm, and pretended I had spent some stolen time exploring the lanes of Colley and environs. Oh, that lovely sunken lane and its fleshly environs!

DEATH OF FATHERS

Perhaps she might have come with me then, perhaps not; and perhaps I should have risked any hurt to avoid that final hurt which I shall never be part of and which I can only partly comprehend. If the brat had been mine, and had died, oh I would have been hurt, for me, or Skarfe, but I would not have been destroyed. Not like Galer was—just hurt. I could have survived, could have closed down another area of my mind and let it function external to the recognisable self. No, Skarfe wouldn't have come . . . you see, she let me make love to her because . . . no, that's wrong too, she fucked with me (because she did it too, didn't just let it be done to her) to demonstrate, if you like, that she was still her own person. So if I had told Galer, she might at least have gone away from him, and the baby would have been a dead bastard, not a dead Detheridge, all the dead Detheridges.

But, you see, I am Jenkyns; I do not believe, as Galer at least used to, that evil does not exist except as negation of goodness. Because then Nigel, as I saw him, would not have existed. But the body and self exist. But if Galer is right, why did his son die? I do not guess because I dare not. The 'I' limits all. I do not know the answer to my question. End of lecture on the nature of tragedy, from which dependeth evil. In the old sense of hanging. Thereby hangs an evil, ho, ho. Avoiding the end of the story, I am. Unless the only end is I don't know. Thus speaks Jenkyns, raising hands to overburdened head. I do not know. Sound of trumpets, ladies and gentlemen. I do not know.

Part Three

Silence

*Down, Derry-down/
O let an old man rest.*

Ezra Pound, Canto LXXXIII

15

That Sunday I had lunched with Skarfe and Galer. In the afternoon Skarfe and I stayed at home, while Galer went off somewhere for a walk. We drank coffee wildly, gossiped a while, then got out the chessboard; I had been teaching her to play for the last few weeks – she was getting very bored with being pregnant, poor girl, and so I thought that a game as boring as beginner's chess might amuse her. In the event, she was a good pupil, quick to spot the bluff and double-bluff, and it intrigued me not only to see her respond to the intricacies of the game but also to see how far I could take each game, allowing her so much advantage that it would please her and not so much that she would realise that I was easing her along. Occasionally I noticed that she went away from me for a while, somewhere into herself, like a person in a trance, almost as if she had caught the habit from her man; I would sit very quiet then, pretending to think about my next move, until she stirred again and I knew that she was ready for the world again.

Until, one time, she didn't come back; I sat for a long time, concentrating on the board – I had in fact finished the game and had started another one in my head, against a maniacal opponent who allowed his pieces subtle variations in move – and finally looked up. I saw then that this was a new way of going away, one I hadn't before seen in her – or anyone for that matter – as if she were holding herself deliberately into herself, somewhere down there in the darkness.

"Are you all right, Skarfe?" I asked. What words we find to speak when a world begins or ends, what marvellous original words! As if in reply, she got up quickly from her chair and fled across the room, as quickly as a person eight months' pregnant can flee. Grace personified, still, all that absurd jangling movement, the belly thrusting her forward, knees flowing, bright hair flowing. And then I saw on the chair where she had been sitting a bright stain of blood, and realised what her stillness had been. I went after her then, of course; she was in the bathroom, and the door was locked behind her.

"Skarfe," I called again, "Skarfe, are you all right? Are you bleeding badly?"

No voice from inside, and I began to panic. I hammered on the door and shouted at her to let me come in to help her. Then she opened the door and came out; she had wrapped a towel around her waist, and I suppose that she must have stuffed a towel under her dress to staunch the bleeding. She held herself very still in the open doorway of the bathroom. "The baby's started, I think," she said and then in sudden panic reached out and grabbed me, a tall girl holding her hands hard on my shoulders. "Jim, I'm bleeding badly."

"Quickly. Don't worry, but be quick. I'll get you to hospital. My car's outside . . ."

But I could see her catch hold of herself again in her mind; I could see it as if a cloud had suddenly obscured the sun, and the wind seemed to stall, and the world to stagger. "No," she said. "No. You've got to find Galer."

"But we don't know where he's gone, and you know how difficult it is to find him when he's walking." I was panicking badly myself now and had to catch hold of my own mind to make it stand still for a moment. "It's much more important to get you to hospital quickly."

"No," she said. "I want Galer. You must find him, not

anyone else, you. Get someone else to take me—phone an ambulance or a taxi or something."

I was out of the flat before she had finished her sentence. If she wanted Galer with her, she would have Galer. I would find him somewhere. But first I had to find someone whom she would let take her to hospital; I don't like blood at the best of times and blood from there somehow seemed more terrifying than from anywhere else. The Headmaster's house was the nearest to the Studies Centre, three hundred yards across the brilliant green lawns of late autumn. People panic in different ways, I'm told; my own involves an excitement of the senses as if I were high, a piling up of the senses so that there are no boundaries any more—the trees are gold falling from my fingers, the wind giant strides across the grass, the white and grey and tinged pink of the clouds sound like breathing in my lungs. Three hundred yards I ran, panicking Jenkyns like a god of perceptions.

Thank God the Headmaster's wife was there. She is a Very Superior Person, Mrs Losden, all nose and chin and grey hair—she treats everyone, even her Superior Husband, like a small boy who has dirtied his pants. But in crises she is magnificent, and perceptive too. She took in my garbled flap of words without a question, got her coat, car keys, shouted to her shotten husband, and came with me across the lawn, striding big like an angry bird.

"Why didn't you take her yourself?" she demanded as we went.

"She wouldn't let me . . ." I began.

"I s'pose she wants you to find her husband—walking again, is he? Bloody typical," she said, then, so that I would understand that I was included in the typicality, "all men the same—never anywhere when they're wanted." Sober, I might have answered her with something rude like, 'And I can't say I blame them,' but all I could think at that moment was 'Thank

God for a bullying woman.' "Good," she went on grimly, looking at me. "Well, you just find her husband and bring him to the hospital. Let him suffer a bit too."

When I tried to go upstairs with her, to help get Skarfe down and across the lawn to the garage where she kept her car, she wouldn't let me. "Pooh," she said, "the girl can still walk; there's always some blood, and it never stopped anyone from walking. You get off at once and find her husband." I might have imagined it, but I fancy she was saying "Shoo" to me then too, as if I had been a silly hen who was fussing round a nest that she, farmer's wife, wanted to raid. Anyway, I shooed; I wanted no more blood and I wanted Galer nearly as much as Skarfe did.

God knows how I found him; it took me more than an hour, hurling the Green Monster up and down every country lane within miles, stopping at every sign that said 'public footpath' . . . , peering across the fields, once or twice shouting and waving frantically to strangers, mistaking them in the distance for Galer, and they stared across the fields and hedgerows at the lunatic in a green car. In the end I found him quite close to St Michaels, walking along the main road from Burston, hands in pockets, striding big on the grass verge; I got him into the car, turned it round, and drove madly to the hospital the other side of Burston. Being Galer, he did not panic at my news, though to tell the truth I did not mention how bad the bleeding had been. There would be time enough for him to find that out. He sat nearly as still in the front seat as Skarfe had done in her chair, while I fiddled with the choke, jabbed at the accelerator, changed gear and even (God help me) flashed my headlights in an effort to make the Monster do more than its regulation 35 mph. God knows where Galer had gone to then; somewhere back into his past and away into his future, I expect, when the world would be populated solely with Detheridge sons.

SILENCE

Lady Headmaster was still at the hospital, looking a little more grimly flustered than I had left her; months later, she told me that Skarfe had bled all over the back seat of her car and that she had had to scrub it for hours to get the stain out. I don't think she had realised that I had meant what I said when I told her that Skarfe was bleeding badly; I think she thought I meant that Skarfe had had the show of blood that most women have at that time. She must have known already how bad things were; she is another one of the kind who wrings lost fledglings' necks, I suppose, and she didn't bother to hide her worry from Galer or me. "I won't stay," she said. "I'm glad you're here. There's nothing more that I can do now—Jenkyns, you will let me know what happens, of course."

"Of course."

She turned to Galer. "Well, young man," she said, "I hope your wife and baby will be all right." Not, you will note, the usual optimistic burble that people use—'I'm sure they'll be all right' or 'Doctors are very clever these days,' or anything like that. Just straight, 'I hope . . .' I walked out to her car with her, partly I suppose to show her that I had more or less recovered from my panic. "Rotten business," she said to me as she got into her car—the usual phrase of her class, I suppose, the one which you use to describe the death of a cow in a bog or the putting down of a favourite dog, as well as for the worst that can happen to any man or woman; but not a bad phrase really. When she was safely in the car, she looked through the window at me, rolled it down, and said, without any mannerism or pretence, "Look after him, Jim, won't you?" Then she drove off at high speed, forcing some poor little petulant Morris Minor to brake hard to avoid being smashed by her Rover and only just avoiding a mother who was trying to cross the road with a pram and a small boy tugging at her hand. I hadn't even known that she had known my name.

I went back inside to find that Galer was sitting stonily in the corner of the waiting-room; he hadn't asked where Skarfe was or how she was and was obviously expecting someone to come to tell him what was happening. All he had done was to give his name to the porter at the reception desk. I had already caught enough of the mood of the place to realise that fathers and friends were considered an even lower form of life than patients, and so went out in search of news. The porter at the reception desk had obviously been specially chosen for the job because he was totally unintelligible, either in an advanced state of paranoic schizophrenia or had a cleft palate, because what he seemed to be saying and the places to which he pointed were completely at variance. Certainly, when I went where he pointed I ended up in the gents; I suppose that's what most fathers want when they are waiting. So I stood in the corridor outside the waiting-room and waylaid everyone who passed me. "Excuse me," I said in my sweetest voice, "can you tell me where I can find out about Mrs Detheridge?" The first three people I asked went straight past me without even shaking their heads; so I stood in the middle of the corridor and asked again. That way at least they had to swerve to get past me, so that I knew my body was still material, even if my voice had got lost somewhere between my vocal chords and their tympans. Finally I stopped a young man in a white coat–a houseman, intern, or whatever they are called–by grabbing his arm. I had given up sweetness by then and tried the Detheridge growl. "For God's sake," I said, "I can't get a word of sense out of anyone. Can you tell me what is happening to Mrs Detheridge; she was brought in here an hour ago?" Either I frightened him with my growl or he was too inexperienced to realise that fathers and their hangers-on were meant to be ignored, but he did find out something. He went off down the corridor, through those great swing doors designed so that stretchers can barge through the middle, and into a room on the right of the doors. He came back five minutes later, just when I was beginning to think that my growl had failed.

"Your wife's in there," he said to me. Poor bloke, how was he to know that she wasn't my wife? "She's in labour, and there are doctors with her."

"Look," said the non-husband. "I'm not her husband. He's in the waiting-room. Will you come to tell him?"

"Oh no, I can't do that," he said. "We are not meant to go into the waiting-rooms, not unless someone is ill there." Someone had been getting at him, I could see; he had probably had a five-minute lecture on the techniques of confusing fathers and friends of patients.

So I did my disciplinarian's act: I stuck my face down into his pale childish one and threatened him. "For God's sake, man, don't be a fool; it won't take you two minutes to tell him what's going on." It doesn't often work, my disciplinarian's act, even with boys, but it worked now—he must have been at a well-disciplined school, that young man, because he came like a lamb to Galer in the waiting-room.

"He's seen Skarfe," I announced to the stony man in the corner. "She's in labour."

He stood up then; he seemed to have grown even bigger in his waiting, and inside he must have been ablaze. "Where is she?" he demanded.

"Down in the labour ward," the houseman said. "She's in second stage labour."

Galer didn't ask what that was; perhaps he knew already—I didn't but it sounded terrifying. "Can I see her?" he demanded.

"I'm afraid not," the houseman replied. "Usually we let fathers go in, but in this case . . ." his voice tailed off. I could see that he realised that he had done the forbidden, which was to give an outsider an idea of how serious a situation was. Before I could stop him, the little lamb scuttled out of the waiting-room. I thought for a moment that Galer was going to go after him, but he stopped at the door and looked through the glass windows down the corridor. Bloody twit, that houseman; and bloody twit me, to have brought him in at all. We were caught now in half-knowledge that was worse than the fear of not knowing. So we waited there, Galer standing looking down the corridor, Jim/John Jenkyns, no-one's father himself, sitting sprawled in an uncomfortable straight-backed chair; God knows we waited, how long God knows, but the light outside died and the darkness swarmed down like a flock of great birds with grey-black wings and eyes like street-lights ...

* * *

He had been sixteen when his youngest sister, Sarah, was born; he had sat up late the night before with his parents, because he had worked at his books all afternoon, and he and his father had talked while his mother had knitted placidly in a big armchair in the corner of the room. What had they talked about? The war perhaps, or where they planned to walk that summer, or his father's hopes for better conditions for the very poor of England. The new baby was a week overdue, but his mother, calm mother, on her eighth pregnancy and fifth child, was waiting in perfect passivity; she hardly spoke all evening, except once when she thought she heard Mary cry and asked Galer to go upstairs to see if she were nightmaring, but sat and watched her husband and her first-born son talk of all manner of things. At ten-thirty John Detheridge had suggested that Galer go to bed, if he was to cope with school the next day; and Galer had gone quietly upstairs to sleep.

At four o'clock next morning his father had come into the room which Galer shared with Harry and had woken him; "Come on to the landing," he had said, "quietly so that you won't wake Harry—I have something to tell you." Galer had staggered half-asleep but excited on to the landing, where his father had shaken his hand and had hugged him; he had another sister, born two hours before—she and her mother were happily asleep in the hospital. Mrs Detheridge had come downstairs at midnight with her small suitcase packed for her stay in hospital, to tell her husband, working in his study, that the baby had started. Sarah had been born an hour later, safely in the hospital.

It had been the only time that his father had been allowed to stay with his wife the whole time one of his children was being born; before the war, he had told Galer, hospitals were not keen on having fathers around. And how he had regretted having waited so long—his wife had been marvellous, he said, refusing gas, smiling at him between the pains, and he had stood at her side and had held the gas ready for her and then had held her knees to give her something to push against; and the midwife had let him look to see the baby actually being born, that small wet compact body slowly pushed out of her mother, his wife, Galer's mother, mother of the world! How he had exalted, like a man who had waited all his life to see a miracle and who had now seen it.

Galer and he had whispered their way downstairs, and he had wrapped his old army greatcoat around Galer's shoulders, and they had sat in the bay window of the drawing-room; his father had opened a bottle of champagne which he had been saving for this celebration, and they had sat together and had drunk champagne and his father had talked. How he had talked! Words upon words, worlds upon worlds, flowing like blood through the arteries and back through the veins, massing in the heart and then flowing out again. He told Galer of his own birthnight, how the midwife had come through the snow to help the wives of two neighbours, of how he had left the house and had walked halfway across the county, walking right through the night and the early dawn, and had come back at dawn to hear a baby crying in the house and to find his wife fast asleep after her night-long labour. He had walked up and down the passage rocking his son to sleep in his arms, his first-born son, dream of dreams; and sixteen years later Galer sat in the bay-window with his father, drinking champagne, glass for glass with his father, until the bottle was finished and the first light of dawn slithered up to the window. Galer tried to stand then, but he was light-headed and had staggered and would have fallen if his father hadn't caught him. His father had picked him up then, as if he were a child and not a big young man of sixteen, drunk on champagne for the first time in his life, and had carried him upstairs to his bed and hours of sleep, right through the morning and into mid-afternoon. He had come downstairs then, with his head aching and his eyes bleary, to ask his father why he had not been woken for school; and his father had laughed at him until he had laughed too, and then told him that he had phoned the headmaster of his school after breakfast that morning to tell him what had happened.

"You mean that you told him I was drunk," Galer said, horror-struck.

"Of course," answered his father. "You wouldn't have wanted me to lie, would you? But I told him why and that it was all my fault, and I'm sure that you'll find that he doesn't hold it against you."

His father had been right. When he went to school next morning, the Headmaster had called him aside after morning prayers and had asked him, quietly and smiling, whether his head still ached. "Will you please congratulate your father on his new baby?" he had said as he went away from the sixteen-year-old Galer, the first-born and the re-born.

* * *

Look across this room, Jenkyns, now. Where is Galer now? He is standing there, in the far corner of the waiting-room,

SILENCE

standing looking down the corridor, and I am near sleep, but I see him there, and wonder where he is now. Where now, Galer the rock? On which I construct. Too big to be a saint, too big for this room, too big for Jim/John Jenkyns. Waiting for news of his son. Passive; yet I notice that the other men who are gradually filling this room keep away from him. Do they smell death in that corner? Yet they sit near me, and I too smell of death. And somewhere down the corridor, through that door where he looks all the time, if he looks anywhere, his son is being born. Yes, Galer's son; oh, perhaps I started him, but Galer's son without question. Thoroughly Galer's. Even if he's born with my face, my hands, my feet, Galer's son still. Created there, not here. Love Skarfe? Oh yes, I love Skarfe, wherever she is now, bleeding in a room down that corridor. And perhaps she loves me too, because I am easy, because I am Jim/John Jenkyns, because I am not Galer Detheridge. But none of those trivia matters now; Galer's son's mother Skarfe is, Galer's wife, and the feelings of the present are too small to be counted. How could we contend with all that past, all that future? Yes, love Skarfe by all means; and love Galer too, love Galer's father, love his son, born, unborn, it does not matter which.

So, ladies and gentlemen, if you can still understand what my half-sleep says to you, witness this: I hereby renounce all rights in that child, except the right of love, because that child, whether it is born or not, is the child of his parents and I love his parents more than I love Jim/John Jenkyns himself. Peroration, my friends, peroration complete: I love, therefore I . . .

* * *

Looking down the corridor from the glaring light of the waiting-room, down towards the wide doors and further to the room where his wife and child were, Galer seemed to see his father walking up through the dark and the light towards him, tall thin, man, loose-limbed, grey-haired, grey-faced in his tiredness, but smiling to greet his first-born son after their brief parting. World without end, that was the prayer, the grace that stayed. And when his own son was born, would his father come down the corridor to him, long-dead man in the old black cassock they had buried him in, carrying the child in his arms, asleep after his brief breathing in of the light. And what would he say, dead father? 'I go on, you see: I don't die, I didn't die, I won't die. Here is your evidence for immortality; look at those eyes, first-born son, look at those eyes, the shape of them. Look at the curve of that cheek, the cleft of that chin. Look at me in your first-born son, look at yourself in your son, my first-born son.'

* * *

Anyway, you just have to go on waiting, not hoping, not understanding, not knowing. Maybe it is a condition of perfection, this kind of waiting. A condition of something certainly, whatever. I remember when I had my university breakdown, when that steering wheel tried to kill me and the road hit me in the face, I had a vision of the Warneford as hell. The modern versions of hell—lunatic asylum and concentration camp. Or perhaps call them Hades, because there are some people who think that asylums are holy places. I met a psychiatrist once at a party in London who got me talking about the Warneford; he said, quite seriously, that the psychiatric hospital was the modern version of the mediaeval monastery—the place you retreat to when the world grows too great for you. Not for me; the next time they get me into the bin they'll have to carry me, and I'll do my feeble best to make them strait-jacket me too. Look, there goes one of the minor devils, all in white starchily rustling; and here comes a major one, male, with instruments in the pocket of his devil's white robe, and bloodless sterile hands held carefully before him. I suppose that's why the gas-chamber and the medical lab are the places people dwell on when they describe concentration camps; it's scientific horror . . . Yet death by hunger must have been just as bad as the death under the knife or the death under the things they called showers.

And what are Galer and I here? Two of the damned, he for too much of the wrong kind of love, I for my hackneyed sin? And all those other men who sit here, restless or joking or whispering or looking at all the lovely nubile girls in the magazines and the lovely nubile devils rustling up and down the corridor, because they haven't slept with their wives for the past month or so, and won't sleep with them again for another month? I could go, of course; Galer doesn't need me here, and Skarfe will want him when she wakes, not me. Galer could always phone when it is all over and I'd come to fetch him. So it can't be Hades, not yet at any rate; we shall wait, Jenkyns old man, we shall wait, wait perfectly. A condition of torment may be perfection, of course, Jenkyns, old self. Death, old man, is a condition of perfection too.

* * *

Came the crisis. I don't know how he realised, but Galer beckoned me from my corner over to where he was standing, looking down the corridor; there was a spate of activity in and out of the doors of the labour ward which the houseman had told us Skarfe was in, nurses hurrying out and doctors hurrying in, doctors trotting out and nurses trotting in. Then one of them came down the corridor, a nurse dressed in delivery clothes, long greenish overdress and cloth overshoes, green bonnet and white mask, pulling off the face mask as she came. She looked in at the waiting-room, but then went on hurriedly to the reception desk, where she consulted with the porter, who pointed across the hall back to the waiting-room. The nurse came back, stopped this time, pushed her head through the door, and said, "Which of you is Mr Detheridge?"

"He is," I said, pointing at Galer standing next to me.

"Oh good, you're still here, are you; we didn't know if you'd gone home," she said. "Will you please stay, the doctor says?"

Galer began to growl something at her, so I spoke quickly. "He had no intention of leaving," I said, and that minor devil in her green robes looked at me and said, "And who are you, may I ask?"

"A family friend," I said firmly. What a little tart, a rude little greenish tart, and I was about to ask what her name was, when she interrupted me to say, "You had better stay too," and with that she was out of the door again, officious little behind bumping at her robes, down the corridor and out of sight.

"There's no point in being rude back," a fat-faced man in a chair the other side of the room said. "I've been here four times now," and he held up four fingers to emphasise his prowess. "And if you try being rude back, they just make life beastly for your wives. I complained to the Committee of Management once . . ." and he shook his head soundlessly.

So we stood for a moment, Galer and I, and then suddenly Galer said, "I'm going to see Skarfe." Before I could stop him, he moved across the waiting-room and out of the door.

"They'll forbid him to visit his wife," I heard the fat-faced man say sadly as I went after him. I didn't catch him until we were through the wide swinging doors half way down the corridor, and I didn't have time to speak to him, simply caught his arm to stop him going through the door of the delivery room on the right. It was the first time in my life that I had tried to stop him physically, and I was surprised at how easy it was. But it could have been only surprise on his part, or perhaps he stopped only to get his balance. Because he turned round and hit me then, not with his fist, but with the base of his hand, his hand open, his elbow straightening like a piston, and crash into my mouth, and I was on my back on the floor against the wall of the corridor. Just like that, no pain, no pain at all, just the surprise of suddenly seeing the world from floor level like a crawling child must do.

That's how I saw into the delivery room. Galer went through the middle of the double door, hands pushing the doors open each side of him, and holding them open there, his arms outstretched, while he watched what was happening, holding them apart so that we could both see, though he must have already forgotten me lying on the floor behind him.

Have you ever seen a delivery room? It's more or less like an operating theatre, I suppose, though they don't have the table right in the middle of the room, but at one side, so that they have room for the things they may need for the baby – respirator, cot, bath, scales, and so on. The actual table is a bit different too; the light above it is not central but is angled so that it shines from the bottom, and above the table there are straps hanging from the roof for the woman being delivered to hang her legs in if need be, and apart of course. Otherwise there are the normal things, a big container of gas next to the table, transfusion equipment, and so on. And nurses and doctors standing around the foot of the table, some working there, some apparently only watching.

But the big thing is the blood; oh, you think there's no blood in a delivery room? Well, I've seen inside one, and I can tell you that there is blood enough to satisfy a vampire. Perhaps doctors aren't so afraid of blood being lost these days, because what their patients lose from one place they can replace from another. Certainly they were pumping blood into Skarfe, because there was a big jar of it in the transfusion unit, and you could see the red of it running down the tube that led into her arm. But it wasn't only that blood I saw; it was the blood at the other end, blood on her legs, blood on the table, blood on the gloved hands of the doctors, blood on the overdresses of the nurses, and I suppose that what one of the nurses was mopping at under the table was blood too. Skarfe—it must have been Skarfe, though it could have been anyone—lying in a grotesque parody of a sexual posture, body flat, legs high and spread wide, and blood was her lover, and then the doctors were taking something from between her legs; I suppose that everyone was so concerned with that that they didn't notice Galer standing in the doorway, and the thing they took out of her, pale and bloody, and . . . well, it could have been a baby; it could also have been a man's heart, or a monstrous bloody penis, or . . . So I saw it, framed by the open doors and Galer's massive body looking in on wife and child.

One of them must have seen us then, because an attendant doctor and a nurse rushed to the doors and pushed Galer out and down the corridor. He let them. They took him into the waiting-room and the nurse stayed with him, lecturing him I suppose. The doctor came hurrying back to me; I was on my feet by then, unsteadily in the middle of the corridor, mopping at my mouth with a handkerchief and spitting blood into it.

"You tried to stop him and he hit you?" the doctor asked a trifle unnecessarily, given the state of my mouth. "Are you waiting too, or are you with him?"

"A friend," I lisped.

"Here, let me look at that." Firm medical hands smelling of soap took hold of my jaw, tipped my head back, and an expert firm finger hooked my lower lip down. "Oh," the doctor said, "it's not too bad—it'll swell quite a lot, but it doesn't need stitching." He let go of my jaw and stepped back. "All in the line of friendship," he joked weakly. "Fathers do get hysterical in these situations, and usually the bigger they are, the worse they are. Much worse than the mothers." I suppose they are used to dying, doctors are; it's only to us that they seem callous. But now he looked towards the waiting-room and said, "Poor bugger; how's he taking it?"

"Taking what?" I asked. I knew perfectly well; I suppose that I had known for hours, but I wanted to hear it said firmly.

"Hasn't anyone told him yet? I thought that was why he came down."

"Told him what?"

"The baby's dead, I'm afraid. It died inside, some time ago; it didn't have a chance, poor little devil – the worst case of *placenta praevia* I've seen for years. *Placenta praevia*'s what we call it when . . ."

"I know," I interrupted him. I wanted no more horrors.

"We managed to save the mother though," he said. "Twenty years ago . . . I say, are you all right?" I must have swayed a little or whatever it is that one does when the walls tumble down on one. Because I had seen, suddenly, that it would have been better for Skarfe if she had died in there.

"Yes," I said, though I was grateful for his hand holding me by the arm. "I'm all right now. It's just the blood." I knew what I meant, but he thought I meant my mouth, because he answered, "It will stop soon."

"Look," he went on, "if nobody's told him, the father I mean, well, perhaps you should – I mean, somebody's got to, me if you don't, and at least you're a friend."

I didn't answer him directly. "Can you tell me one thing?" I asked. "What would the child have been? What sex was it, I mean?"

"Oh, it was a boy," he answered me. "Not that it makes much difference now." He paused. "Will you tell him, then?"

Again I didn't answer but mopped busily at my mouth. He must have taken my silence to be acquiescence, and perhaps I intended that he should. I left him then and walked slowly down the corridor, through the swinging doors and towards the waiting-room. The nurse must have decided that it was safe to leave Galer by now and she had gone away, and I could see him sitting alone in the far corner of the room, straight-backed, stony faced, eyes shut against the glaring light. I stood looking at him through the glass for a long time before I decided. No, I would not tell him. I had let the doctor understand that I would, but I would not tell him. I could not bear to tell him what he must have known already, that his son was dead before he had breathed, that his son had not been born at all.

Galer did not see me standing there and he did not see me go away. I went out into the dark car park and stood beside my car, fumbling for my keys. It was all so simple really; if I had ever loved Skarfe, the love had died while I lay there on the floor of the corridor with the taste of blood in my mouth and a vision of blood and more blood through the open doors past Galer. There was nothing left in me, except the knowledge of what I did not know. There was no love for Skarfe, there was no son for Galer, there was no father for anyone. In front of me were the bright glaring lights of the hospital, behind me the dark line of trees that edged the car park, dark trees only a fraction less dark – or more dark – than the dark of the night sky.

* * *

After the doctor had told Galer that his son had been born dead but that his wife was going to recover, though she had lost a great deal of blood, and that he should be able to see her in an hour or two when the anaesthetic had worn off, Galer sat silent for so long that the doctor thought that he must have fallen asleep; so he talked in whispers to the other fathers in the room so that they should not waken him. Until Galer, hearing their whispers like the whispers of the dead, stood up, pushed past the doctor, and walked outside the building to where the dark had gathered. He stood there, a big man tied to his own mind and his own body, looking out into the darkness, and when the doctor came after him to ask if he were all right, he did not bother to answer. What was it that the stone had said? What had the dead man in the waves said? Had they voices at all, or was it just the sea that he had heard? The man in the sea had dreamt of a forest, the stone in the sand had dreamt of the sea, and the stone in the sea had dreamt of nothing.

"You will be able to have more children," the doctor said almost fiercely, trying to make this man see that one death would not change the progress of a world. "Your wife is going to be perfectly all right, and there's no reason that she shouldn't have more children."

"No," Galer said.

"That's not true," the doctor said again. What was one death, after all? There were so many deaths, so why should one death be all that important?

"No," said Galer again, and then turned to the man to say, "Go away, go away, for God's sake. I'm all right, if you'll only leave me alone." The doctor went. He looked behind him from the steps but kept going until he disappeared into the building again.

It was necessary to say "No." He did not understand why, but it was necessary. He said it again out loud. "No," to the air perhaps, or to the dead people who gathered about him, and again, "No." There was nothing left now, the nothing of absence, and the nothing that was before anything. Fathers and sons, dead; wives and children, dead; there would be no more children, no more marriage, no more fathers, no more love. His father was dead and his son was dead. Nothing before and nothing after. There was only the dark line of the trees that jagged and hammered at the dark of the night sky.